The sight of his muscles shining with sweat shot a hot tingle of appreciation right down the middle of her

For an instant she could not tear her gaze away.

His soft chuckle warned her that he had noticed her fascination. Iana immediately shut her eyes, cursing herself for her wayward thoughts. She ignored his offer of assistance.

When she dared to look again, he had retreated to the edge of the water and begun wading in, his back to her. With a will of their own, her eyes immediately focused upon his uncovered nether cheeks. "Och, my sweet lord," she breathed in absolute awe.

"Oui?" He looked over his left shoulder and raised one dark brow. *"Qu'est-ce que c'est?"*

What is it? he asks. Iana scoffed. *Lust* is what it was. Pure, unadulterated lust. And she should be *ashamed* of herself...!

Acclaim for Lyn Stone's recent titles

The Highland Wife

"…laced with lovable characters, witty dialogue,
humor and poignancy, this is a tale to savor."
—*Romantic Times Magazine*

Bride of Trouville

"I could not stop reading this one…
Don't miss this winner!"
—*Affaire de Coeur*

The Knight's Bride

"Stone has done herself proud with this delightful
story…a cast of endearing characters
and a fresh, innovative plot."
—*Publishers Weekly*

ISBN 0-373-29188-4

THE QUEST

Copyright © 2001 by Lynda Stone

This edition published by arrangement with Harlequin Books S.A.

® and TM are trademarks of the publisher. Trademarks indicated with ® are registered in the United States Patent and Trademark Office, the Canadian Trade Marks Office and in other countries.

Visit us at www.eHarlequin.com

Printed in U.S.A.

Please address questions and book requests to:
Harlequin Reader Service
U.S.: 3010 Walden Ave., P.O. Box 1325, Buffalo, NY 14269
Canadian: P.O. Box 609, Fort Erie, Ont. L2A 5X3

This book is dedicated to those independent "Cato Girls," Louise Pope, Mary Dunlap and Ruth Mimms, my mom and my aunts. Also to the heroic "Cato boys," Earl, Green and Walt.

Equally as dear and deserving are my dad, Harlen Perkins, my stepfather, Preston Pope, and my uncles and aunts by marriage, Raiford Dunlap, Calvin Mimms, Corinne, Alice and Jolene Cato.

I thank you all for the invaluable lessons you have taught me through advice and example. How else would I have recognized love when I found it?

Chapter One

West coast of Scotland, 1340

The taste of his first defeat grew no less bitter with his arrival on these shores, thought Henri Gillet as he climbed out of the disreputable vessel they had commandeered. He dragged his long legs through the sucking, thigh-deep waves. "Pay the man, Ev," he called out over his shoulder.

The squire tossed a small pouch of coins at the disgruntled fisherman and then struggled through the bitterly cold surf to where Henri waited on the deserted, rock-strewn shore.

"Where are we, sir?" the lad asked while he shook himself off and shivered. Though Everand strove hard to erase the trepidation from his voice, Henri knew he surely must fear what was to come. Truth told, he feared it himself, though not for the same reasons.

He needed to reach safe haven so that the boy would have a chance at survival. At the moment, Henri was not certain he could manage that. His own chances were meager at best. Doggedly he placed one foot before the other and steeled himself against the grinding pain. The bleeding wound just below his ribs ached less than the hurt in his heart. He had lost everything.

If he died, he must account to God. And if he lived, he must face his father. In his mind, there was little difference. Not that he expected harshness in either case, for both had treated him benevolently thus far and would again. And that would be far worse than any punishment they might inflict. A bitter brew, indeed, was defeat.

He had not caused it. In fact, he had done all within his power to prevent it. And yet, he still felt accountable, responsible somehow for losing what had been entrusted to him. The lives of those who had followed him when he'd been called to war were forfeit. All gone. All drowned, save young Everand.

"I know this land. We are not lost," Henri finally assured the squire. He experienced a sharp stab of guilt that he had dragged this young man so far from his home in Sarcelles to fight against the English. And to a near watery grave when their ship sank off the coast of Portsmouth. Even so, the fourteen-year-old lengthened his short-legged stride to keep in step. Eager as a hound pup to please the master, even now. Henri shook his head at the earnestness of youth.

"You should rest, my lord. That wound of yours worries me." The squire did not mention that Henri had begun to stagger and show signs of weakening. Loyalty and compassion had been bred in this boy's bones, Henri thought. For that reason alone, he had chosen Everand Mercier, a deceased cloth merchant's youngest, to serve him. What a fine knight he would make one day, despite his size.

"There should be a settlement not far up the coast. We will bide there and send a message to my family," he told the boy.

"We have little coin left to hire anyone for that, my lord," Everand informed him. "Will it not involve their traveling near the width of Scotland?"

Henri halted and pulled the silver chain from around his neck. He also removed the ring he wore on his smallest finger, and shoved both pieces at the squire.

"If death takes me, use the chain and pay someone to cart us to Baincroft Castle in the Midlothian. The baron there, Lord Robert MacBain, will notify my father. He will have a care for your future."

To his credit, Everand did not argue or offer assurances that death was impossible. He knew better. He only nodded and asked, "What of your ring, my lord?"

Henri smiled and reached out to lay his hand upon the small, bony shoulder. "The ring is yours to keep. Tell Lord Robert and my father that I would call you my son."

Everand blushed and laughed with disbelief. "I, my lord? Look at me! I am as light as you are dark! That aside, they will never credit that you sired such a runt even if you were old enough at the time to have done so! Which you were not," he added wryly. "I doubt me you were even…tall enough at the time."

"*Tall* enough?" Henri chuckled in spite of himself, for his head had grown light as air. Ev could always draw a laugh from him, even in the darkest hour.

Though he knew the night was not yet near, the landscape seemed to darken and waver against the horizon. Henri sank to his knees and sat back on his heels. "Tell them, all the same. I claim you. Lord MacBain will accept this. He is a brother to me, yet we share no bond of blood."

"But, sir, you cannot mean to deceive your family into thinking I am your bastard," Ev argued.

"Of course not. Never think I would ask you to deny your legitimacy, Ev, or the good man who sired you. But I mean to adopt you here and now if you do not object to it. While you can never be heir to my title, you will inherit a portion of my personal wealth. You deserve that for all you have done for me."

"Then I thank you, sir. Though you are too generous."

Henri sucked in a pained breath. "I fear you were right on one issue, Ev. A rest might be in order." He grasped his side and felt the sticky wetness warm his palm. After days of this, he must be nearly bled out.

He gave what he felt could be his final order. "Go and find that village and fetch a cart for us, Ev. I will wait for you here."

Then Henri lay down on his good side and watched Everand's short legs pumping nearly knee to chest as he raced up the coast to seek help. When the lad became a speck in the distance, Henri muttered a brief prayer, closed his eyes and welcomed sleep. For however long it lasted.

"Begone from here and leave me be!" Intrigued as Iana was by the young fellow who had constantly bedeviled her for the past half hour, she was not inclined to hie herself off with him on some wild errand of mercy. She had been busy all day in preparation for leaving Whitethistle. There simply was no time for this.

She shifted the sling bearing the sleeping child to a less awkward position on her back, lowered the bucket into the well and waited for it to fill. If she washed their clothing now, it would dry before nightfall. They could leave the village before sunrise.

Pity for the young lad's plight prompted her to speak as she began tugging on the well rope to draw up the wash water. "I have heard there is a healer a league or so north of here. Get her to go with you."

"You *must* come," he insisted, impatiently shifting from one foot to the other. "Thus far you are the only person I have found who understands a word I say. Does your husband speak my language, too? I will explain our plight to him so he will let you come. He would be glad of the reward we offer, would he not?"

"I have no husband," she replied. "Nor do I have time to waste upon some wounded vagabond. Now, off with you." She picked up the bucket and turned to go.

"We are not mere wanderers, I swear. Sir Henri will die if I do not bring him help. Please!"

None in this godforsaken place spoke any French at all, that much was true, Iana granted. Even should this lad make himself understood, no one hereabout would trust him. Earnest as he seemed, what woman in her right mind would go blithely off down a deserted beach with him when he might have older friends waiting to ravish her or worse?

Yet she could see for herself that the boy was no beggar, nor did he look to be an outlaw seeking sport. His clothing, wrinkled and ruined as it was, possessed a richness foreign to these cottagers. His speech indicated a worthy education and his manner indicated gentility. She did not truly doubt he was what he declared, some knight's squire.

Iana set down the bucket again and faced him, hands on her hips. It troubled her to think she could save someone with a few moments of her time and a handful of herbs, when he might otherwise die. "How far away did you leave this fine master of yours?"

"Only a short distance," he assured her. He lied. She could see it in his eyes and rebuked him with her expression. "Very well, then," he amended, shamefaced, "I admit it is a good two hours' walk."

"Two *hours?*" Iana threw up her hand and rolled her eyes. "Why me? Why would you think I know aught of healing?"

He perched his hands on his skinny hips and struck a superior stance. "Most ladies are taught such, are they not? How else would they care for the people in their charge? Please, lady. I would not ask, but he is sorely injured and needs to be stitched. I will pay you well."

She eyed him shrewdly. "You call me *lady*. If you believe me that, why would you think I need your coin?"

The sandy-haired youth drew up to his full yet meager height and looked her up and down, judging. "Your demeanor and your speech betray your birth, even though you dress little better than a peasant," he observed.

He glanced around at the nearby cottages of daub and wattle. "And you live here. I would venture you have fallen upon hard times. Through no fault of your own, I am certain," he quickly added.

His last words disclosed his doubt of that, and he avoided looking at or mentioning the sleeping child. She had told him she had no husband. He probably thought she had disgraced herself with some man, and been cast out of her family for it. Not far off the mark concerning her station and her exile, she admitted, though he had the cause wrong.

"Sir Henri and I reward good deeds, I assure you," he said.

With a few coins of her own, she could more easily quit this cursed village where Newell had left her to stew in her rebellion. For days now, she had been thinking that anywhere short of hell would be preferable to Whitethistle. Though she had nowhere to go and no way to get there, she had been about to attempt it in her desperation.

She knew if she did not, she must give up wee Tam. Newell would never allow her to keep the bairn once he found out about her, and none of the villagers would take the poor babe. Surely God had sent this young man to provide the ready means for her escape.

"How much will you give me?" she asked, trying not to sound too eager.

The boy withdrew a finely worked silver chain from inside his salt-crusted doublet for her to inspect. "This," he offered regretfully. "It was to finance our journey east, but I suppose it will do us no good if Sir Henri dies from his hurt. Tend him and you may have it."

Her eyes grew wide at the richness he held. She could separate those links and easily support herself and Tam for months to come. As quickly as that, she decided. "We must return to my cottage first and gather my things. His wound is a cut, you say?"

Relief flooded the boy's eyes. "More like a gouge. Not terribly deep, so he tells me. We bound it up, but it has kept bleeding off and on for nigh a week now. Loss of blood and fever have weakened him, but it has no stink of decay." He winced. "Yet."

Iana nodded and led the way to her cottage. As luck would have it, none of the villagers were about. The men were busy fishing and the women preparing meals this time of day. Even the young ones had their chores. So much the better if no one noticed her leave with this young stranger.

It would take no time at all to collect her sewing implements and the few things she could not leave behind. Tam wakened as they entered, so Iana removed her from the sling and fed her the last of the bread and milk. She then set the child upon a small earthern pot. The lad made a hasty exit and waited outside.

"There, sweeting," she crooned. "There's my good Thomasina! Ah, you're a braw lass, are you not?" Iana took a few moments to clean the child all over with a cloth and the water she had just drawn, and dress her in a fresh linen gown.

The large brown eyes regarded her with such trust Iana felt tears form. She brushed her palm over Tam's dark, wispy curls. "No one will part us if I have aught to say to it," she assured her. "You have lost too much this past month, as have I. Now, here we go, love," Iana said as she set the pitifully thin foundling within the sling she had fashioned and wrestled it around to hang against her back. The burden had become a true comfort to Iana this past fortnight, a bit of warmth in her cold isolation.

The mother had died from a coughing sickness, pleading with her last breath that Iana take the child and help her survive. Little Tam had been near death herself, though from starvation rather than the illness that felled her mother.

Iana knew nothing about them other than the child's forename and that the mother had been forced to leave the village some months before. Iana had found the two in the woods while gathering herbs. None of the villagers would speak of the mother, and they shunned the child as though she were a leper.

Other than her light weight in the back sling, the babe was no trouble. She ate when food was offered, relieved herself when Iana helped her, and she never cried. Judging by the number of teeth she had, Tam must be near two years of age, though she looked only half that and she could not walk. The first night when Iana had lifted the babe in her arms, Tam had reached up one hand, touched Iana's cheek and uttered one faint mew like a kitten. Aye, Tam was hers now.

Iana looked up to see the boy reenter the cottage.

"Oats," she muttered briskly, grabbing up the draw-string sack that held her supply, "and usquebaugh." She handed the youth the jug to carry. The strong spirits would serve as well as any medicaments she could borrow from neighbors.

No one here had much use for the herbs Iana favored for treating wounds and sickness. They mostly relied on animal parts and old Druid remedies. The forest was full of better things. Iana added what she thought she'd need to her sack. The old healer at Ochney had been a good teacher. Iana only wished she had been able to remain there past her girlhood to learn more from her.

She bundled the few clothes she owned inside her shawl and knotted the ends together. Once she had sewn this knight's wound, she would set out immediately for Ayr, the nearest good-sized port. A few silver links from the chain she had accepted from the young squire would gain her passage on the first ship leaving Scotland. Mayhaps to the Isle of Eire. She had heard that it was beautiful there and the folk a friendly lot.

Iana cared not where fate took her so long as it was away from here. If her brother found that this exile of hers had not taught her a lesson and changed her mind about wedding Douglas Sturrock, Iana did not doubt he would resort to much stronger measures. He had warned he did not wish to beat her into compliance. Little did he know what scant effect that would have. As if beating her once would make her accept a lifetime of beatings. Toads had more brains than Newell. The things his wife had told Iana about him indicated he had become nigh as dastardly as her own husband had been. Iana could scarcely believe it of her brother, but his own actions lent truth to Dorothea's words.

Becoming wife to Sturrock offered about as much promise as had her first marriage. Iana might survive it if Newell forced the match, but wee Tam would not. The defenseless orphan would be left alone here to die. Now Iana had a way to avoid that, a definite chance of successfully saving them both.

The thought of that sped her steps so that the lad had to scurry to keep up.

"There was a battle at Portsmouth, you say?" she asked out of curiosity. "Have you French already invaded England? Where is this city?"

"The southern coast, lady. We had fired the place and were away home when the ship began taking on water. We signaled the nearest of our vessels, but she did not respond. Before we knew what was happening, we listed sharply and many went over the side. Then she sank like a stone."

He paused, took a deep breath and then continued, "Sir Henri was injured by a broken spar. He fell against it as he released the barrels tied on the deck. We thought everyone might use those to float, though we saw no one else doing so. We believe all thirty souls perished, save ourselves."

Iana shook her head and clicked her tongue in sympathy. She had no political leanings whatsoever, but it seemed a shame so many should die in any cause. Scotland had always sided with the French, of course. Her own King David had sought asylum in France the past few years while Bailliol, friend to the English king, had usurped Scotland's crown.

Here in the west country, it mattered little who ruled. Life went on the same as ever. But she would break away from here before the day was out and make her own way in the world.

No one at Ochney Castle would know where she went. Newell would come in three days to ask whether she was ready to surrender her will in the marriage matter. The thought of him discovering her mysterious disappearance made her smile with satisfaction.

They had trudged along for some time when the boy, Everand, suddenly passed her at a run. "There! There he lies! Come quickly, lady. Hurry!"

She watched him drop beside his master and tenderly lift the man's head upon his knees, cradling the face as though feeling for fever. Soon she stood directly over the two and looked down upon the man she was to care for.

Not an old man, as she had imagined. She guessed him to be thirty years, mayhaps a few past that, but not many. He was a large fellow and darkly handsome. Blood loss accounted for the sickly pallor of his skin beneath the short, thick beard. Sand coated one side of the long dark locks that must reach his shoulders when he stood upright. He was unconscious, maybe even dead already.

"Move out of the way," she instructed the squire as she knelt. Carefully, she untied the sling and set the baby behind her on the sand. To the boy, she ordered, "Mind the child for me if you wish me to do this."

Iana tugged aside the blood-soaked clothing and began to pull loose the wrappings around the man's midsection.

"God have mercy," she muttered when she saw the angry wound. She spoke to the lad again. "Gather some wood and build a fire. It looks as if we shall be here for a while." Though she knew it would be wiser to leave within the hour, Iana could not bring herself to desert this knight or to rush his care.

He opened his eyes, but she could see that he did not focus well. Fever, she guessed.

"Take the boy to Baincroft. Anything you want," he mumbled in her own language.

"And leave you here like this?" she asked wryly. "I do not think your little man would allow it."

He blinked hard and his lips lifted in either a pained smile or a grimace. "No, I suppose not," he mumbled. His accent proved faint, but there was no mistaking he was French. "Then I thank you for...helping." His eyes drifted shut.

Iana uttered a mirthless laugh. "You might want to delay that gratitude, sir. I am about to deal you more pain than you already bear."

When the boy returned with the dry deadwood, she found her flint and tow to make the fire. When she'd accomplished that, she fished a small metal bowl from her belongings and handed it to the squire. "Fill this with seawater." Then she sat back to wait, snuggling the silent Tam against her side.

Henri struggled to hold his gaze on the woman's face as she worked upon him. Efficient as a moneylender counting coins, he thought, while she removed his tunic and bathed his body in the seawater Ev had fetched for her.

The sting of the cleansing troubled him little more than the constant throbbing pain he had endured for days. When she glanced worriedly at his face, he summoned a smile, knowing she would think him brave and stoic. His small deception pleased him, having a lovely woman believe him so. In truth, he was half-dead already and quite well used to the agony of dying. He would make a good end of it. Not one whimper.

She lifted a small container to pour some liquid over his wound. The excruciating fire of it tore a groan from his throat.

"Felt that, did you?" she asked. "It will get worse."

He clenched his teeth to trap the blasphemy that almost escaped. As reassurances went, hers was not welcome.

She put the jug of that same liquid to his lips and bade him drink deeply. He did so more than once, immediately realizing that it was the Scots' famous water of life. It burned his throat as viciously as it had his wound. He'd had this stuff before and knew a blessed numbness would follow, a drunkenness from which he might never wake.

"'Twill take a few moments to work upon your senses," she told him. Then she set the jug aside and took out a needle the length of his smallest finger. To the eye of it, she guided a full ell of thread.

"By the saints," he muttered. "You'd sew me with pikestaff and rope?"

"Aye, and glad of it you'll be," she said, adding ruefully, "but not right soon."

The languor offered by the spirits began to envelop him in its warm cocoon. The sun was setting now. He could see the last rays of it dancing across the waves. Idly, he wondered if he would ever see it rise again. No matter. "Have your way then, madam."

His eyes closed of their own accord, though he'd faintly hoped to expire while gazing upon her striking features. He forced them open again to see whether he had imagined her beauty. She looked the same.

Strange to find such a one here in the hinterlands. Though he had seen a good portion of Scotland in his day, he had never come this far to the west. For some reason he had imagined there would be only tall, ruddy maids with wild, matted locks and thick, sturdy limbs.

Unruly Viking stock combined with the fierce warring spirit of the Old Ones.

Not this woman. She appeared almost delicate, her movements graceful as those of a nimble hart. Her skin brought to mind fresh cream reflecting firelight. Sparks glinted in the depths of her sin-dark eyes each time her gaze caught his own. If only he could see her hair. Smooth, silken and long enough to reach her waist, he imagined, though she had it properly covered so that he could not even guess its true color. Dark, he thought, because her brows were. How he would love to see her hair, run his fingers through its smoothness. Oh well, he supposed he would soon be past pleasures of the flesh.

He turned his head slightly, and there was Ev, sitting cross-legged beside the fire. In his lap sat a small, thin, ethereal creature with eyes the size of walnuts, peering at him curiously. A child? Where had it come from?

It looked unreal, its eyes old, its mouth frowning, its body nearly wasted away. The sight of it made him want to curl an arm around it and shelter it. As though he had sent that silent message to his squire, Everand did so in his stead. The boy's act comforted Henri as nothing else could have done at that moment. A fine knight Ev would make one day, he thought yet again.

Henri looked back to the woman, wondering whether he had conjured up both these strangers. The fever fogged his brain, he decided, giving him visions of both hope and despair. The one of hope seemed more real to him, definitely healthier, and he clung to her winsome visage.

He allowed his lids to drop once more, content to hold her image for as long as his mind worked. Drifting into permanent oblivion, entertained by such a vision, possessed great appeal.

Suddenly he jerked and howled, "God's *nails!*"

She quickly flinched away from his upraised arm, the needle held aloft in front of her. "You must hold still!" she said firmly.

He followed the taut line of thread and saw it attached to the raw edge of his skin. If he was not dying already, she would surely kill him on the spot.

"I shall hold him down," he heard Everand say in a deep voice, as though he were a man full grown and oak sturdy.

Henri almost laughed aloud at the idea of small Ev rendering him immobile. Instead, he upended the jug and downed the remainder of the strong brew that promised surcease from his torture. He was already drunk, but not drunk enough.

"Go to," he gasped to the healer. "Everand will restrain me. He has more strength than his size allows."

Henri knew he must lie still and bear it without moving, or else Ev would lose face. At least one of them should retain some dignity before their lovely benefactress, and Henri knew he had already forfeited his own.

At long last, she announced, "There, 'tis done."

Henri tasted blood in his mouth where he had bitten the inside of his cheek. He turned his head and spat as soon as Ev released his arms.

Again, he spied that child of the ether, the one he had imagined before. It sat upon the sand, silently sucking upon one finger, those large, hopelessly sad eyes trained upon him still, weeping inwardly without sound or tears. Was it a shade awaiting the release of his soul?

Never in his life had he wished to faint. Now certainly would be an excellent time for it. Talons of fire gripped him like the sharp, unrelenting claw of a dragon.

The woman pressed a cool, wet cloth to his face and moved it gently as she spoke. "You must sleep now. I shall return anon with a litter and remove you to a place of shelter. Likely 'twill rain before morn.''

"Will I live?" he asked, doubting even she could save anyone so damaged and untended for days. The fever had caught up with him two days ago and raged worse as the hours passed. Now it had him seeing ghost children and thinking death might be welcome, after all.

She did not hesitate in answering him honestly. "Anything is possible. I have done all that I can do. The rest is up to you and God."

Henri reached for her hand, grasping the long, slender fingers as tightly as he could. "You will not leave us then?"

Indecision marred her brow, then vanished, to leave a look of resignation. "Nay, I will not. Your lad promised me the silver chain in return for my care of you."

"Alive or dead. That was to be the offer," Henri bargained, hearing his own words slur. "You will see me to my brother's home…either way." When she looked as if she might object, he added, "It is too much silver for so few stitches and a meager taste of spirits. Be fair."

For a time she considered his words, then she nodded, replaced her implements within their sack and pulled the cord tight to close it. "If you live, I will tend you until you can do for yourself. If you do not recover, I shall wrap you, pack you in clay and transport you to the place you wish to go. Your squire will show me the way, aye?"

Henri heard Ev's sound of protest and turned to him, though he also spoke for the woman's information. "Go east and cross the Firth of Clyde. After you pass the hills on the far side, ask directions either to Baincroft or the castle of Trouville."

"So be it," she declared, then pulled her hand from his, rose and turned away.

"A moment more, madam," Henri rasped. "I would know your name."

She looked over her shoulder and, after a brief hesitation, told him. "Iana...of Ayr."

"A free woman?" he demanded gruffly, though he would not retract the offer even if she were not. He only needed to know whether they would be followed by some irate laird intent on recapturing his comely healer.

"Free?" she asked, puzzled, as if the word were foreign to her. A light dawned in her eyes, even as he watched. "Aye, I am that," she said then, "free as a lark. And I fully intend to stay so for as long as I live. I shall see you to this place called Baincroft, and your family will reward me by giving me work to do."

Trusting that Everand would be in capable hands, Henri surrendered to his fevered dreams.

Chapter Two

Iana instructed the boy to mind Tam for her, and hurried away into the night. She had warned him that his master's fate rested upon how well he minded the child. His lack of reluctance for the task surprised her and made her feel guilty for the untruth. She hated lying.

It was no lie she had told the knight, however, saying that she was free. This heaven-sent bargain of his had granted her that freedom. He did not need to know how *long* she had considered herself unfettered, now did he?

Iana felt fairly certain she could keep him alive, and devoutly hoped she would succeed in doing so. The wound was not deep, nor had it festered. However, the loss of blood or fever might well take him yet, unless she dosed him heavily with herbs and kept him warm and dry for several days before attempting to travel.

It certainly would be more advantageous for her if she did not arrive at his brother's home with a dead body. Besides that, she rather liked the lad, Everand, who doted on his master and was kind to Tam. Iana did not want to see him grieve.

Taking the man to her cottage at the edge of the village was not possible. He might be discovered there. If it became known that she entertained a man within her temporary home, her brother would likely do more than beat her when he found out. And if they remained there until the knight was fit to travel, it would be time for Newell to come for her answer. They had but three days to get well away.

'Twould be best if they repaired to a nearby cave. She knew of one that would suffice. It was where she had planned to go with Tam and hide from her brother until he gave up searching. Getting the knight there would be the problem. He could not walk and she had no beast for him to ride. Her only recourse was to obtain one somehow.

Or why not three? She'd pay no more dearly for them than for a single animal if she were caught. Hanged was hanged. Besides, she did not fancy trudging the breadth of Scotland with Tam on her back, dragging the knight on a litter with only the help of a lad.

The nearest village to Whitethistle stood at least two leagues distant. She knew it well, for it rested upon the estate of her dead husband, the demented old lout who had never given her anything before he died other than two years of abject misery.

His family had taken all of her jewelry from her and kept her dowry as well, so surely his cursed sons by his first wife owed Iana something for enduring their father without complaint. There should be at least three mounts enclosed in a stable somewhere thereabout.

Iana lifted her skirts and quickened her pace. If she was to become a reiver tonight, then she had best be about the business of it before good sense took hold.

Henri opened his eyes to total darkness. There were no stars above him. No moon. Nothing. For a moment, he believed death had claimed all but his awareness and the ever-present pain. He sensed he was enclosed somehow, not out in the open. Then he heard Everand's almost inaudible snoring nearby, interspersed with the distant, soft whuffle of a horse. Was this a stable?

"Ev?" he whispered.

A cool hand brushed his brow. *The woman.* He drew in her scent, that of sweet grasses and the underlying essence that marked her gender. "Where are we?" he asked.

"In a cave," she answered, her voice dulcet and comforting. She placed something to his lips. "Chew upon this. It will aid your rest and cool your fever."

He accepted it and tasted green bark. Foul stuff, but given that she had sewn him up and rescued him from the elements, he granted her that modicum of trust. Henri chewed for a few moments, then removed the bitter residue from his mouth.

"We leave here come morning," he told her.

"So eager," she commented with a soft laugh. "I fear it will be at least another day before you are well enough to ride, good sir."

"I have sailed the entire length of England in worse condition. I daresay a few days on horseback will not prove any more life-threatening."

"As you will, then," she replied softly. "But now you must sleep, sir."

"Henri," he whispered, groping about for her hand until he found it and threaded his fingers through hers. It helped to feel grounded here in this dark place, so he would not go flying off into the beyond. The feeling of hanging suspended in purgatory when he'd awakened must have affected him more than he realized. "My name is Henri."

He realized he must be more fevered than he thought, to invite this informality with a woman. Even his mistresses did not address him so, and he had never before encouraged such a thing. However, she thought him but a simple knight, apparently. That made sense, for when they had set out upon their voyage, he had instructed Everand not to call him "lord." Most of the time Henri preferred the simplicity of being a knight among other knights, instead of the heir to the Trouville dynasty. It afforded him more friendship and camaraderie. He definitely wished a friendship with this woman, he thought with an inner smile.

"I am Iana," she said.

"I remember. *Iana*," he added, for no reason but to say it, tasting her name on his tongue. Like honey, it sweetened the bitter taste of the bark. "Your father is called Ian, I would wager."

"My grandfather," she replied. He could hear the smile in her voice.

"I know an Ian," he told her idly, his words slurring as his mind grew heavy with fatigue. "A rogue, he is."

Again, she laughed, a mere flutter of sound that soothed him immeasurably. "Rest now...Henri," she advised softly.

The sharpness of his aches had subsided. The coolness of her palm seemed to draw the heat from him. "Magic," he commented, smiling into the dark.

He listened, imagining he could hear her heart beating a steady rhythm, or mayhaps it was his own. A horse whuffled again and Ev made a sleepy sound of protest, likely in response to a dream. For the first time in weeks, Henri felt safe enough and well enough that he could willingly embrace sleep without thinking of death.

* * *

"These are *your* horses, lady?" Everand demanded. He stroked the neck of the smallest mount, a mare who tended to nip.

She shrugged. "They are now."

He grinned impishly, showing fine white teeth and dimples. "You stole them, did you not? I knew it last night when you returned after so many hours. Did you kill someone for them?"

"Of course," she said, then wrinkled her nose at him in jest. Iana held tightly to the rope attached to the large cob, allowing only enough slack for the horse to bend its neck and drink from the stream. "In truth, I left a link of the silver for payment."

With her free hand, she patted the knight's chain, coiled within the sack attached to her belt, and took pleasure in the clinking. "When the moment arrived to take the beasts, I found I could not become a thief."

"Aha," he acknowledged with a sage expression. "An honorable soul. I *do* admire that in a woman."

The lad's sudden transformations from child to jaded gentleman and back again amused Iana. 'Twas hard not to laugh at his pretentiousness. "How old are you, Everand?"

"Fourteen summers. And you, lady?"

She did laugh then, but answered him honestly. "You should not ask such of a woman. I am two and twenty."

He looked aghast. "I swear by the saints, I would have guessed not more than ten and seven. How well you wear your years!"

Iana could not contain her mirth. "An accomplished flatterer. I *do* admire that in a man," she declared, giving him back his compliment. "Now come, we must get these mounts back inside that cave ere someone happens along and sees us with them. I should not enjoy swinging from a gibbet!''

"But you paid more than their worth," he argued. "What is to fear?''

She turned to lead the cob and the roan back to their hiding place. "Aye, but I did not strike a deal with their owners. It may be they were not willing to sell. Now hurry along, your master will be waking soon and wonder where we are.''

Everand paused to fill the wooden bucket Iana had appropriated from the stables where she gleaned the horses. Hauling that with one hand and leading the mare with the other, he followed her.

"Two and twenty, eh? You said you have no husband. Have you never wished to marry, lady?'' he asked as they walked. Though he had had the care of Tam the night before, he still avoided mentioning the existence of the child, who now lay nestled against Iana's back.

"No, I never wished to wed, but I did so all the same,'' she answered curtly, unwilling to lie to the boy, but also disinclined to share her tale of woe. If he and his master knew the entire story and the plans her brother now had for her, they might well leave her behind to avoid trouble. "My husband perished last year, and I will speak no more of him.''

"Aha,'' the lad said, "so this is how you became impoverished. Poor lady. You should marry again, this time to one who would have a care to provide for your future. And that of your child,'' he added, commenting for the first time on Tam's presence. Iana supposed the fact that he now thought the bairn had a father made her acceptable enough to mention.

"'Tis none of your affair,'' she snapped. "Be silent ere I box your ears.''

"Ooh, a woman with pluck," he crooned in that too-adult voice of his. "I also like *that* about you."

The impudent little nodcock. Iana was still shaking her head when they arrived back at the cave.

She had chosen well their place of concealment. The hollow extended deeply into the side of the hill, its opening a crevice barely wide enough to squeeze the mounts through. The interior widened to a cavity nearly the size of her small cottage, offering plenty of room to house the horses. Through another narrow passage there lay a chamber half the size of the first, but still adequate for her, Tam, the lad and his master to sleep without crowding each other.

She had dared not build a fire inside. If there existed an opening for the smoke to waft out, it might be spotted. If not, they would surely choke on it.

The only light within their sleeping chamber was a small oil lamp that she had brought from the cottage. How she would replace the oil when it burned away, Iana did not know. She had left it burning, half-full, so that the knight—Henri, she recalled—would not awaken in darkness while they were gone.

"Water, berries and dry oats," she announced to Everand and the man, who had dragged himself up to sit against the wall of the cave. "That must do for today."

The knight's gaze immediately locked upon Tam, whom Iana could feel peeking over her right shoulder. He said nothing about the child, but looked somehow relieved and puzzled and disappointed all at once. Shifting slightly, she felt Tam curl into a ball against her back, hiding herself.

"Why can we not buy food?" the squire demanded, plopping down beside his liege. "You have the silver. Your village is nearby."

Iana sighed. How could she explain why they must remain hidden without giving them the real reasons? If she were indeed a free woman, what was to stop her from adequately provisioning them for the trip and setting out upon it without this subterfuge?

The knight's bargain was that she deliver him to Baincroft in return for the silver. If they did not want to trouble themselves with a runaway lady whose brother might be offended enough to punish them if they were caught together, she would be forced to relinquish what was left of the valuable chain, and remain behind. Newell surely would find her then, she would be wed and Tam would likely die when taken away from her.

Iana busied herself apportioning the food as she considered whether she should lie. She could sell the horses and go her own way. But no doubt the owners would be looking for them, expecting the one who took them to try to sell or barter them somewhere. Women did not make such trades or sales. She would be conspicuous, and therefore remembered.

Newell would track her that way as surely as if she left a trail apurpose. No, she must remain with this knight and squire, travel with them for her own protection, and do so in secret. Her brother would be searching for a woman alone.

They both watched her, waiting for her to answer. A half-truth, then, she decided, a play upon their knightly inclinations to protect the weak.

"There is this cruel man who wishes me to marry. If I simply disappear, mayhaps he will forget I exist. However, if he hears that I have acquired silver, the greedy fool might chase me to the ends of the earth." Her brother might do that anyway.

And Douglas Sturrock might, as well. She still did not

know what Newell had promised the man to make him consider the match. Her youth and beauty were gone now, and Duncan had left her nothing, not even her dower lands.

Neither knight nor squire said a word. They merely watched her as though waiting for her to continue.

"This is why I brought you here instead of to my cottage," she added. "This man would see your presence there as a challenge. I do not wish to be taken by force and made wife to a man who would mistreat me and this child. Nor would I wish you harmed on my account. So we must hide."

The one called Henri stirred slightly, resetting to make himself more comfortable, she supposed. His measured words surprised her. "This fellow you speak of has not forced you to it yet. And I know the law here prevents wedding a woman against her will."

"Aye, true enough," she replied. "But there are many ways to bend one's will, especially a woman's."

"Some men are not kind to their wives, that is true." He seemed to consider that before he asked, "But why would you worry for the child? Surely this man would not risk the wrath of your husband's family by harming it. A clan war is nothing to court, so I understand."

"The child is not of my husband," she answered, offering no explanation.

"Ah, I see." He cleared his throat and seemed at a loss for words after that.

The boy spoke instead. "Whose child is she?"

Iana pressed her lips together and looked away. Then she declared defiantly, "Thomasina is mine."

"What would you have done had we not arrived and given you means to hie yourself away?" the knight asked her.

There was a very good question. Iana shrugged and grimaced. "Eventually surrender, I suppose."

The lad laughed gleefully and slapped his upraised knee. "Ha! When the snakes return to Eire."

"What mean you by that, Ev?" the knight demanded.

Everand turned to his master and explained in a condescending voice as he shoved his upraised palm in her direction. "Here stands a woman who has buried one husband, endured living in a hovel among peasants, and breached propriety by sleeping in the wild with two men. She also stole away three mounts from sleeping villagers. You believe such a brave spirit would lie down for some sluggard without stones enough to have taken her already?" He crossed his skinny arms over his chest and tossed her a wink, then added sagely, "I think not."

Iana saw the knight bite back a smile. "Two *men* in the wild?" he repeated. "I would say that alone qualifies her as most daring. As you say, it appears she has spirit. Now eat your berries, Ev, and govern that mind and tongue of yours."

The lad readily obeyed, wearing the smug expression of one who had divined all the answers necessary when no one else present was wise enough to do so.

"You seem much better, sir," Iana observed, desperate to change the topic of their discussion. "How fares the wound?"

He lightly touched the wrapping, which remained free of new blood. "Painful, but healing, no doubt. I feel much stronger after sleeping for so long. Again, I thank you for your care and for agreeing to accompany us."

She measured out the oats into her metal pan and added water to soak them soft. "I shall need more than the silver as reward for tending you on your journey," she dared tell him.

His narrowed eyes warned her against greed, though she did not think what she would ask counted as that.

"I will require employment in this new place. You must speak for my skills with this lord of Baincroft who is your brother."

"In all truth, we have no blood tie, save that we share a half sister. Our widowed parents wed when we were but lads. So we have a bond forged early that is as unbreakable as true kinship. Robert will make a home for you and the babe at Baincroft if that is your wish."

If they could only reach the other side of Scotland, all would be well, Iana thought. Newell would never think to look for her so far afield. But the chain's rich links would not last forever. "I must have your promise of this work, sir, for I shall have no other means of income once the silver you gave me has been used up."

He looked offended that she would demand his word. "I give you my vow that I will ask my brother to make a place for you. However, he might already have a healer in residence. If so, I do swear that I will provide for you myself."

"For what services?" she asked, sorely afraid she could guess. His brother was a lord, which meant he must be the younger, making his way as best he could fighting for the French. Such a one would not hand out his hard-earned coin in charity any more than she would whore for it.

Everand growled a suggestive chuckle. Apparently, the thought of her working on her back had occurred to him as well, but the knight's hand on the lad's arm cut short whatever he might have said.

"Whatever services you choose to bestow," Sir Henri answered. "Have I offered by any look, word or deed to besmirch your honor?"

Iana would not be put off by his lofty indignation. Men, noble or ignoble, were not to be trusted. "Nay, I'll grant that *you* have not."

She flicked an accusing glance toward Everand, who certainly *had* done so. He had the grace to lower his impudent gaze as she continued, "However, you are in no shape to offer me insult at the moment. How am I to know what you might expect of me once you are hale? I should make clear at the outset that I will be beholden to no man, be he gentleman or rogue. Find me work, sir, of an honest nature or I shall be obliged to call you knave to all, and 'twill be your fine honor besmirched, not my own!"

She immediately saw she had pricked his anger to a rolling boil, damn her quick tongue. Now he would want to be quit of her for certain. Desperate, she attempted to sweeten his temper. "I beg you do not take offense, sir...Henri. A woman with no defender must needs use what means she has to enforce—"

"Cease this foolish prattle!" he barked. "I have no designs upon your person, lady. And I can see you *are* a lady. Or *were* at one time. Rest assured, you have nothing to fear from me."

"And the cub?" She nodded toward Everand. The lad's fair head jerked up, and he glared at her in disbelief that she would even think to fear his advances. Or mayhaps he was simply offended that she had called him cub.

She noted the quiver of Henri's lips, as though he had squelched a sudden burst of laughter. In an instant, he had schooled his features into a mask of solemnity. "Everand will not offer you abuse. My son does as I bid him do."

"*Son?*" she and Everand asked in unison.

"Son," Henri repeated, looking directly at the lad. "I

have told you I would call you mine. You wear my signet. Why do you question me?''

''Well, you are not going to die now.'' The lad's voice
cracked, betraying his uncertainty.

''So much the better. You'll not be orphaned twice in
the space of a year.''

Evarand cleared his throat and sat straighter, twisting
the gold signet ring he wore on his middle finger. ''I am
unused to it is all. My apologies, sir…Father.''

''Accepted. Now give this lady your promise to protect
her body and her virtue, so she will not suspect you of
plotting evil deeds against her.''

Everand turned to Iana and scrambled up so that he
knelt before her. ''I so promise. You have naught to fear,
lady.''

''My eternal gratitude, Everand,'' she replied formally,
struck by the silliness of his gesture. He was so small,
she could flatten him with a slap if he dared to touch her,
which she was certain he would never do in any case.

''That's settled then,'' Everand announced, scooting
back to sit beside Sir Henri. The lad shrugged and
grabbed another handful of the berries as he added in a
deep, gravelly voice, ''I never care to sport with unwilling wenches, anyway.''

Henri collapsed in a fit of coughing and Iana laughed
outright. Everand chewed his berries and smiled.

It boded well, she thought, that fate had sent her these
two. In truth, she had no fear of the knight. She could
outrun him easily in his condition, and probably even
after he had recovered. He was of such tall stature, she
doubted he would prove very agile. The lad, she liked
immensely, impertinent as he was. He was scarcely old
enough or big enough to offer any true threat.

Though she admittedly found Henri handsome and

possessed of a quick wit, Iana had no intention of granting him any favors, now or in future.

That devil's minion, James Duncan, had soundly cured her of wishing to cohabit with a man for any reason, be it lawful matrimony or otherwise.

Now there was no need to worry. She had decided. She was free forever of any man's will.

Chapter Three

Henri spent the afternoon alternately testing his strength and resting from the effort. His fever had abated that morning, only to return at nightfall.

The lady Iana did not seem overly concerned about that, but still dosed him as she had the night before.

Though he had many questions about her life in the village and why she was there, he did not ask them. Nor did he demand to know the paternity of the child. If it were her bastard, that would explain why she had lost favor with her own family and that of her dead husband. That certainly would be cause for her banishment and her mean existence. Henri did not want to know of it, he told himself. He did not wish to think of her as less than a lady.

She had saved him and he owed her his kind regard, despite anything dishonorable she might have done.

He could not fault her care of him in any way, for she was most solicitous. At times, too much so to suit him.

"I detest this bark," he complained, popping a piece into his mouth when she insisted.

"Willow cools you and also reduces pain," Iana explained. "I do swear 'tis nothing short of wondrous how quickly you are mending."

He had to admit he felt better than he had since the ship sank. "What else have you to make me well again?"

"Tomorrow I hope to find yarrow to ease the soreness." She handed him a wooden cup filled with water. "Drink this when you've finished with the bark. Then go to sleep."

"Must I sleep, too?" Everand asked plaintively. "I'm not wounded."

Iana smiled at him. "Aye, if we are to get an early start, we should all have plenty of rest."

Well before dawn they emerged from the cave into the dewy darkness and began their journey. Henri ignored the stinging pains in his side, made worse by the slow rocking motion of the wide-backed bay that carried him.

Lady Iana had advised them to travel silently, but he saw no point in it. No one would be about this time of morning. Those with any sense at all would still be sleeping.

The waning moon barely gave off enough light to keep them from riding straight into the tree trunks. Soon it would be gone altogether in that darkest hour before the sun rose. Then, he supposed, they must ride with their hands before their faces to avoid low-hanging limbs.

"Do you think her suitor will give chase when he finds her gone?" Ev whispered from behind him. "We are hardly armed for a fight."

Henri turned slightly to answer. "Very likely he will follow. In his place, I would. She is a comely woman."

Everand's soft, knowing chuckle made him smile. The boy had only recently shown any interest in females, but when the notion that he liked them struck, it had done so with the force of a battle-ax.

"What are we to do if that happens?" he asked Henri.

"Stand against him. Give her time to flee with the babe. I have my dagger and you have yours."

Everand scoffed. "Mine is hardly larger than a paltry eating knife."

"And you well know how to use it, not only at table," Henri reminded in a chastising tone. "A blade is a blade, Ev. Remember your training."

"Silence!" The order came from the lady. "You'll be heard from here to the coast."

Had she been listening when he'd called her comely? Henri wondered. She was that and more. Aside from that beauty, he had to admire her strength of purpose. For a woman, she certainly had proved resourceful. Left alone to fend for herself and that poor mite of a child, she seemed to seize every opportunity. Henri was happy he had provided one for her. He much feared what could have happened if she had continued to live there unprotected. Of course, he planned to see that she had what she needed to live comfortably after this.

He had her to thank for his life. Surely he would have died if she had not agreed to help and had not stopped his wound's bleeding. Even then, he might well have perished from this cursed fever had she not found a place of shelter and fed him that thrice-damned bark.

Who was she, really? Highborn, he strongly suspected. No peasants, few free men and almost none of their women should be able to speak such excellent French. She had been tutored by someone, and none too briefly, at that.

Her frequently imperious manner indicated she had once held a position of some power, one important enough so that she fully expected to be obeyed when she issued an order. That supported her tale of the dead husband, a noble one with a household for her to direct.

Then again, she might have been a player or singer, one of a troupe of jongleurs who had only observed the behavior of nobles and thought to copy it. They traveled much, which could explain her French. Surely that had not been her lot of late, with a babe in tow. Of course, she might have been some lord's leman who had acquired these attributes from her generous lover, got with child and been cast off by him.

Henri realized he might never know the truth about her, for he surely owed her the right to keep her secrets after all she had done for him. Yet curiosity bedeviled him as they rode for what seemed hours on end.

He had not been on horseback for several months, having spent that time at sea. Aside from the increasing discomfort of his wound, muscles unused for that while screamed in protest of the long hours riding bareback.

Soon he did not care who Iana was or what untruths she might have fed him. All he wanted was for her to cry off this journey for a while, so he would not need to ask for mercy. He had little pride left as it was.

The tantalizing burble of the stream they had followed since they'd left the cave beckoned powerfully. How good it would feel to lie down and wallow in the coolness of it. He had yet to wash the sea salt from his body and his clothing.

"We must rest and water the mounts," he declared when he could bear it no longer.

She turned with a look of concern and immediately reined in. "Are you bleeding?"

Henri almost lied, certain it would be worth it to rip open his wound if that was what it took to get him off the horse. "No," he snapped, as he leaned forward, slid one leg over the bay's back and quickly dismounted before she could object. He grabbed on to the mane when his traitorous legs buckled beneath him.

He noted with satisfaction that she had a similar problem. Though she obviously knew how to ride—another clue that she was no underling—it was clear that Iana had not sat a horse lately for any length of time.

"You should have stolen saddles as well," he told her, softening the rebuke with a forced grin.

Ev hurried forward and took the reins of Henri's bay. "At least she managed to bring the tack, sir," he declared in defense of her. "We might have had to make do with ropes of braided grass."

"This way," she ordered, dismissing Henri's complaints as unimportant. Limping a bit, likely due to the weight of the babe, she led her roan mare through the trees to a very small clearing beside the shallow stream. "We shall rest here for a short while."

What was her bloody hurry? Another mystery to solve. If the man who wished her hand in marriage—if such a one truly existed—were persistent enough to trail after her, he would still need time to discover that she was missing. She had been gone only one night and half a day.

Henri looked up through the trees. It was just before midday. "We should wait until the sun is not directly overhead," he advised, "else we could err in our direction."

"Oh? Very well," she agreed reluctantly. "Sit. I will portion out our food."

She untied the cloth from around her shoulders and set the child upon the grass. It did not move, like a fawn protecting itself by its immobility.

Henri observed it closely for some moments, reluctantly meeting the wary brown gaze it fastened upon him. He offered his finger to grasp. "Have you a name?" he asked softly.

"Her name is Thomasina. Tam," Lady Iana informed him. "She does not speak."

"Is she ill?" he asked, quite concerned about the too slender limbs and protruding belly. Even the child's dark hair grew in thin and wisplike. "Does she eat well?"

A sharp "aye" was the only answer he got as Iana busied herself with the victuals. What did that mean? he wondered. Aye, she was ill, or aye, she ate well?

"So, Tam," he said softly, offering her his hand, palm up. "What a gentle sprite you are." The baby ignored his overture, but her lips parted as if she would utter something. Then she suddenly ducked her head and stuck her finger in her mouth.

He liked babies, though he had seen few of them since his sister was born some sixteen years ago. Alys had been nothing like this one. As he recalled, it had required three nurses, taking shifts on guard, to keep that rapscallion confined to the keep. He could still remember her ear-splitting screeches when things did not go her way. The memory made him smile.

Iana shoved his share of the food toward him, cupped in a large leaf.

Oats and berries again, fewer than last eve, he noticed. "Suppose I catch some fish," he offered.

"With what?" she asked curtly. "And if you managed that miracle, should we eat them raw? We cannot risk a fire to cook them."

"Why not?" Ev queried before Henri could form the same words.

"Because...because someone might see and come to

inquire who we are and why we are here. I did take these horses. We would all be hanged for thieves if the owners did not find, or else chose not to accept, the silver I left them in exchange.''

Henri knew that was not the real reason. She truly feared someone else was coming after them. ''I shall deal with your erstwhile suitor if he troubles you,'' he assured her.

She laughed and rolled her eyes, clearly not trusting that possibility. He could not recall a time when anyone doubted his prowess. That stung, especially in light of his recent loss of dignity before this woman.

Henri withdrew the long, wicked dagger from his soft leather boot and raised one brow. *Question that, if you will,* he dared silently.

''No man wields a short blade better, lady,'' Ev told her.

Iana paled at the sight of it. Many had done so before her, for different and more urgent reasons.

Once she recovered, however, she warned him. ''Even that weapon would not be proof against his sword. He wields it well...so I am told.''

Sword? Then this man who might come after her was knight or noble for certain. This did not surprise him. ''I have yet to taste defeat at any man's hand,'' he declared. *Only at the hand of the elements, the sea,* he mutely added, the thought neatly dashing his pride. He replaced the knife in his boot.

For a time, he looked away from her and across the brook, seeing nothing, his mind on the men who had died in service to him. A small comforting warmth nestled softly against his left hip. The tickle of small fingers touched his hand where it rested against his thigh.

''Tam?'' he whispered, and looked down. When he

glanced at her mother to see whether she minded, he did not miss the unshed tears in her eyes. Yet she was smiling. It made no sense, but then nothing much had since he had set sail from France.

After a while, Iana reached for the baby and settled her on her skirts. He watched the feeding as if they were two strange creatures he had come upon in the wild.

"How anyone can enjoy that is a true source of amazement," Henri commented when Tam had finished eating. He poked at his portion of the food. "I hate oats," he muttered, staring at the offensive handful of grain. "It is the one thing about Scotland I truly abhor. *Everyone* eats oats. Munching them dry makes me feel like neighing and stamping my feet."

To his surprise, Iana laughed, charming him unexpectedly with the sound and sight. "Do as I did. Add water," she advised, inclining her head toward the brook.

He frowned down at the grain. "And make glue? I am of the opinion it sticks together the sides of one's stomach so it does not feel so empty. The sole purpose of the mess."

Henri leaned over and scooped up a bit of water from the stream. "A bit of mud for more crunch. Several minnows," he said. "*Voilà.* A veritable feast."

Stuffing his mouth full, he chewed with determination and very real dissatisfaction.

Iana giggled like a child, covering her mouth with one hand. Above it, her eyes twinkled merrily. A beautiful, clear brown, they were, like the finest ale. And just as intoxicating.

Henri thought he might go to extravagant lengths to see her laugh again. The sight and sound of it did something strange to his insides, like lifting his heart in his chest, making it feel light as a feather.

How long since a woman had dosed him with instant happiness? Too long, obviously. He smiled, completely forgetting his aches and the taste of oats.

It was then he noted Ev, frowning at Iana, at him, and again at her. With the quickness of a woodsprite, the boy abandoned the reins of the two mounts drinking at the edge of the burn and dashed off into the woods.

Ah, the old green-eyed monster, Henri deduced. Question was, did the boy resent his attention to Iana or was it the other way round?

Since Everand had been the one to find Iana, he might well imagine he had first claim to her regard. She was a beautiful woman and Ev had only just discovered the joy in having one of those nearby.

Then again, the boy had held the place of primary importance in Henri's life these past few months. First keeping Ev alive in the dread battles at sea, then being kept alive by him after the shipwreck, had forged a bond Henri honored most highly. Enough to call Everand his son.

In either case, this was no time to allow friction within their threesome. They had a long way to go together.

Iana rejoiced that Tam had begun moving about on her own instead of merely sitting or lying where she was put. It spoke well for the knight, Henri, that he had not rebuked the child for her interest in him. Even so, Iana did not believe he would suffer it for long.

When they had eaten and rested for a while, she ordered the others to remount and they continued on their way, riding east and still following the stream. Having a source of water eliminated having to carry that with them, and the less the mounts had to bear, the faster they could travel. Iana had no guess as to how long it would take them to reach the place called Baincroft.

"Look, there is smoke up ahead," Everand announced. They could clearly see several plumes of it rising above the trees.

"A village," the knight observed, though they could not yet see any dwellings. "We could stop there for the night."

"Nay!" Iana objected. She wanted none to see them. Newell might ask after her here, and so determine which way they were traveling. "We must not. They will surely be wary of strangers, especially you, sir."

"Why?" he asked, sounding almost offended.

"You are foreign, for one thing, and obviously no common wanderer."

He regarded her with no little suspicion. "You know we must find milk for the child and food for all of us. We cannot survive on berries for the rest of our journey, and the oats are almost gone, are they not?"

She could not deny it. They might deal with their hunger if need be, but the bairn required sustenance. "Aye, well, you two should remain out of sight. I shall go into the village alone and beg what they can spare."

"Take the babe," Everand suggested. "They will not refuse you then. She looks near to starving."

Tam had been near to it, Iana admitted to herself. Poor wee thing came so close. If only she could tell these two how much the child had improved in the days since her mother had died, they would be astounded. It broke Iana's heart to think what might have happened.

"Tend the beasts," she instructed as she dismounted. "I shall go ahead on foot and see what might be had."

They complied, though Sir Henri did not seem to like the idea. She knew that had more to do with her issuing the order than with what she had told them to do. He did not strike her as a man used to acting on anyone's demand, especially a woman's.

"Have great care," he warned her. "Call out if you are accosted."

And what did he think he would do about it if she were? Come rushing to her rescue? As it was, he swayed on his feet as though cup-shot. She approached and reached up to feel his face.

He smiled down at her as if she offered him a caress. "Not much fever," Iana said, making clear her reason for touching him. "Go and lie down over there on the banks. Have your lad fetch you a drink. The bark is in this pouch." She handed him the small bag containing the willow cuttings. He grimaced as he took it, then grinned at her.

She set off through the thinly treed forest in the direction of the smoke. Once out of sight of the knight and squire, she knelt upon the ground and removed the silver chain from the pouch at her waist. With her small blade, a large stone and a great deal of effort, she separated another link of the chain. Concealing the remainder of her treasure, she carried the link in her hand.

The villagers viewed even her with suspicion. She could only imagine how they would have greeted Henri and Everand. Only when she pled for their mercy did they reluctantly fill a sack with coarse bread, a bit of cheese and more oats. Her tale of being recently widowed and left with nothing but a sickly child stirred little sympathy. Only when she surrendered the silver did they agree to give her a skin filled with goat's milk.

When one of the elders eyed her greedily, she made up a tale of how she had found the silver link among her husband's things and had saved it until she became desperate.

Once she had their offerings, Iana hurried off into the woods in the opposite direction of where Henri and the squire waited. Walking hurriedly and stopping on occasion to see whether she was followed, Iana circled around the village.

"Success?" the squire asked as she approached.

"Aye," she told him, holding up the heavy cache of food and skin of milk. "They proved generous."

"Do not tell me," Henri warned, making a comical face. "More oats?"

She laughed, but mirth died when she noticed what he was wearing. Rather, *not* wearing. "Where are your clothes, sir? You'll catch your death!"

He drew Iana's small, woolen blanket closer around his body. "They are clean and drying upon yon bush," he said, inclining his head toward the swiftly running stream. "Free of salt and sweat, as am I, thanks be to God."

She struggled not to look upon the solid muscles of his shoulders, chest and legs. Never had she seen a man quite so well made.

The squire's hair was as wet as his master's. So were his chausses and shirt, though he still wore his.

"Fools, the both of you!" she fussed, stalking over to plop down beside the inviting water. "Do not blame me if you sicken and die."

"This is high summer and the weather is warm enough," Henri argued, "and for the first time in near a se'ennight, I feel cool."

"And what of your wound?" she demanded.

"I removed the wrapping. There is no bleeding and

your stitches seem well set. See for yourself." He opened the blanket to show her.

Iana hastily averted her eyes, but not before she saw that he was still wearing a loincloth to cover his private parts. A wicked spear of disappointment pricked her. For shame, she castigated herself, to be so curious about the body of a man she barely knew. Even had they become the best of friends, she had no cause to think about *that* part of him.

"Cover yourself until I have time to repair what you have doubtless undone," she snapped. Treating him as she would a wayward child seemed the best defense against the attraction she felt toward him.

She ignored Everand's snickering as he relieved her of the food and drink, and the three of them went to sit near the water to eat.

Iana released Tam from her back, rolling her weary shoulders and sighing with relief. Henri gently scooped up the child and set her in his blanket-wrapped lap. "Have you hunger, *chérie?*" he asked. "Shall I feed you?"

"I will do it," Iana argued.

Henri looked up at her, apparently concerned. "No, I think not. You need to rest yourself. How are you to look after us if you fall ill of exhaustion?"

He turned to the boy. "Ev, make a small fire and prepare the fish."

"Fish!" she exclaimed. "How did you get—"

"Tickled them," he answered. "If one remains very still, it is a simple thing to do."

She shook her head even as she hurriedly snatched away the flint from Everand. "I do not wish to hear any tall tales. And I've told you we cannot have a fire."

He took the implements from her hand and gave them

back to his squire. When his large fingers brushed hers, she froze in place, too stunned by their effect upon her to protest.

''Now rest yourself or bathe or sulk, whatever you wish to do,'' he said firmly, ''but we shall have a fire and proper food. I have decided.''

The sudden spell broken, Iana glared at him. *Imperious idiot. Overbearing oaf. Foolish frog.* Though she said naught aloud, she willed him to read the insults in her eyes.

He ignored her, switching his attention to the sack of food. ''Now what shall we feed our wee fairy? Sops of milk, eh? Does that sound tasty?'' he crooned to the babe.

Little Tam looked up at him, wide-eyed. The only moves she made were to tilt her head and raise a hesitant hand to touch his chest. The child seemed spellbound by the huge knight. Small wonder, Iana thought. If she were not so canny about the true nature of men, she might be enthralled herself.

But he was only a man, even more imperious than the usual male. She had no reason to hate this one, and in fact did not. However, she had excellent cause to deny the prickle of fascination he roused in her. And if she were wise, she would quickly regain the role of leader in this expedition. Otherwise, she might find herself trailing along in his wake, doing his bidding just like his squire.

Son, she reminded herself. He had recognized the lad, which was more than most men did when they had sired one out of wedlock. Waiting this long to do so counted against him in her estimation. Everand was half-grown already. Of course, the delay might have been wise if the mother had wed another who mistook Everand for his own. And Henri had said something about the lad being orphaned once already. For now, Iana would give Henri the benefit of the doubt.

She watched the boy arrange the fish upon skewers and lay them across the stones he'd stacked around the small blaze. How long had it been since she had eaten a meal prepared by someone else? Well over a month, she figured.

As much as she hated the admission, Iana did not enjoy fending for herself. Her brother had been right about how difficult that would prove for her. She'd had to learn how, and it had not been an easy thing. After spending her entire life being waited upon, she found little joy in the menial tasks of cleaning, washing and cooking. Still, she much preferred that to being owned by a man who had the power of life and death over her. Duncan might have provided maids aplenty to keep her hands soft and her back straight, but he had nearly killed her twice.

With hardly any thought to what she was doing, Iana prepared a cup of milk and tore out a soft portion of the bread. Dipping bite-sized pieces of it into the milk, she offered them to Tam. The bairn sat in the knight's lap, leaning forward to take the food.

"Eats like a baby bird, does she not?" Sir Henri said with a muted chuckle. "I wonder when she will attempt to fly."

Iana smiled at the baby. "When she is ready. With help, she will stand for a few moments now. And she did creep over to where you were sitting last eve. That is much more than she would do a few days past."

She reached out and took Tam from him and stood the babe upon her feet, carefully supporting her shaky stance. After a moment, Tam's spindly legs gave way. Iana held her close and praised her.

''What is wrong with her?'' Sir Henri asked in a quiet voice.

''I do not know,'' Iana answered honestly. She thought it must be lack of proper food and the fact that Tam had been carried about all her life instead of learning to walk. It could be something else, an illness the child had been born with or a combination of fear and deprivation that caused her to be so. ''But she is getting better, I believe.''

He looked both sad and hopeful. Why would he care? Iana wondered. Why should it matter to him whether the babe improved or not? She had seen men totally indifferent when their own female children perished. Despite her intentions to avoid it, Iana's heart warmed toward this gentle knight who looked upon a peasant's babe with concern in his eyes.

She smiled at him, only to see his expression change on the instant.

''Someone comes,'' he announced in a whisper. ''Sit where you are and do not move. Ev, crawl to your right and hide behind those bushes. Keep your blade ready, Son.''

Before Iana knew what had happened, the knight had disappeared silently into the brush to her left, the blanket he had worn left in a wad upon the ground.

She sat alone, Tam in her lap, the fish slowly browning over the small fire nearby. Abandoned.

The racket of someone approaching, leaves crackling underfoot, terrified her into action. She did the only thing she could do. Tumbling Tam upon the wadded blanket, Iana quickly picked up a rock the size of her fist and turned toward the sound of the intruder.

Chapter Four

Her back to the stream, Iana stood, feet braced apart, her skirts concealing Tam from whatever might emerge from the forest. Be it animal or man, she prepared herself to dash out the brains of it, should it dare approach. She sucked in a deep breath and held it as she hefted the rock in her hand.

"Eh! Here, Woad. I thought she'd be headin' fer th' water."

The greedy-looking man from the village plowed through the brush, grinning at Iana, showing gaps where his front teeth should be. He was enormous, his stomach hanging over his belt, his legs like tree trunks. She did not recall his being so dreadfully big.

A mere ghost of a fellow, skin and bones and stringy white hair, followed him into the small clearing.

The large, shaggy-haired one propped his hands on his hips and wrinkled his brows, attempting to menace her, she supposed.

"We'll be havin' the balance of that siller now, lass. Dinna be stingy wi' it."

Iana shook her head, glaring at him.

"If ye've nae more siller, then we'll see what else ye'll

offer us fer our trouble. Got treasure under th' skirts there, ha' ye, lassie?''

"You'll have naught from me," she declared. Where the devil was that knight? Henri might not be able to defend her, but the least he could have done was left her his knife. She weighed the rock again, balancing it, adjusting her grip. It would have to do.

The ghostlike one crept forward even as Shaggy stepped closer, tsking at her weapon as if it were but a pinecone she held.

Suddenly the bushes behind the two men came alive. Henri and Everand burst through, blades flashing hither and yon like rapidly struck sparks off flint.

Howls of rage sent birds flying, small beasts scurrying. Iana almost stumbled backward over Tam. Quickly she crouched, scooped up the babe and hid behind the nearest large tree so they would not be trampled.

Openmouthed, she watched. Lightning-quick steel sliced through worn homespun and leather as if it were butter. The two blades were everywhere at once with no pause.

Next she knew, the two thieves stood bare as the day they were hatched, cowering, whining, hands shaking as they covered what they considered their most valuable parts. Iana trembled with laughter and relief.

Henri, still wearing only his loincloth, teased the chest of the shaggy one with the point of his dagger. Truly, the reiver looked a proper beast, with dark hair covering his shoulders and even his back. A ghastly sight.

"Your hide would make a warm pelt, I'd wager," Henri observed in a menacing growl, slowly shaving a blade-width's path across the area over the man's heart. He then wiped the blade upon the man's bushy beard. "But it would take years to leach out the stink."

"Please, sar," Shaggy begged, "we didna mean nae harm. Let us gae and we'll stay gone."

Henri turned to Everand. "What think you, my friend? Should we kill them here, or let them go, and give chase? Do you fancy the hunt?" He nodded as if greatly looking forward to the taunting, giving Everand a clue to the answer he expected, since the lad kenned only French.

Everand bobbed his own head, wearing a look of glee, his small knife holding the ghostie's chin as high as it would go.

"Twenty paces lead, then. Give us a good hunt and we'll make it a clean kill. Lie down and whimper, I shall skin you alive. Can you count?"

"Aye," Shaggy croaked, his eyes wide with fear. Ghostie whimpered.

"Off you go on the count of three! One...two... three!" Henri shouted and gave a war whoop any Highlander would envy. Everand chased through the bushes behind the men, shrieking like a banshee all the while.

Iana fell back from her kneeling position, laughing so hard her sides ached. Tam clung to her like a frightened kitten.

Henri crouched beside them, his smile wide. "You are all right, I assume."

"A-aye, I am well," she gasped, hardly able to catch her breath. "How in heaven's name did you *do* that?"

"But a game," he said modestly. "It is better played with swords, but we made do well enough."

"I should say so! They'll not slow down right soon, if ever."

He stood and held out his hand. The sight of his muscles shining with sweat shot a hot tingle of appreciation right down the middle of her. For an instant, she could not tear her gaze away.

His soft chuckle warned her that he had noticed her fascination. Iana immediately shut her eyes, cursing herself for her wayward thoughts. She ignored his offer of assistance.

When she dared to look again, he had retreated to the edge of the water and begun wading in, his back to her. With a will of their own, her eyes immediately focused upon his uncovered nether cheeks. "Och, my Lord!" she breathed in absolute awe.

"Oui?" He looked over his left shoulder and raised one dark brow. *"Qu'est-ce que c'est?"*

What is it? he asks. Iana scoffed. *Lust* was what it was. Pure, unadulterated lust. And she should be ashamed of herself. Not only ashamed, but terrified to be thinking what she was thinking. Not for promise of paradise should she entertain desire for any man. Such would be her undoing and that was a fact.

"Nothing," she replied, still a bit breathless, keeping her gaze firmly locked upon the tree beside her. "I was about to offer up a prayer."

"Say one for me, if you will," he beseeched, his voice rife with amusement.

Just before he disappeared beneath the surface, she thought she heard him say, "Best pray for colder water."

For the next two days, Henri did as Iana instructed most of the time, giving good reason whenever he had to object. It was obvious to him that she had traveled little in her life, for she pushed the mounts too hard and, as long as Tam's supply of milk lasted, forgot about obtaining food for the next meal unless reminded.

She always went alone, as she had before, into a village when they passed one. There she would somehow obtain a loaf of bread, a bit of cheese and another sack of the damned oats.

Now and again she would halt her mare, slip off and disappear into the woods for a short while. Only answering nature's call, he had thought at first. But she would also return with a few sprigs of plants to tuck inside her pouch. Later, when they stopped to rest, he would be required to swallow her harvest in one form or another or have the leaves crushed and pasted upon his wound. It seemed she was more than adequate in her chosen work, for he felt better each day. The fever was completely gone now and he experienced only slight twinges when he moved about too swiftly.

Every time she touched him and each time he felt her eyes upon him, he cursed his ungallant thoughts. The more his body healed and grew freer of the pain, the more it bedeviled him with its growing insistence upon getting closer to her.

He owed this woman his life. How could he offer her the insult of seduction? True, she was a widow, one with her honor intact. Or so she said. There were times he believed it wholeheartedly, but then there was her child to consider. How had she gotten Tam without putting aside that decency of hers at least one time in her life? He supposed she could have been taken by force, but he shoved aside that abominable thought, deciding he had much rather she had gone willingly to any man, rather than believe she had suffered that.

Though he did sense she was wary of him, it did nothing to discourage his desire. He wanted her so badly he ached with it.

Everand had immediately filled the space Henri deliberately put between himself and the woman. The boy's constant chatter and exaggerated chivalry annoyed him. He who had always been indulgent toward young squires and their follies of the heart, and he who had also never been jealous in his life. Not even of his unfaithful wife.

"How long before we reach Baincroft, sir?" Ev asked him as they rode.

Henri shrugged. "Well, I know how long it takes to travel from Odun in the Highlands to Baincroft. My brother fetched his bride from near there last year and told me of the time involved. Judging by his journey and the maps I studied long ago, I think we must travel about half that distance. It depends upon how long it takes to find crossing at the Clyde. Our passage around the hills beyond will slow us down even more, however. Three more days is my guess," he told Everand. "Mayhaps four."

"There is a ferry north of Largsmuth," Iana informed him. "We should reach that before tonight."

"You have traveled this way before, then?"

"Aye, once," she admitted, "though I have not been any farther east than Largsmuth."

Henri rode on silently, questioning whether he had any right to ask more about her life and what had brought her to that village where Ev had found her. Thus far, she had not welcomed his curiosity and simply ignored him when he asked anything about her past.

"You must have lived near the Clyde when you were wed," he said in an offhand way, excusing his prying, since he did not phrase it as a question.

"Nay," she answered, not looking back at him.

"When you were a lass, then," he guessed again.

She remained silent.

He smiled to himself. One more piece of the puzzle slipped into place. She was not Iana of Ayr, as she had told them. Ayr was a coastal town not far from where they had come ashore, if he recalled his maps aright. Her girlhood home was near the Firth of Clyde. She'd not denied it. And her grandfather's Christian name had been Ian. She had let that slip when he was ill. Once he reached Baincroft, he would inquire if anyone there knew a nobleman named Ian who lived near the Clyde.

Why it seemed so important to find out exactly who Iana was, Henri could not say. Possibly because he could not abide a mystery. Then again, it might be because he desired her so fiercely and wanted to know just how available she was to him with regard to her station in life. Unworthy thoughts troubled him, so he dismissed them.

"What is the cost of crossing at Largsmuth?" he asked, determined not to indulge his prurient interest in her any further.

"A schilling, I believe. My bro... I cannot recall the exact price," she snapped.

Henri smiled. Another slip. She had been about to say brother, he was certain of it. If her brother had been with her at that crossing, he must have been escorting her somewhere, likely to the man she would wed. Women had little cause to leave their homes, otherwise. So it was probable that she had traversed this route in reverse, in order to become a bride. Her husband had died, so she had told Ev. Why had her family not come for her if she had been widowed and left with nothing? Were they all dead?

It seemed that the more answers he obtained about his Iana of Somewhere Nearby, the more questions he found arising.

Iana had dreaded this part of the journey. Left to her own devices, she would not have risked passing this way, near Largsmuth, but would have taken ship on the west coast and gone to a place unknown. Though it was unlikely anyone hereabout would recognize her as sister to Newell, it certainly was not impossible. He had many friends in the area who had visited their home and met her as a girl. Despite all that had happened to her, she had not changed overmuch in looks, save to grow taller.

Sir Henri had taken the lead when she stopped to adjust Tam's sling. Now he led them directly through the town. Iana kept her head bowed, cutting her gaze right and left, thankfully seeing only strangers.

Largsmuth proved an odd mix of buildings, some wattle and daub, some quite wonderfully constructed of wood. A few of the latter boasted hinged half-walls, let down, propped upon supports and used as tables to display wares of the shopkeepers.

The remainder of the silver chain lay within her pouch, begging to be spent upon a decent gown, shoes that were not encrusted with mud, and soft-scented soaps to soothe her skin. She sighed and rode on, knowing the folly of spending for things she could do without.

"Ah, I see an inn up ahead," Sir Henri said, turning. "We shall sleep there tonight."

Then, as if he had read her mind, he added, "And purchase new raiment in these shops, of course. We should not arrive at my brother's keep looking the part of beggars."

Everand cleared his throat and eased past her to halt next to his lord. "Sir, we haven't any coin for that."

The knight looked back at her, smiling confidently. "Lady Iana will graciously allow us some of the silver from the chain, and I shall repay her the instant we arrive at Baincroft."

"Nay," she said, shaking her head. "I say we shall

not stay here the night, nor shall we spend my silver upon fripperies, sir.''

His smile disappeared. ''You would grudge us this, lady? I had not marked you as miserly. Do you not believe that I will compensate you? I remind you, we did save your silver from the thieves, did we not? You would have none of it, were that not so.''

He had her there. Had it not been for him and the lad, she would have nothing left now, not even her honor. Iana looked around her, keeping her face half-concealed by the rough wimple. She saw no person familiar to her. What could it hurt to rest her bones upon a feather-stuffed bed for a change?

Happening upon someone who knew her face worried her as much as spending the silver. She would not have to go about in the town once they had secured rooms in the inn. Sir Henri could buy what they must have. These townfolk would not remark much upon the fact that he was French, as would have those in the small villages they had passed. Many foreigners must travel through a city this size.

''Very well,'' she agreed reluctantly. ''Make for the inn.''

He gave a firm nod and urged the bay on down the cobbled street toward the two-story building with the hanging sign.

''Lead the mounts through that alley,'' he ordered Everand, pointing to the space between the inn and a cloth merchant's stall. ''There should be a stable in back. See to our beasts yourself, for I do not trust strangers to feed them properly.'' He turned to her and waited.

For a moment, she did not realize what he expected of her. Then she remembered. Sighing, she untied the bag containing the chain and plopped it in his outstretched hand.

"Merci," he said, and smiled reassuringly. "I will repay you, Iana." In seconds, he had forced apart several of the links with his knife blade.

Iana's heart sank when he tucked the entire pouch inside his doublet instead of giving it back. Less than half the chain remained since she had paid for their horses and every sackful of food she had begged from the local populace 'twixt here and the coast.

"Follow me, my lady, and remain close," he warned. "There are likely to be ruffians hanging about the public room."

She did as he asked, for she had never stayed in an inn before and did not know what to expect once they entered. When she had traveled this way with Newell, Dorothea and their retainers, they had carried their own tents, furnishings, servants and victuals.

When Henri led her inside, she saw that she had been wise to heed him. Several men gathered around a chest-high bench, laughing and toasting each other, well on their way to becoming drunk.

Sir Henri nodded amiably to them and hailed the publican. "We would like rooms," he informed the man.

"You only need the one," the bearded proprietor told him. "'Tis large and will sleep four. Two beds."

Henri looked down at her. "One will do." Something in his eyes warned her not to protest his decision. In truth, Iana had no objection at all. Propriety had been cast aside the moment she had found him, so that was not an issue. More importantly, one room would cost considerably less than two.

She winced a bit when he handed over two of the silver links. One should have been enough.

"We require one night's lodging, enough food to carry us through three days travel, milk for the child and stabling of our mounts. Also, bring us three buckets of hot water as quickly as you can warm it." He had not lowered his hand after turning over the silver. "I will have three marks in change."

Two of the men at the bench stopped drinking to watch the dealings when the publican laughed at Sir Henri. "You jest!"

"No jest," Henri declared softly. The look in his eyes held a warning and his smile had ceased to be. "Three marks, no less. Else we shall take our room elsewhere."

The innkeeper turned away, hawked and spat. With a shrug, he reached into a purse at his waist and withdrew the coins, dropping them into the knight's hand. "Aye, well, times is hard."

Henri waited a moment longer, raised a dark brow in challenge to the men who were watching, then followed the publican up the stairs.

Iana almost grasped the tail of his doublet in her worry over being left behind. This was a frightening place, she thought, and the men looked hard-edged despite their previous mellow mood. She now understood her brother's abhorrence of abiding in public inns.

Everand joined them before they had settled in. "The stables are more than adequate, sir," he reported. "I saw to the feed. The man there says his master will beat him if he does not curry every animal, so I let him do it."

"You will judge whether he has made a proper job of it before you sleep," Henri instructed. "For now, you remain here with Lady Iana and Thomasina while I see to our other needs. Bar the door and do not open it unless you hear my voice direct you to do so. I shall return before they send someone with our food and water for washing.''

"As you wish," Everand replied, then added, "Father."

Henri smiled at him, a singular expression that spoke of his affection for the lad. He said nothing, only placed a large hand on Ev's shoulder and gave it a fond shake. Then he left.

Everand quickly dropped the heavy bar across the door into its fittings and turned to her, crossing his arms over his chest and leaning back against the portal. "You need not fear, lady. I shall guard you with my life. And your babe, of course."

She might have laughed at him for pretension, had she not seen what he could do with a knife. "We are glad to have your protection. Tam and I thank you for it."

He pushed away from the door and came to sit upon the bed where Tam lay sleeping. With one finger, he awkwardly pushed an inky wisp of hair off the child's cheek. "She does not have the look of you."

"Nay, she does not," Iana admitted.

"I had a small sister," he said softly, in the voice of the young lad he was instead of the deliberately deepened tone he used most of the time. After a long hesitation, his gaze still resting upon Tam, he added, "She died with my mother."

Iana felt her heart twist just watching his remembered grief. "I regret your loss, Everand. And then your father died, also?"

He nodded, still not meeting her eyes. When he answered, he seemed almost lost in his thoughts. "He wasted away with grief, I believe. He wanted death. My brothers were all gone, my mother and sister, as well. There was only me. When Lord Henri came one day to select cloth for his new court garb, my father pleaded with him to offer me employment.''

He glanced up, the corners of his mouth tipped in a sad smile. ''You should have heard the plaudits my sire heaped upon my head whilst asking that boon, lady. I feared never to live up to his praise of me. Wishful lies, most of it, yet Lord Henri accepted it as truth. I refused to leave home until my father breathed his last. Then my new master came for me and made him his squire.''

''And now his son,'' she added, sitting down at his side, pressing her hand on top of his. ''I'll wager both your old father and your new feel great pride in you, the one in heaven and the other who directs your life here.''

He shrugged with modesty. ''I pray it is true, though I have unworthy thoughts betimes.'' He glanced up at her from beneath his long lashes. ''And, like your poor Thomasina, I do not seem to grow properly.''

The urge to comfort the motherless boy overwhelmed her. Iana put her arms around Everand and held him to her, brushing a kiss upon his brow. ''Take heart, Everand. My own brother remained much smaller than his years should have made him until he was near sixteen. Then he quickly grew near as tall as Sir Henri.''

''You cannot mean it!'' Ev exclaimed, pulling back from her, his large eyes rounded with hope. ''Shall I, do you think?''

''Wait and see,'' she advised, pinching his cheek lightly and giving it a pat. ''And even should you not attain such great height, it matters not at all. *Deeds* make the man, Everand. Always remember that. Your deeds will speak for you, not your size, nor your wealth, nor your way with words. Deeds are all that matter in life.''

He inclined his head thoughtfully. ''So says Sir Henri, or something to that effect. I suppose I must believe it.''

There came a scratch upon the door then and he leapt up from the bed, his hand on his knife hilt, doubtless hoping for a chance to perform the heroics of which they had spoken.

"Who goes?" he demanded in his deepest voice.

"I bring your supper," a man declared. The iron handle of the door moved downward, but the bolt held fast.

"That is not the publican," Iana whispered.

"Come back later," Everand ordered loudly. Then, very quietly, he said to her, "It must be one of those ruffians thinking to steal from us."

After a few moments of silence, something heavy banged against the door. The bolt shook in its fittings. "Mercy, he means to break it down," she gasped.

"Take the chamber pot and stand to one side of the door," Everand told her. "Aim for his head if he breaks through. I'll finish him off with my blade."

The man rammed against the door again. Iana grabbed up the heavy clay pot and ran to her station. Everand gripped his eating knife and assumed a fighting stance.

With the third blow, the entire portal came off its rusty hinges and collapsed into the room. Iana struck swiftly, threw her full weight behind the swing of the pot and connected with a solid thunk.

Stunned, the brute just stood there, his weapon drawn back to strike.

Everand flung his knife and lifted a stool, tossing that as well. The blade struck true, to the left of the rogue's breastbone. His beefy hand grabbed it just as the stool hit his head. With little more than a groan of dismay, the man toppled like a felled tree, landing flat upon the door itself. The wicked short sword bounced out of his hand with a clang and landed in the corner.

For a moment she and Everand just stood there, frozen

with the shock of their success. Then the lad's lips kicked up in a semblance of a smile and he shrugged. "We did it!"

"Do you think he is dead?" Iana asked. Everand walked over to the man and nudged him with his boot. He did not stir.

Together they knelt and rolled the brigand off the fallen door so that he lay on his back. Everand retrieved his trusty knife, grimaced at the bloody blade, then wiped it clean upon the wretch's filthy jerkin.

Iana felt the man's neck vein for a heartbeat and found none. Blood welled out of the vacant wound in his chest and stained a dark crimson circle upon his yellowed sark. If they did not move him soon, they would have a puddle upon the floor.

"We've killed him, I think. What should we do now?" she asked.

Everand bounced to his feet, went to the doorway and leaned out into the corridor.

Apparently, the noise of the fracas had drawn no attention. Or it was possible happenings of this sort were so commonplace they did not merit anyone's notice.

The lad stepped back, looked down at their attacker and blew out a sigh. "Could we lift him high enough to get him out the window?"

"I believe so," Iana said. "He is quite large, but there are two of us."

"Then we should tidy up. The landlord will not be pleased by this, I am quite certain."

Iana agreed with that. Even if they could prove the man intended to rob them—which they could not—they would have to stay here until there was an inquiry into his death. She did not want to think what might happen to them, since they could not prove he had meant them harm.

Together they struggled to drag the man toward the window that opened to the back of the building. With the greatest of effort, they managed to get his upper half through the opening, then tumbled him out and watched him land upon the ground between the inn and the stables.

"Do you think anyone will guess we threw him out this window?" she asked in a whisper. "What of the stable lad?"

"Busy inside there with our mounts. There's no one about to have seen us do it," Ev assured her. "Likely whoever discovers him will believe he was accosted down there in the back dooryard."

Iana stared down at the man for some time to see whether she might have been mistaken and he would bestir himself after all. When he did not, she finally turned away.

Everand was grunting, diligently trying to prop the door back into place, so she went to assist him. Together, they got it upright within the opening, though they had no way now to secure it. At least it would afford them a bit of privacy. If anyone else came along, they would stop and scratch or knock, instead of walking right into the chamber.

"What of the blood on the outside of the door?" she asked, wringing her hands to keep them from shaking.

Ev patted her arm. "Do not worry. There was little on it. He mostly bled when I took out the knife. There by the window where we lifted him is the worst of it."

"I will take care of it," Iana declared, gathering up her scattered wits and berating herself for her weakness. If a mere lad could deal with all this, then so could she.

She unpacked the remainder of the rags she had brought for use as bandages, and wiped up as much of the gore as she could. So stained the raw wood was after many years of occupancy and abuse, the smears left were hardly noticeable.

Amazingly, wee Tam had slept through the entire incident. All in all, Iana felt things had worked out much better than they might have done. They had given a right good account of themselves, she and Everand, and Iana decided not to bemoan the fact that the cursed lout had met his end here. Had they not been successful, they might be the ones lying dead.

"The chamber pot was a fine idea, Ev," she told him, her voice less steady than she would have liked.

"It was, was it not?" he acknowledged pridefully.

"Aye, I admit I was not quick enough to consider it. And your aim with the blade was true as a marksman's arrow. I commend you."

"Resourceful, that is what Sir Henri says I am." He shrugged as he helped her pick up the pieces of broken crockery that littered the floor. They tossed the shards onto the small blanket she had spread upon the floor to collect them. "He always says that about me."

Iana sighed, feeling rather numb now that her heart had stopped hammering so hard. "Does he ever mention humility, by any chance?"

Ev cocked his head, thought a moment, then shook it. "Not that I have ever heard."

She could believe that rightly enough. Finished with their task, they gathered up the ends of the blanket and carried it to the window. No sooner had they tossed out its contents than they heard a loud knocking.

Suddenly the door fell flat into the room with a bang.

Iana jumped clear off the floor and Ev cried out a warning.

Henri stood in the opening, fist raised and mouth agape as he stared down at the unhinged panel of boards.

Chapter Five

As he entered, Henri dropped to one side the bundle of goods he had bought. "What the devil is this? What happened to the door?"

"We had an unwanted visitor, sir," Everand announced cockily, "but we managed to entertain him without you." He nodded toward the window.

Henri rushed across the room and looked out. A man lay in the rear dooryard unmoving; another knelt over him. Had the injured one jumped from the window?

"Did he harm either of you?" Henri demanded, still looking down upon the intruder, watching the one who had found him drag him away.

"Not at all," Iana answered, "though I fear the chamber pot is done for."

"Makes a fine weapon, sir," Everand said proudly, "and our lady wielded it well."

Iana nodded, accepting the compliment.

Henri turned, incredulous. "You struck him and he leapt out the window?"

Iana and Everand looked at each other before facing him again.

She was the one who explained. "When we would not

let him in, he broke the door down. I hit him, then Everand crowned him with a stool and sent a blade straight to his black heart. Together we tossed him out.''

Henri's awestruck gaze caught upon the unfamiliar short sword that lay abandoned in the corner of the room. A chill ran up his spine and he shook his head, still disbelieving. ''You mean he...? Why, he might have...''

''Aye,'' she agreed. ''But no matter. 'Tis done and he is gone now. I was thinking we should be away, as well. And soon,'' she added.

''Yes, that definitely would be wise,'' Henri muttered, his mind still fixed upon the intruder and what could have happened during his brief absence. He would not leave them alone again for any reason.

Iana was right. They needed to quit the inn and travel on immediately. Injured as he was and not at full strength, he was hardly geared for defending them against anything other than the most inept of miscreants. Certainly not the vagaries of Scottish law. There were certain to be repercussions.

''This is not good,'' he growled. ''Not good at all.''

Everand took offense. ''I used my blade as you taught me. And our lady was most brave, sir. I fail to see how you can take us to task for—''

''I do not reprimand you, Ev,'' Henri declared in a carefully controlled voice. He drew in a deep breath and tried to calm his thoughts. Everand's use of the knife could prompt dire consequences. ''He is dead, is he not?''

''Aye,'' Iana answered, for the first time appearing shaken now that the heat of the encounter had begun to fade. ''I...I believe he was dead when we threw him out.''

Henri paced, worrying his bottom lip with his thumb

and forefinger. "He was a local man. I saw him drinking with the others when we came in. The publican has not come up or sent anyone to investigate the noise?"

"No one has come, sir," Everand said. "Could the innkeeper have sanctioned his friend coming up to rob us?"

Henri nodded. "Probably. For all he knows, we are French travelers who would not be missed did we simply vanish. We would be wise to do just that since we have slain one of their own. They might not be convinced that we had good reason for it."

"Aye, I thought the same," Iana agreed.

He picked up the short sword the man had dropped, quickly collected the bundle of clothing he had bought for them and two of their packs. "Hurry, Ev, bring the rest. Iana, get the child. We had best go now before they raise a hue and cry."

"Would they hang me, sir?" Ev asked, scrambling to gather their things. "The man was bent upon harm, after all."

"Sir Henri is right, Ev. Let's not tarry to find out," Iana said, already shrugging into the sling bearing the babe.

Tam had wakened, though she remained unnaturally silent, as always. Henri could swear he saw fear in the child's huge, dark eyes. He smiled at her to try to dispel it.

"Come, then, let us be off," he said softly to Iana and Ev, so as not to frighten Tam more.

Together they filed quietly down the stairs. The innkeeper was not present below, though several other men were busily lifting tankards and quarreling amongst themselves.

As naturally and unhurriedly as possible, Henri led

Iana and Ev outside and around the building to the
stables, which were now deserted except for the horses.

Moments later, they rode away from the inn. He kept
their pace slow so as not to draw attention. Darkness was
approaching and the shops were shutting down. There
were fewer people about than when he had been out before.

Henri hoped their departure went unremarked, at least
until they were safely away.

"Which path to the ferry, my lady?" he called over
his shoulder.

She pointed and he led them in that direction, urging
his mount to a trot. He hoped the ferrymen would willingly make one more trip despite the dwindling daylight.
He did not like to use force.

It could very well be that nothing would come of the
incident. The townfolk might bury the wretch and forget
him within the hour. But Henri recalled how concerned
the kneeling man had seemed. If the publican had known
his drinking companion was going to their chamber, and
then later found the blood streaks in the room let to them,
Henri feared there would be the devil to pay if they were
caught.

Scots loved their vengeance, even against one another.
Any opportunity to exact it upon three outlanders might
excite them to a frenzy.

Iana watched from a safe distance while Henri arranged their crossing. More silver changed hands. Too
much of it to suit her. By the time they got where they
were going, she would be destitute again. But the thought
of facing a charge of murder made her mind it somewhat
less.

Henri had promised to see to her support, but she knew very well what that meant.

In all truth, she did not trust herself to remain indifferent to his lust. Or hers. She imagined those wondrously long-fingered hands upon her, his beautifully shaped lips claiming hers, the mounded muscles of his chest hard against her while he...

Shamefaced, she jerked her gaze away from him, realizing only then how hungrily she watched the man whenever she was certain he would not notice. Something about him drew her as inexorably as a wave to the shore. Something she knew she must fight with all the will she possessed. Anger at herself made her almost ill.

Even if he did not require her body in payment for any support he gave her, she would still be beholden to him. Living upon his generosity would require her to live her life exactly as he demanded. No pleasure would be worth that indignity. That right she would grant to no man, even one as chivalrous as he seemed, or as outrageously handsome as she knew him to be. She'd had more than enough of living beneath a man's thumb.

Only for the duration of this journey would she allow him any say in what she did. He knew the way to where they were going and was obviously more accustomed to travel. It only made sense to accept his direction. Once they'd reached their destination, however, Iana meant to reassert herself as a free woman. Employment would insure her status, and he had promised it.

When he beckoned, she rode forward and dismounted beside him and Everand. They led the horses aboard the large conveyance, which dipped and swayed dangerously with the lapping of the wavelets. The surface of the firth seemed rougher than when she had last crossed it.

Her brother had told her that the water narrowed and

grew shallow in this place, hence the placement of the ferry service.

In the hazy, golden twilight, the other side did not appear that far away. It seemed one could almost swim the distance if the waves were calmer and the water not so cold.

The ferry was a wide, flat-bottomed vessel with sides almost shoulder high, constructed to transport horses and cargo as well as passengers. Two ferrymen stood by to man the sail and two others wielded long poles to push the boat out of the shallows. With the three mounts and seven people aboard, it seemed crowded.

Iana shivered. She did not like boats. The last time she had crossed this way, she recalled the motion of the waves making her quite sick. Water lapped hard against the sides. The sails were not yet unfurled, and the pole-men pushed hard to gain deeper water.

No sooner had they begun their voyage than Tam began to wriggle a bit against Iana's back, a certain signal that she needed to get out of the sling. There was no putting it off. The moment Iana knelt, Everand hurried to her side and lifted the baby out.

"Bless you, Everand," Iana said with a smile. She took Tam in her arms and stood up, patting the baby's back to sooth her. Unsteady on her feet with the ferry undulating beneath her, Iana leaned against the side for support. "Can you find her wee convenience for me?"

To his credit, the lad did not protest the indignity of fetching the small lipped bowl.

Suddenly the large bay whinnied and danced to one side, upsetting the packs. The kneeling Everand tumbled backward against Iana, jolting Tam right over her shoulder and past the railing.

Iana screamed. Henri, who must have seen what happened, vaulted over the rail into the water. The polemen halted. Everand would have gone in the water, too, had Iana not grasped his tunic and held on with both hands.

"Sir!" he cried, struggling to get away from her. "He'll drown, lady! Let me go!"

Iana clutched him around his middle and dragged him down to the deck of the ferry. "He cannot save both of you! Be still!" she shouted.

One of the polemen carefully worked his way to the spot where Henri had gone in, leaned over the side and reached down. The ferry rocked, but remained in place. Iana clenched her eyes shut and prayed. Ev had gone limp in her arms, sobbing like a child. Moments passed like hours.

"Here, mon!" the ferryman shouted down. "Grab onto the pole! 'At's th' way. Hand th' wee'un up ta me."

Iana then released Everand to assist, hoping the lad had collected enough of his wits not to leap after his master.

An instant later, the ferryman plopped a soaked Tam into Iana's arms and turned back, reaching over the side again, lowering a rope and shouting instructions to Henri.

The baby shivered violently as Iana enveloped her, trying to blot the freezing water off the child with the tail of her gown. Half her attention remained on the knight's rescue.

The ferry seemed to dip when Henri climbed over the side with the aid of the ferryman and Everand. He landed on the deck with a thump and immediately scrambled toward her on his hands and knees.

"Is...is she...alive?" he gasped, reaching out to place a shaking, wet hand on Tam's back.

In answer, the baby let out an earsplitting cry that ended in a racking cough.

"Thanks be...to God," Henri muttered, and collapsed.

"See to him, Everand," Iana commanded, her own voice choked with tears of relief. "See to your da."

The poleman grunted and resumed his station, leaving them to recover as best they could. Everand found the pack with Iana's one blanket and quickly wrapped it around Henri.

Iana scooted over to the side wall of the ferry, sat back and continued to cuddle Tam, who seemed to have come alive after her accident. She squirmed and cried as readily as any child might when treated to such a dunking in icy waters.

Iana wrestled the babe out of the wet, clinging shift she wore and wrapped her in the soft, thick wool of the abandoned sling. She crooned nonsense to reassure the baby and soon Tam quieted, sucking rhythmically and noisily on her cold little fingers.

Miracle of miracles, Iana thought, they were all safe. At least for the moment. Surely to God they had endured enough for one day.

"How is he?" she asked Everand.

"Alive," Henri answered for himself as he struggled to a sitting position and clutched the blanket closer. "Only half-frozen. Thomasina?"

Iana dropped a kiss on the curls plastered to the baby's head and lay her cheek where she had kissed. "She's warming. Did you hear her? She cried."

He chuckled gruffly and sniffed. "They heard her in Paris, I would wager."

Everand gave a short bark of laughter, then dissolved into tears again, his shoulders shaking. Henri embraced the lad and held him close. "Come, lend me some warmth, Son. I think we must swear off water altogether, you and I. It has not brought us much luck, has it?" He spoke softly, making foolish jests, soothing his newly acquired offspring much as she soothed hers. In the gathering darkness, their eyes met over the heads of the children, and Iana suddenly wanted to weep.

As he spoke to Ev, she heard love and affection in his voice, a voice that reached inside her and strummed something that had lain unresonant all her life. A desolate sense of yearning closed over her as surely as the waters had enveloped Tam. She wondered whether Henri could save her from drowning, too, if she dared to let him try.

As they disembarked, Henri parted with yet another piece of the silver, thanking the ferryman profusely for helping him save the child. Henri knew he would have survived, but he doubted he could have managed to get Tam back on the ferry without assistance.

Finding her in the water at all had been a mere stroke of fortune. Had she not been wearing that loose white gown of hers, Henri knew he would not have spotted her. Thanks be to God, the garment had billowed out around her just beneath the choppy surface. He had grabbed for it the moment he hit the water.

It felt as if he'd swallowed half the firth. His side ached abominably and his head felt likely to split. And he was as damned cold as he had ever been before. They would have to camp somewhere nearby. Henri knew he was not the only one who needed rest.

They loaded the packs upon the horses, and he assisted Iana onto her mount. She now wore Tam's sling in front of her, the better to warm the child against her breasts. The poor mite had fallen asleep at last after crying most of the way across the water. Henri patted her small bottom through the wool and grinned up at Iana. "She might never willingly take a bath after that adventure."

"I daresay she will not," Iana said, smiling down at him.

"The fright seems to have loosened her tongue," he observed. "Has she always been silent before this?" He rubbed the child's back gently while he looked upon Iana's shadowed features.

Instead of answering his question, she looked toward Everand. "Your squire needs sleep, sir, and 'twill soon be dark as pitch. Mount up and let us find a place of shelter if you will."

Henri nodded in acquiescence and turned away, sorry that Iana felt the need to be so secretive about her daughter. Most mothers wished to speak of little else but their children, yet Iana rarely mentioned her own. Nor, it seemed, did she wish anyone else to do so.

The fact that Tam had been conceived outside the bond of Iana's marriage would explain why she refused to talk much of her, of course. Because of that, Iana had obviously been cast out and forced to live the way she had.

Women could be righteously executed for infidelity, but usually were not, especially if they had not willingly betrayed their husbands. As a rule, they were set aside instead. Banished to a convent or simply turned out in the cruel world to survive as best they could. The same could happen to a girl of nobility who had not yet been married or betrothed and found herself with child.

He prayed that neither of these things had happened to Iana, but there were no other reasons he could imagine for her circumstances. Any fool could see she had not been born or reared as anything other than a lady.

She said she had been wed, but somehow, she did not seem fully awakened to the pleasures possible between a woman and man. She wanted, but she obviously feared that wanting. So he wondered if she had made up the husband. Yet, if she bothered to do that, why deny that Tam was the child of that fictional union?

He gave up on the puzzle because he was simply too exhausted to struggle with it at the moment.

"Must we cross those mountains, sir?" Everand asked, pointing toward the rise of the Carrick Hills.

"We shall head north," Henri told him, "where they are not so steep, though it will take longer."

"Nay!" Iana exclaimed. "We shall not go north."

She sounded rather vehement about it, he thought. Henri looked over his shoulder. "Why?"

"Be—because I do not wish it."

Henri did not argue. Neither did he agree. "Then we shall camp in the meadow up ahead, near the trees. Morning is soon enough to set our course."

He suspected the reason she did not want to travel north was fear of encountering someone who knew her. Family, he guessed. Iana was from near here, Henri felt fairly certain.

They made camp within the shelter of the trees, as he directed. Iana seemed as weary as he, and Everand looked nearly dead on his feet.

"You build the fire, Ev. I shall see to the horses. Lady Iana, if you have the strength left, find me clothing in that bundle I purchased in Largsmuth. There is also a small garment there for Thomasina. You and Everand may save yours for our arrival at Baincroft if you like, but Tam and I should get dry and warm lest we sicken."

"You purchased things for us?" she asked, sounding none too pleased by it. "We had no need."

Ah, so she still begrudged the silver, did she? "I found a merchant's wife willing to sell some things newly sewn for her own use. Inside her husband's booth, I saw her stitching upon a child's bliaut and asked her if she had aught else. Happens she did and made me a fair price on them," he explained. "The garb for myself and for Ev did not come dear, for it is not new. I dickered for it and there is silver left. What I have used, I shall replace. I told you so."

He thought he heard her scoff.

"You doubt me?" he asked, wishing he had the stuffing left to be angry, but he did not.

She said nothing, but laid the babe upon the soft grass and went about doing as he had asked. Tossing his new shirt and chausses upon the ground at his feet, she then quickly dressed the child. Curling up again in the nest of her woolen sling, Tam sucked upon her finger and closed her eyes.

He watched as Iana pulled up several handfuls of grass and began rubbing down her mare. The strokes she made were leaden.

"Well, what do you wait for? Go," she ordered, flinging out one hand, "change out of those wet things and I shall finish here."

"Fine. Do so!" Henri let her. Damn her for not taking his word about the silver. Contentious wench. He scooped up the dry clothes and marched off.

To be perfectly fair, however, he had not told her of his wealth. She had no way of knowing he was other than a knight come straight from a sea battle with naught but that chain, his squire and the clothing on their backs. If he made her aware of the fact that he owned several estates in France and was heir to yet another fortune, she then might trust he would not leave her begging.

If she believed him. Why should she, though? Few noblemen took to the sea unless they were traveling from one shore to another for business or pleasure. They hired captains and crews and fighting men to go to war. Only, when the king had called upon him, Henri could never have sent his men to do what he would not.

Well, once they reached Baincroft, she would see. His father and Rob would loan or give him whatever he needed in the way of wealth. Then Iana would understand that she'd never had cause to worry. He would look after her and make certain she did not have to toil the way she had been doing to survive.

He could well imagine what a vision she would be, bathed in fragrant perfumes, clothed in rich fabrics and bedecked with jewels.

A pity he could not take her as his mistress, Henri thought, but she would never consent to that.

Why not? asked a wicked voice within his head. *She could hardly have a stranglehold on virtue if she has betrayed her vows and borne a bastard.*

No, he would not decry her, even silently, without knowing for certain. And he could hardly ask her if it was true. If it were not, the insult would be too great. If it were, she might feel forced to lie about it. Best he leave the matter be. And leave *her* be, he added for good measure, before he put a foot wrong and insulted her past forgiving.

He stripped off his wet clothing and donned the fresh, wishing he could have saved it for his arrival at Baincroft instead of having to wear it now and sleep in it for several nights to come.

Henri raked his hair off his brow and smoothed it behind his ears. His beard had grown so that he must look a fright. Tomorrow morn he would sharpen his blade and shave. Rob would never let him hear the end of it if he arrived home looking like the beast he felt at the moment.

Home. Baincroft seemed exactly that to him, despite the much richer abodes he owned in his native land.

Though he'd been fourteen when he arrived in Scotland, it had been the first real home he had ever known.

Yes, his father's brief exile had proved a godsend for them both. Lady Anne became the mother Henri had never had and her son became his brother. Those halcyon days cavorting around Baincroft and becoming part of a loving family remained the happiest of his life. They sustained him even now.

How he had hated to leave and take up his duties in France when the time came! But his and his father's people there had needed a lord. Now he would soon be back within the family fold. Loved and fussed over. Teased and mocked. He could scarcely wait to get there.

These thoughts brought guilt, however. Iana could not look forward to such joy. Her family must be even nearer than his own at the moment, yet she feared seeing one of them even accidentally, or so it seemed.

She would be taking up her life in a strange place with no friends, knowing no one, save Everand and himself. And she clearly did not trust *him* at all.

If he were the knight he had sworn to be, he would do all he could to ease her way, to protect her and make her less vulnerable. He should tell her all about himself and how he could well afford to provide for her and little Thomasina. Even if she did not believe him, she might at least have hope that he was telling the truth.

He stole out of the darkness toward the fire, noting Everand had fallen sound asleep on the grass beside it. Tam lay asleep, wrapped in the sling, her long lashes lying like little fans upon her soft cheeks.

Iana watched him approach, her dark eyes heavy-lidded with weariness.

"Are you hungry?" she asked, her gaze sharpening as she inspected his new clothing.

"Starving," he admitted, settling down beside her and accepting what she offered. "Ah, there's cheese left. I shall fashion a bow and hunt for us in the morning. We can spend a day or so here and rest."

"Nay, I would go on," she said firmly. "And I would like us to travel straight through the hills, not to the north."

Henri did not answer her immediately. He finished eating and drank his fill of the water she had brought from the firth in a wineskin.

"Well, what say you?" she demanded.

He sighed and brushed his hands together to rid them of the crumbs. "The way through the hills is shorter, I grant, but it would be difficult traveling, much of it afoot. I cannot see that we would gain much time."

"Nor would we be found if the townsmen send someone after us."

Henri met and held her guilty gaze. "And neither would we chance encountering your kin, who live to the north of here, am I right?"

Her lovely eyes widened with surprise before she jerked her gaze to one side. "Leave the matter be, sir. It is naught to you."

"Is there no hope that you might reconcile yourself to them?" he asked gently, thinking how families could quarrel vehemently, then be woefully sorry until things came right again. Until one or the other of the parties made the necessary overture.

"None," she declared, and got up to walk away.

"Iana, wait." He followed, laying a hand upon her shoulder when she stopped. Moving closer behind her, he leaned down and brushed the side of her cheek with his lips. How soft her skin, how sweet. "Forgive me. I did not intend to pry out your secrets."

"Did you not?" She jerked away from him and turned around, shaking with rage, her eyes flashing in the firelight. "My life is my own, do you hear? My *own,* and dearly bought! If you do not accept that, we part ways here and now and be damned to you, sir! No man will force my hand again!"

"Whoa!" he exclaimed, throwing up his hands. "Do not tar me with that brush. When have I ever sought to force you to anything?"

She shook her head, wrapped her arms across her chest and rubbed her shoulder where he had grasped it. He knew he had not gripped her hard.

"Do you fear me, Iana?" he asked gently. "Please do not. I would never harm you by deed or word." Again, he stepped closer and took her face lightly between his palms. "I vow it."

She swiftly backed away, leaving his hands outstretched in midair. "I am not afraid," she snapped.

But she was. He could detect it in her voice as well as in her actions. Was it his touch that terrified her so? Had she been so mistreated by some man that she feared them all alike?

He might never know. Why was it that he felt so compelled to find out?

"I admire you, you know," he said, changing tactics. He found he craved her trust, a thing she did not grant to anyone, as far as he could tell. Maybe its rarity was what made it seem so precious. "Not many women could survive the way you have done. I know not what you endured before we met, but this journey alone would have sent most of the women I know into fits and faints." He smiled at her, wishing to regain what ease together they had attained before this outburst.

"I never faint," she muttered, her head lowered. Her

hands still gripped her shoulders, looking as if they were the only things holding her upright at the moment.

"Nor resort to fits, thank God," Henri said, laughing when her head jerked up and she glared at him. "Your recent outburst does not count. That was but a strong defense of your privacy."

She had the grace to force a smile and nod.

He took pity. She badly needed rest, much more than he needed to pursue the mystery of her former life. There would be days yet in which to do so.

"You should go and lie down now," he suggested, "and I should do likewise. It will prove arduous making our way through those hills tomorrow."

"Through the hills," she affirmed, giving him a glowing grin of gratitude for finally granting her the choice of routes.

Since he had restored her good humor, Henri decided to risk asking a favor of her. As they walked together toward where Tam and Everand lay sleeping, he stopped her with a light touch to her elbow. "Tam has her woolen sling and Ev has the blanket. Would you sleep beside me?" he asked softly. "Only for the sake of warmth?"

She stiffened as if he had slapped her. "I would not sleep beside you or any man alive! Not for *any* reason!"

Chapter Six

Iana expected either laughter or anger at her pronouncement. Men did not choose to believe it when a woman refused them, and if they did, it made them furious to the point that they oft-times became violent. But Henri did not mock her now, nor did he threaten her in any way because of her outspoken denial of his request. He only looked at her with an expression that might have been regret or sympathy. She welcomed neither, but supposed she preferred both to his scorn or a blow to the head.

"As you will," he said softly, with no trace of humor, and inclined his head in a gesture of gracious defeat. "Rather, as you will *not*. I do beg pardon if I offended you, but I was only thinking to ward off the coldness of the night."

Iana managed a nod in acceptance of his apology, then retreated to the place where Tam lay sleeping.

Henri puzzled her. She had never met a man like him. Not once had she seen him in true bad temper. Even when he had sliced away that would-be thief's clothing and sent him tearing through the woods in terror, Iana had detected a note of amusement beneath Henri's threats. Thank God, the thief had not noticed. Whenever

Henri spoke curtly to Everand or to her, it was clear that only fear for their well-being prompted the sharpness of his words.

Her attraction to him frightened her. All she needed was to succumb to lust at this stage of her life. She, who knew precisely where sweet words and sweeter needs could lead a lass. Next she knew—if she did not keep her wits about her—she could be begging a living for herself and *two* bairns.

"Sleep well, my lady," he whispered from where he lay on the far side of his squire.

"And you, also," she replied. After a long moment's hesitation, she added, "Thank you."

Surely he would understand that her gratitude extended well beyond his courteous wish for her good rest. She now trusted he would not force himself upon her, though she had worried he might, once he was no longer suffering from his injury and the resulting fever. At the moment it was herself she did not trust to lie beside him for the sake of warmth.

Something within Henri beckoned to her with an insistence Iana found almost impossible to deny. Henri was kind. And witty. He was of an even temper and he truly seemed to care sincerely for other people. She knew well that what drew her to him involved infinitely more than his strong and winsome body.

Yet there was that, too, she had to admit. Iana sighed as she found herself wondering what loving would be like with a man such as Henri. Her experiences as a wife had offered her no pleasure at all and too much pain to forget. Instinctively, she knew it would be different with Henri, but how different?

He seemed gentle enough when not aroused, but would passion turn him rough and hurried? Would the greedy demands of the body bring out the very worst in him, as it had with her husband? And as Newell's wife vowed had happened within their marriage? Would Henri hurt her, or would he give her the pleasure she had once dreamed a man might?

Curiosity was driving her mad, but she could not afford to give in to the powerful need to know. To do so would mean relinquishing her independence. If she allowed Henri to take her, there would be consequences beyond the possibility of begetting his child. He would make himself responsible for her whether she objected or not. He was that sort of man.

Where she lived, every move she made, every coin she spent and even the clothing she wore would again be dictated to her. She would have no choices at all, about anything in her life. After the brief bit of freedom she had grasped as a widow, Iana could not allow it.

She pillowed her head upon her arm, curled herself around Tam and tried to ignore the chills she so easily might have avoided by accepting his offer. When at last she drifted off to sleep, she nestled back into the solace of a wondrous dream, one in which she found no reason at all to oppose his nearness.

In fantasy, they fit perfectly together in both belief and body. There was no master, nor mistress, nor struggle for autonomy. Only the keen pleasure of give and take, and afterward, a warmth and comfort so heavenly, Iana never wished to wake.

Henri nudged Ev with the toe of his boot and whispered, "Wake up, slugabed. Fetch us some water while I rekindle the fire. Look what I found."

Ev cracked one eye open and peered up at him. Then he came fully awake and grinned. "Eggs!"

"Shh. Yes, we shall feast upon those and the partridge that provided them. I wish to surprise our lady and wake her with the scent of roasting fowl. Hop to if you are hungry."

Henri laughed softly at Ev's hurry, and then set about preparing the meal. First he whittled a point on a long branch of green oak he had collected, then stuck two forked limbs into the ground on either side of the fire upon which he would rest it. Next he plucked the bird free of its feathers and neatly gutted it for cooking. Efficient as he ever had been at this, Henri thought proudly.

The task reminded him of his boyhood at Baincroft, when he and Rob would go a-hunting for days on end, doing for themselves, acquiring new abilities aside from the taking of game.

They learned many skills not generally associated with the sons of nobility, such as cooking, washing their clothing and making weapons or traps of whatever they could find. In turn, they had become Crusaders forced to live off the land, outlaws evading capture or knights errant seeking the Grail. What joyous days those had been. And in what good stead those adventures had placed him now.

He glanced fondly at the sleeping woman and child, glad of his ability to gift them with such a simple thing as a decent meal.

The wary Iana probably would suspect him of trying to seduce her with food. The wish did cross his mind that she might show her appreciation by becoming more friendly, perhaps granting him a kiss. Eggs for a kiss, then. But a fat, tasty partridge should bring more, he thought, grinning at his private jest as he skewered the bird upon the stick.

He knew very well she would starve before she allowed him to kiss her. Neither had she permitted him to warm her in the night, but he had arranged that nicely enough, anyway. In her sleep, she had not minded at all how close he lay. She might even laugh did she know the discomfort he had suffered by having his way and yet not having it, but he was not about to tell her.

Humming beneath his breath, Henri positioned the fowl to cook and sat back upon his heels to await the water Ev would bring to boil the eggs. Henri was good at waiting, when it suited him to do so.

Again he looked at Iana, relishing the sight of the long, golden braid he so seldom got to see. During the night, he had carefully worked loose her wimple just to have this lovely sight when the morning sun rose. Even the dawn's weak rays gave her a beauteous luster he enjoyed immensely.

The color of her locks continued to surprise him. With her dark eyes and brows, the hair should have been some shade of brown. Yet it held the rich patina of burnished gold. Fascinating. Henri shook his head, still smiling.

She was so lovely. Much of that loveliness shone from the inside, of course. Her compassion and bravery, together with the way she looked, stirred his desire in a way no woman had affected him before.

All the others, so easily won, with so little wooing, were as nothing compared to her. Her lack of immediate and enthusiastic surrender might be playing a part in his determination to possess her, Henri admitted to himself, but he did not care why he wanted her so. He only knew that he did, and more so every hour that passed.

The delicate scent of her, the remembered touch of her small nimble hands on his body as she treated his wound, haunted him constantly. The riddle of her past only added to her mystique. He loved a mystery.

He could never marry her, of course. If he took another

wife, it was bound to be a French noble's daughter. That was expected. But if Iana should come to love him, Henri could see no shame for either of them in an arrangement of the heart.

Certainly she would endure no more public censure than she would here in Scotland as an outcast woman with a child. He could take her with him to France and keep her in splendor there, give her the best that life had to offer. He would recognize Tam as his, Henri decided, just as he planned to do with Everand. The daughter of a future *comte,* bastard or not, would fare very well indeed when she was old enough to wed. He made a mental note to mention that to Iana.

Ah, yes, even life here in the wilds was good this morn, and soon to get better. He would win Iana's trust, make her recognize that desire he saw in her eyes, and he would have her. She would be well worth the wait. Then she would never have to worry again what was to become of her and her child. Iana would be his to cherish.

Iana did not wish to open her eyes. She had been dreaming of a feast the likes of which she'd not seen for months. The heavenly smell lingered, permeating the air all around her. She stretched her arms wide and drew in a deep breath before wakefulness could dispel the imagining.

"Good morn, my lady," Sir Henri greeted her.

She blinked at him, then saw what he was doing. "Bless you! You have found real food." In a trice, she crouched eagerly beside him near the fire, the better to savor the delicious aroma.

"Look there," he whispered, staring past her shoulder, his eyes full of wonder.

Iana turned and saw Tam unsteadily creeping across

the grass toward them on her hands and knees. She gave little grunts of frustration now and again when she happened on a rough patch and lost her purchase.

Laughing with sheer joy, Iana held her arms wide and beckoned to the child. When she glanced at Henri, she saw his fierce look of pride, as if he were responsible for Tam's new venture. In a roundabout way, Iana supposed he was. Had he not tempted her away from the babe by the prospect of this unusual repast, Tam might not have bothered testing her mettle. At last, the child had come to life. Her fall into the firth seemed to have awakened her from some sort of spell.

"She will be walking the next thing we know," Henri said proudly.

"Aye, of a certainty," Iana agreed, scooping Tam up in her arms and rewarding her with a hearty kiss. "There's my good lass. Oh, you are so brave!"

"So she shall have her reward," said Everand, who sat on the opposite side of the fire. He nudged a small bowl that Iana had brought for mixing herbs into the glowing coals. Iana saw that it contained three quail eggs covered with water, and nodded her approval.

"I met a family of travelers when I was firth-side getting the water," he informed them. "They spoke to me but I could not understand their words."

Iana's gaze quickly collided with Henri's. "Those people will surely speak of such a meeting. What if they are bound for Largsmuth and mention it there?"

She set Tam down, rose quickly and began to gather their things. "We must leave here before we are found."

Henri remained where he was. "I agree we should go soon, but not on the instant. Even if they do as you fear, it will take them some time to find the ferry and make their way across the firth. By the time they do that, and

on the unlikely chance they happen upon someone looking for us, we shall be well into the hills. Do not worry.
Come, sit you down again. We are almost ready to eat
and there is surely time for that.''

They could not be away quickly enough to suit Iana.
She hardly took the time to properly appreciate the meal.
Only when they had mounted their steeds and put a
goodly distance between themselves and the banks of the
Clyde did Iana draw an easy breath.

She worried as much over being found and forced to
return to Largsmuth as she did about any retribution for
that man's death. She remembered that her brother Newell acted as a magistrate in important matters, and she
much feared that the town might be within the realm of
his responsibility.

All day they rode, halting only to rest the mounts and
quickly attend to their own needs. Iana suspected that
Henri merely wished to arrive at his brother's home as
soon as humanly possible. He did not seem worried in
the least that anyone from Largsmuth would give chase.

"The going is quite harsh, but I did try to warn you,"
Henri told her.

They had found it necessary to dismount in order to
negotiate a particularly wicked slope. Everand's horse
slid several lengths and almost toppled before regaining
a tenuous footing.

When darkness prevented further travel, they stopped
for the night, only to rise with the dawn and be off again.
Again, her sleep seemed filled with dreams of heady
warmth and pleasure. Yet they did not give her the ease
and comfort such dreams should have done. She awoke
feeling a vague dissatisfaction she could not, or did not
want to, put a name to. Her entire body hummed with it.

Iana felt cross on arising. As they rode, she had cause

to appreciate the time when Tam had not voiced her disapproval. Now the child made her presence known quite regularly, babbling, whimpering and weeping outright. She also wriggled around within the sling like a wee fish on a hook.

Iana even imagined Tam had taken on weight. She was eating more than ever. Mayhaps it was only that she no longer lay still like a lifeless poppet. Iana was infinitely glad of that, even though the babe was now a trial to carry for any length of time.

Henri offered to relieve her of her charge a number of times, and Iana finally agreed. Every time she relinquished Tam and the sling to him, his hands would brush hers. Once he even dared to place those hands upon Iana's shoulders and rub the aching muscles there. The delicious sensation made her sigh and wish for more.

His knowing smile promised he would gladly give it, did she but ask. The incident reminded her of playing near the fire as a child, poking the glowing embers with a stick. The sparks flying then and now were dangerous to her well-being, Iana quickly realized. She had a name for that feeling she now awakened with each morn in his company. However, desire, like an out of control blaze, should be discouraged unless one wished to risk everything.

Halfway through the second day, Henri drew rein and waited until they rode abreast. "The worst is behind us."

Iana could see for herself there were now only gently rising hills, hardly worthy of the name, before them. "Where are we? Do you know?"

Henri nodded and urged his mount to a walk, even as he searched the horizon before them. "I am almost certain Kelso must be some leagues distant, to the south.

Baincroft is northeast of there, a good half-day's ride by my reckoning.''

"Should we not follow the next beaten track to a village and ask the way?'' Iana inquired, clicking her tongue and nudging her exhausted mare with her heels.

"Once the land flattens, I shall know where we are,'' he assured her.

Iana exhaled sharply and shook her head. "I knew it. We are lost.''

"We are not,'' he argued. "I am never lost.''

Iana stifled a smile. "Aye? Well, you did travel up the wrong side of Scotland to get where you are going.''

He gritted his teeth. She could see the muscles clenching in his jaw. "There was an excellent reason for—''

"There, sir!'' Everand interrupted, pointing. "I see smoke, too much for a campfire. Shall we ride for it?''

Several plumes of gray were barely visible in the distance.

"Very well,'' Henri said grudgingly. "Our supplies have dwindled and we should find milk for Thomasina.''

They turned their mounts southeast and increased their pace to a trot. In the sling upon Iana's back, Tam made a humming noise, apparently fascinated with the way the bounce of the mount affected her voice. The sound elicited a chuckle from Ev and banished Iana's weariness. But it was Henri's smile that caused her heart to flutter.

The village bustled with activity. It appeared fairly prosperous compared to the places they had seen along the way. Women gossiped round the community well, while a gaggle of children chased one another in a game of some sort. None of the people wore rags or seemed thin from lack of food. The housing looked to be in good repair and the animals seemed well fed.

Henri drew up before a gray-bearded man who sat in

front of one of the newer cottages, whittling. "What is this place called?" he asked the old fellow.

"'Tis Tharlstane," the man replied, squinting up at them.

Henri dismounted. "We would purchase a meal here if you have victuals to spare. We have silver."

The old man laid aside his blade and the length of wood. Wiping his hands upon his rough woolen tunic, he rose to his feet. "Marta!" he shouted toward the open door to the house.

A round-faced woman stuck her head out. "Aye? What is it, Da?"

"We've paying guests. Milk th' goat," he ordered, then crooked a gnarled finger at Henri. "Get yer woman and wee 'uns offen the beasts and coom inside."

Henri assisted her down as Everand slid nimbly off his mount. Without being told, he led the horses around the side of the cottage to tether them there so they would not deposit their leavings out front.

"I be Abel Sanquhar," the man told them, considering Henri with a knowing nod. "And ye'd be ken of Trouville, aye?"

"I would. You know my father?" Henri bent his head to avoid knocking it as he entered the cottage.

"Aye, the *comte*'s well known hereabout. Me and my lads helped him raise his keep some years back. I did a muckle bit o' carving for 'im. Sit yerself, missus," he ordered Iana, while he went to a shelf to fetch several wooden bowls and spoons.

A loaf of freshly baked bread sat cooling upon the smoothly sanded table. Iana's mouth watered at the smell of the stew cooking over the fire. Next to the bread, old Abel placed a half round of cheese.

"How far is it to Baincroft?" Henri asked as he took

Tam from Iana. When he sat upon the bench, he placed the baby in his lap. Tam rested her small arms on the tabletop and stared curiously at their host as if she, too, awaited his answer. They might have been father and daughter, so close were their coloring and expression.

"Quite a ways. Good half-day's ride," he said. "Got dealings with MacBain, have ye?"

"He is my brother," Henri said with a ready smile, obviously delighted that the journey was almost over.

"Call 'im that, do ye? I knew his da, too," Abel said with a snort. "Rotten sod and that's a fact. Puir lad of his went daft on account of it."

"He is not *daft*," Henri said through his teeth. "Lord Robert is as fine a man as you are ever like to meet. He cannot hear well due to a fever he once had, but he is lacking in no other way, I assure you."

"Hmm. Deaf, then." Abel shook his head as he ladled stew into three bowls and set them in front of his guests.

Iana wondered what it would be like to work for a man such as Henri's brother. If the poor lord could not hear, how would she speak with him? She had never known anyone afflicted with deafness. But Henri had said MacBain could not hear *well*. She must remember to speak loudly in his presence, Iana decided.

She promptly set aside that question in favor of attending the stew. It smelled heavenly, of fresh meat boiled with turnip roots and fragrant herbs.

The girl came in with a wooden bucket filled with milk. "This be my only grandchild, Marta, named for her mum, God rest her soul." Young Marta set down the milk and curtsied, offering them all a shy smile.

Henri rose halfway in greeting, clutching Tam's stomach in one large palm. He sat again and inclined his head toward Iana. "Lady Iana of Ayr."

"Yer wife?" Abel asked, one bushy brow raised.

"No," Henri said quickly, and attempted to shift the man's attention to Everand. "This is my son and squire, Everand."

Abel ignored that introduction. "Is she yer betrothed, then?"

Impatiently, Henri said, "No."

The old man fastened his gaze upon Tam, then frowned. "Whose is th' bairn?"

"Thomasina belongs to Lady Iana," Henri said. "The lady is a widow."

Iana could see that the man believed Tam also belonged to Henri. He did cradle the child in a protective and proprietary way, as a loving father might. He had even handed her a wooden spoon to play with, and jounced her on his knee.

Old Abel cast Iana a dark and disapproving look. He glanced pointedly at her hand, which bore no ring. A lady, wed or widowed, would have had that if nothing else, to mark her status. "Well, eat and be off with ye, then," the old grouch rumbled.

Everand, oblivious to the mounting tension, tucked into the stew with a vengeance. Marta tore off a hunk of the bread, laid it beside his plate and began slicing cheese for everyone.

"We shall eat elsewhere if our presence offends you, Sanquhar," Henri warned. His expression looked thunderous.

Abel raked Iana with a final look of disdain. "Ye'll be gettin' no better welcome anywhere else," he said. With that assertion, he left them and went back outside.

Henri offered Iana an apologetic frown. "Shall we leave?" he asked softly.

Iana forced a smile to cover her embarrassment. "I

think not. He is probably right about the welcome. We will do as he instructed, eat and begone.''

''You need not worry,'' he told her. ''When we arrive at Baincroft, the people there will not treat us so rudely.''

''Us?'' Iana questioned. ''I am the one who draws the censure. Abel Sanquhar thinks Tam is a bastard and I a fallen woman. You believe it, too,'' she accused.

Henri chewed thoughtfully on a bite of the cheese before commenting. ''You did say she was not your husband's get. What else am I to surmise but that she is your *natural* child?''

Iana shrugged, barely containing her anger. He was right, however. She had given him no reason to think otherwise, but it sat ill with her that he would assume such. ''Surmise whatever you choose, sir. But the truth is, I found Tam in the woods.''

''Yes, of course,'' he agreed politely. And altogether too quickly. He plied her with no questions about which woods or how long ago or what the circumstances were that led her to discover the bairn.

She knew how futile it would be to explain the matter any further. Henri would no more believe the truth than anyone else would.

''Will this affect your arranging work for me when we arrive at our destination?'' she asked stiffly.

Henri hesitated an instant too long before he answered, ''It should not matter.''

It *should* not, Iana thought, but it very likely would.

Chapter Seven

Henri gave Abel Sanquhar one of the coins he had demanded from the innkeeper in Largsmuth. It was far too much, given the amount of food they had eaten, but he had nothing smaller. He felt as if he should box the unctuous fellow's ears instead of giving him silver.

They loaded their belongings on the horses and rode out of the village single file. Curious stares from the villagers followed them as they passed. Henri for one was glad to leave the place behind.

Why the old man's words to Iana angered him, Henri could not say. It should not cause him bother when someone took her to task for bearing a bastard. If she'd had a husband at the time she conceived, she obviously had betrayed him the same way Henri's wife, Justine, had once betrayed him. He recalled having made quite a few remarks on *her* behavior at the time.

The French were a bit more sanguine about such matters, unless they were the ones wronged. Scots could be a self-righteous lot and most unforgiving, even sanctimonious, when they were not directly involved.

Henri decided for certain that he must take Iana to

France, where she would be less likely to encounter any further condemnation.

God knows, Justine had not suffered much of it when she had strayed from her vows. Had she not died, taking Emile's babe with her to the grave, Henri would still have her as his wife and that child as his heir. In truth, he seldom thought of it anymore and wished he could forget it altogether.

Somehow he did not think Iana had actually committed adultery. It was more likely she had never wed at all. If she had, surely she would be wearing her husband's ring, if only for the protection it offered.

She did not behave as a widow, but more as a wary maid unused to men. He supposed she must have been seduced, probably only once, by some scoundrel who might have tricked her into thinking he had marriage on his mind. That would explain her wariness in becoming intimate again even when she felt the desire to do so. And she did desire him, Henri knew. He'd had too many eager lovers not to recognize that particular fire in her eyes.

"Will it not inconvenience your brother's household if we arrive late tonight?" Iana asked, dragging Henri away from his thoughts of her plight.

"We are so close I wish we could go on, but I think we must camp tonight," he answered, absently rubbing his side.

"Does your wound bother you still?" she asked quickly.

"Hardly at all," he answered, smiling at her sincere concern. "Only when I twist a certain way. In another day or so, I shall be good as new. You have tended me well and I thank you again."

She nodded. "Remember that when you recommend me, if you will."

"I shall never forget," he assured her, "and I will gladly give you the credit." For all the good it would do, he was more than willing to sing her praises. She did know her herbs and how to stitch a body so it would heal properly, but that would hardly be enough in her case, Henri feared.

He figured they had roughly two more hours of daylight. It would take twice that to reach Baincroft if the old man spoke truly. Henri did not wish to appear at the gates of Baincroft when everyone was preparing to go to bed. They were not expected and, as Iana pointed out, it would be incommodious.

The land through which they rode now was fairly level and provided easier travel. This part of Scotland seemed more civilized and welcoming. Henri had always enjoyed the verdant place with its fields of heather and gorse, spreading oaks, tall pines and occasional wildflowers.

"Shall I ride ahead come the morn and announce your arrival, sir?" Everand asked. "They would understand me there, would they not?"

"The steward, Thomas de Brus, speaks French, though my brother and his wife do not. I think it best if we ride in together."

With that pronouncement, Henri urged his horse well ahead of Everand's. He needed time to consider how he would explain Iana to Rob and Mairi once they reached Baincroft. He could simply tell them she was a widow and let them assume Tam was born of her husband. But they would still want to know, since she was obviously a lady, why she was now alone and destitute with a child. Hell, he would like to hear her answer himself.

A noble husband would have provided for her before

his death, and lacking that, her family would have taken her in again. Either she'd had no husband at all, or she had betrayed the one she had and been set aside for it and denied by her family. There seemed no other explanation that made any sense, he thought with a disgruntled shake of his head.

Henri hoped the fact that Iana had saved his life would be enough to make her acceptable in their eyes despite everything. They were born and bred Scots, however, and might well have the same reproachful attitude as Abel Sanquhar.

Either way, Henri knew it was unlikely they would offer her employment as he had promised he would ask them to do. That could work in his favor, Henri thought. Then she would have excellent reason to accede to his wishes and come under his protection. What else could she do?

Everand dropped back to ride beside Iana, seeming no more eager than she was to greet a castleful of strangers come the morrow. "I do wonder what my lord's brother will think of me," he said in a low voice, so that Henri could not hear him. "You must have the same worry for yourself, my lady."

Impatiently, he raked a few windblown strands of hair from his brow and sighed. How serious he looks for one so young, she thought.

"Aye, I do worry," she admitted.

Though he had not remarked on it, Iana knew then that Everand had not ignored the disapproval the village elder had offered. "Lord and Lady MacBain are not likely to greet Tam and me with open arms, that is for certain. I truly had not considered that possibility until the old man pointed out the appearance of my circumstance."

"Did you really find the baby in the woods?" Ev asked openly.

Iana smiled and nodded. "I did. Her mother was dying and Tam was nearly dead herself. I promised I would care for her and so I have. She is my daughter now, Everand, just as you are Sir Henri's son."

"You must tell my lord again, the whole of it this time," Everand coaxed. "He will surely believe you. It is admirable, what you are doing for the little one."

Iana shook her head. "Nay, he will not take my word on it as easily as you do. He could think I made up the tale to save myself scorn. Do not fret over it, my friend. All will be well."

"I shall wed you myself and give Tam a father," Everand declared. "As soon as I gain a bit of height and weight, I shall look as old as you. No one will even think to question you after that."

Iana cleared her throat to cover a sudden urge to laugh. It would not do to spurn such a noble proposal, and it did touch her heart that he would offer. "I thank you, Everand, but you have too much yet to do with your life to burden yourself with a family. We will make do on our own. You may call yourself Tam's honorary uncle if you wish. She could do no better than to have a kinsman such as yourself."

He cast her a look that told her he understood the real reason for her refusal. "I shall help you look after her while we are there. Just remember, if life proves awkward for you at Baincroft and you should change your mind, my offer stands."

Iana nodded and smiled her thanks instead of refusing. He would not do as a husband, but if she ever chanced to produce a son, she would wish him to be exactly like this lad.

She would have some of the silver left, surely, though she had not known the cost of things would be so much out in the world. Never had she been allowed to purchase things for herself, so she had no way of knowing.

Even if she had the entire chain or Sir Henri's promised replacement in coin for what they had spent, it would not feed and house her and Tam for long. She needed work.

When darkness had almost descended, Henri reined his mount and waited for them to catch up. ''Here is as good a place as any to sleep,'' he announced. ''The stream will provide us water and means to make ourselves presentable in the morning.''

Iana waited for him to help her dismount. Her back ached from the sling and the baby's wriggling against her. Gratefully, she held on to Henri's shoulders as he assisted her off the mare. He held her, his hands still at her waist, while Everand relieved her of Tam's weight.

Iana watched the lad carry the baby in one arm while he took up the horses' dangling reins with his other hand. He sang a cheerful little song as he led the mounts over to the water.

When she would have pulled away, Henri's fingers tightened to prevent it. His somber gaze met hers. ''I must speak to you of what is to come. Thoughts of it have troubled me greatly since we left the village.''

That sounded ominous enough that she wanted to delay it. ''Let me tend to Tam first.'' Still he did not let her go.

''Ev will see to her for a while. Come, over there beneath that elm is a comfortable spot where we can sit and talk.''

They settled upon a lush blanket of grass, with Henri close by her side, facing her. His right hip brushed her left as he took her hand in his. She wished he would sit farther away so she could think properly. His nearness unsettled her.

"I know of no other way to say this, but to be forthright. I would like to offer you my protection," he declared.

"Imagine that," Iana said, not really surprised. "Your squire was even more gallant. He proposed marriage. Are the French so passionate that they would proposition every woman they meet?"

He did not return her smile. "I cannot marry you, Iana."

"I know. That was not a hint. I would not wed you even if you begged." She tried to withdraw her hand, but he held it too tightly. "Nor will I be your whore. Now let me go."

Suddenly he did so and raked the dark hair back from his face. He pressed his temples with the heels of his hands as he sighed. "Damn you Scots! Must everything be so right or wrong?"

Iana laughed. "Everything *is* right or wrong. In this instance, both things are wrong. I have told you I will belong to no man. I meant what I said." At his despairing look, she tried to explain. "I cannot accept what you offer, Henri, but I suppose I must thank you for the thought."

She had a few thoughts of her own that she would never voice. The images he conjured by his question would plague her forever, she suspected. Lying in his arms with no thought of tomorrow. Kissing him without pause until she sated her longing. Not stopping with kisses. Ah, she had to banish these tempting ideas from her mind before she went mad. Or succumbed, heaven help her.

"It is not enough for you," he said with resignation.

"Nay, it is too much," she argued. "If your brother does not welcome my serving as healer at Baincroft, then I shall find another place to dwell. If that happens, repay me the silver you promised and forget I exist. You are not to feel responsible for me, do you hear?"

He scoffed and shook his head. "How can I not? I owe you my life. I want you more than I have ever wanted any woman. I care for your child. You expect me to dismiss you from my mind like so?" He snapped his fingers.

"Aye, I do!" Then one thing he had said eclipsed all else. "You want me? More than anyone?" Iana whispered, disbelieving.

"Are you so blind you cannot see what you do to me?" he demanded, glancing down at himself. "Can you not feel my desire when I lie behind you each night?"

"When you *what?*" Iana gasped.

"Yes, I have held you, and do not pretend you were oblivious to it. Did I not hear your sweet sighs and hums of pleasure while you feigned sleep? Yet I did nothing that would offend. Not one thing." He turned away from her as if disgusted with himself for his restraint. "No, I treated you with all respect, no matter what you have done before."

"Before?" she demanded through gritted teeth. "You knave! I have done nothing in my life that would give me shame!"

He huffed. "No, I daresay you would justify each time you lay with a man not wed to you. Called it love, did you?" He pushed up from the ground and looked down as if he would spit upon her. "Though you would not lie down and call it that with me, eh? No, I suspect you now have done with all such pretense. Well, so have I! God save me from women in *love*. I have had enough of those to last me a lifetime.''

Horrified, she leapt up and faced him, hands on her hips to keep from striking his insolent face. ''I have never, never lain with a man not wed to me! How dare you insult—''

He mirrored her stance. ''I dare because I know full well no man would render you destitute without good reason. And no family would turn out a nobly born daughter unless they had sufficient cause. I did not even do that to my wife when she—''

''God's truth, you have a *wife?*'' she screeched. ''And you asked me to—?''

''Be my mistress. *Oui!* My wife is dead,'' he shouted.

''You killed her?'' Iana demanded.

''Of course I did not kill her. What sort of man do you think me?''

''One with a head as hard as the standing stones!''

''With a body to match it, thanks to your wiles.'' He glared at her and she glared back.

''My lord? Sir?'' Everand ventured, then in desperation added, ''Father?''

Reluctantly, Henri broke his hostile stare to answer. ''What is so dire that you interrupt?''

The wide-eyed lad handed Tam to her and then stuttered, ''Y-you should n-not shout at Lady Iana, sir. She has done no wrong.''

Henri took several deep breaths, his eyes closed, apparently attempting to gain control of his temper. When he finally spoke, his voice sounded perfectly normal. ''Of course, you are right.'' He hesitated. Took another deep breath. ''My heartfelt apologies, Lady Iana.''

Had he put too much stress upon the word *lady?* Iana thought so, but it had been subtle for all that. ''Accepted,'' she replied diffidently, shifting the silent Tam to one hip.

"It is almost completely dark. Ev, make a fire," Henri ordered calmly. "Make it well away from the water. We do not want to be disturbed by the night creatures coming there to drink."

"Speaking of night creatures," she snapped once Everand had gone off to prepare the camp. "You keep to yourself when we retire."

Henri exhaled and wearily rubbed the back of his neck. "Look, Iana, I truly did not mean all that I said."

"Well, I *did*," she declared. "I meant every single word."

He treated her to a Gallic shrug that made her want to kick him soundly in the shins.

Henri abided by her dictate and slept apart from her the entire night. He regretted their harsh words and knew he had not helped his cause one whit by losing his temper. Soon, however, she would realize that she had no recourse but to accept his offer.

He would never wish to force her into an alliance, but neither could he leave her in strange surroundings to fend for herself and Tam. Rob would look after them, see that they did not go hungry or without shelter, but Henri doubted Iana would accept charity from anyone, especially if it came coupled with disdain. While neither Rob nor his wife, Mairi, were likely to offer her that, others at Baincroft were certain to do so if they suspected she had borne an illegitimate child. This was the way of things.

They had risen quite early, made themselves as presentable as possible and set out on the final two hours of their journey. He tried not to notice how the amber of the new woolen gown he had purchased for her in Largsmuth brought out the golden glints in her hair and made her creamy skin glow to perfection. But he did notice, and had to bite his tongue to keep the praise from slipping off it. She would only throw it back in his face and again decry his use of her silver.

Ev had no such compunction and told her how beautiful she was, earning himself a beaming smile for his trouble. Henri ignored them both, his jaw clenched so hard his teeth hurt.

Soon Baincroft's towers came into view at last. Henri's heart swelled with anticipation as it always did when he arrived here.

He recalled the first time he had come, seeing the place and comparing it to the rich French estates he and his father owned and the royal palaces where he once lived as the young son of the king's advisor. Henri had quickly learned that Baincroft contained a wealth of warmth and welcome that those finer abodes would never possess.

"The gates stand open," Everand observed. "Is that unusual, sir?"

Henri smiled. "Not at all. This is a peaceful place. There are sharp eyes upon those towers, alert to any threat. We will have been seen already, you can wager on that."

Everand sighed. "A pity we do not have your colors to carry so they would know who approaches."

"They will recognize me soon enough. My brother's standard flies, which means he is in residence."

Iana remained quiet and looked extremely wary, as if she dreaded their arrival. Henri felt compelled to reassure her. "Do not fear. You will be welcome." At least at first she would, simply because he had brought her.

In silence, they rode on until a huge charger burst

through the gates and thundered toward them. *Rob*. Henri threw back his head and laughed aloud, held up his arms as if in surrender and dismounted to wait.

His brother leapt off even as his stallion skidded to a halt before them. "Harry, you dog!" Rob shouted, his face wreathed in joy. Henri embraced him gladly and returned the fierce shakes and backslapping.

When they had pummeled each other enough, Rob stepped back, still holding Henri's shoulders, and glanced questioningly in the direction from which they had arrived.

He and Rob rarely needed words to communicate, which was fortunate, since his brother could not hear and spoke as infrequently as possible. Rob admittedly had trouble with Henri's French accent even after all these years. They usually employed mostly hand gestures and facial expressions unless there were others present who would not understand them.

Now he decided to forgo that simple courtesy in the interest of expediency and began to quickly make the signs.

I was at war with the English and my ship sank. My squire and the lady saved my life. We came from the west, over the mountains.

"Hurt?" Rob asked aloud. The large hands gripping Henri's shoulders gentled as his face darkened with concern.

Henri pointed to his side, inclined his head and shrugged, dismissing it as unimportant. He held out a hand toward Iana, who had remained mounted. "This is Lady Iana...of Ayr and her daughter, Thomasina. Iana, my brother, Lord Robert."

Rob approached her mare and bowed. "Welcome, my lady," he said in his deep, gravelly voice, which held no inflection. He winked and smiled at Tam, who was peeking around Iana's shoulder from her sling.

"My lord," Iana acknowledged. Henri had to laugh. It was a mistake most people made, thinking that if only they were loud enough, the sound might get through to Rob. It did not, of course, but it did distort the mouth so that he could hardly tell what words formed upon the lips.

When it became obvious that was all she intended to say, Rob turned to Everand, who now stood beside his horse, twisting the ends of the reins.

"Squire?" Rob voiced, glancing at Henri for confirmation.

"And my son," Henri announced. "Everand."

Rob frowned, a certain indication that he had not grasped the name with its nasal intonation.

"Ev," Henri clarified, executing the two letters with his fingers and repeating, "My son, Ev."

The sharp gray eyes studied Ev for a moment, apparently noting the boy's pale coloring and lack of stature. Rob then returned his steady gaze to Henri, bearing the silent query that was fully expected.

"He is mine," Henri stated unequivocally.

Without another qualm or further hesitation, Robert turned and offered Ev his arm to clasp. "Nephew," he said with simple acceptance.

Henri quickly translated the word and Everand accepted the offer with a firm nod and a laugh of relief. Rob slapped him affectionately on the shoulder and almost knocked him off his feet.

"Best eat more," Rob advised as he remounted and motioned for them to precede him toward the castle.

Henri realized he had never thought to tell Iana and Ev about Robert, though they had obviously gleaned the information from his conversation with Abel Sanqhuar the day before. Sometimes Henri forgot altogether how different Rob was from others.

"My brother cannot hear you," he said to them, facing forward with his back to Rob as he did so. "However, he can see your words and should be able to understand yours even better than ours, Iana, since Everand and I are French. Always face him as you speak and talk as you normally do. Never shout or exaggerate. And remember that he sees much more than most people. If you are not careful, he will divine your every thought even as you think it."

"A frightening prospect," Iana muttered.

Henri chuckled. "You do not know the half. At times I have believed him a warlock."

Her rounded eyes said she had taken him seriously. Again he laughed. "That was a jest. Rob is quite human, but a man of many talents. The greatest of those being his ability to judge the heart of a person. You may trust him with your life if your heart is true."

She said not another word, leading him to wonder whether she feared his brother would find her lacking in that respect. Henri thought it unlikely. Iana had shown compassion in tending his wound and accompanying them here. She was resourceful, brave and possessed of a fine wit. But she did have guilty secrets and there had to be a reason for that.

For now, he wished he could put the worry aside and revel in the reunion with Rob, Mairi and those two rascally nephews of his whom he had not seen for nigh on a year. Tomorrow he should take Ev and ride north to his father's keep and visit his parents and sister.

But could he leave Iana here while he did so? No, he decided, nor could he take her along. His father would pose a great many more questions about her than Rob would do, Henri was certain. Maybe it would be best to postpone traveling there for a few more days. Just until he saw how she would be treated here by the folk of Baincroft and whether she would accept Rob and Mairi's charity.

That offer would not sit well with a woman of Iana's pride. She wanted work. Henri had promised to ask and he would do so, but privately doubted he would meet with any success on her behalf. It was one thing for the lady of a lord to tend the health of the people in her husband's demesne, quite another for him to hire a lady to do so.

Knowing Iana was nobly born, Rob probably would not grant her a paid position at Baincroft as a healer or any other thing. He would consider it demeaning for her to earn her way in the world. As a sworn knight, Rob was bound by God to give a lady aid and protect her. Nothing in the vows mentioned providing employment. Even if she thought to lie about her origin and call herself a commoner, no one had yet lied successfully to Robert MacBain.

Henri felt a stab of guilt that his own offer of protection would do more to demean her person than would her living in a bothy and selling or trading herbal cures and potions. Yet he could think of no other way he could have her.

At present, it seemed she had but two alternatives. She could live upon Rob and Mairi's generosity. That is, if they did not question Tam's birth too closely and deny her because of it. Or she could become Henri's mistress. She might think she could go off on her own and beg for a living, of course, but Henri would never allow that. He did not consider that an option at all.

If he could, he would persuade her to become his mistress, though that would mean leaving Scotland immediately. Neither Rob nor his father would countenance Henri's leman living beneath their roof. They would think less of him, as well, for establishing Iana as that, even if they learned of her former indiscretion.

That consideration left Henri with ambivalent feelings he could not sort out. He wanted her desperately, more than he had any other woman in memory. Yet he could never marry her, for a number of reasons. She had no dowry or link to any royal line, as did he. She was not even French. And, apparently, she had borne an illegitimate child and been cut off from her entire clan for the offense. But if she finally did agree to his proposition, then she would be an anathema to his family. She would never be welcome to enjoy this part of his life, the part that kept him whole and made him who he was.

He looked at her then and his heart ached for her as much as for himself. How selfish he was, Henri thought suddenly. How incredibly venal. His own thwarted desire was as nothing compared to her dilemma. And still she rode straight-backed and regal as any queen, facing down whatever she must to make a life for herself and her little Thomasina.

"I will be by your side, Iana," he said. "Trust in me."

She leveled him with a look, one eyebrow cocked and her eyes narrowed. "The day I trust in any man is the day they lay me to rest. Then I must hope they could manage the burial, at the very least, without botching it."

Henri could think of nothing at the moment that would refute her argument. He had to admit her men certainly had not done right by her thus far, whoever they were.

Chapter Eight

Iana allowed Henri to help her down from the mare. His hands lingered at her waist even longer than usual. The warmth of his palms and fingers through her clothing seemed a deliberate attempt to comfort. His gaze affirmed that was his intent. She did not want him to release her.

When he did so, the loss of his touch left her feeling alone and vulnerable among these strangers. Iana almost reached for his hand, but stopped herself in time, knowing how improper that would appear.

Clouds suddenly rolled over the castle and she felt a drop of rain, then another. A rumble of thunder sounded in the distance. A portent of things to come?

She risked another glance in Henri's direction, hoping for some sign of reassurance, but his attention was for their hostess.

The lady who had come out to meet them waited patiently, holding the hands of the handsomest children Iana had ever seen, two lads as alike as two beans in a pod.

Henri escorted Iana over to the woman and presented her. "Lady Mairi of Baincroft, Lady Iana…of Ayr." His very tone told her he did not believe for an instant that was who she was, but she had already known that. So be it. The truth would have her on the road again, sent back to Newell to do what he considered her duty. A plague on them all.

"Greetings," said the lady as she ran a curious gaze over Iana and stopped at her shoulder.

Tam's head ducked lower, out of sight. Iana could feel the babe's nose pressing against her shoulder blade.

Henri had already stepped closer and brushed a kiss upon the lady's cheek, giving his own greeting. "Mairi, how good it is to see you again."

He quickly knelt and embraced the children, laughing at their eagerness to be first in his arms. "Harry and Ned! Come here, you scamps." He stood and swung them around before setting them down. They squealed with delight and begged for more, but their father made a sign to them that sent the two scurrying away, back into the keep, giggling and trying to outrun one another. Henri laughed at the sight, his great fondness for the boys apparent.

Lady Mairi watched Henri, obviously waiting for him to explain his sudden presence and that of herself, Tam and Everand. He did so in a perfunctory way. "I make known to you my son, Everand," he said first.

After only the slightest hesitation and a quick glance toward her husband, she reached out, took the boy's hand and smiled at him. "What a fine lad, Henri. Everand, we are happy to have ye here." Immediately, she turned again to Henri, a brow raised in question.

"I was wounded after a sea battle off the southern coast of England," he told her. "Everand and I secured a craft and made our way up the western coast. Lady Iana saved my life when I would have died of fever from my wound."

When the lady reached out in sudden concern for him,

Henri caught her hands and hurriedly reassured her. "I am fine now, Sister. Lady Iana agreed to accompany us here in exchange for what silver I had and the possibility of making a new life among your people."

"We owe ye a debt, for his life is precious to us. Ye are a healer then?" Lady Mairi asked Iana.

"I am familiar with medicaments, have delivered two children and I can sew a wound," Iana answered. "I admit that I have never apprenticed to anyone, but have made a study of healing. Also, I must tell you that I do not hold with the old remedies of spells and curing the sick with animal parts and odd objects."

Lady Mairi laughed merrily. "Honest to a fault, aye? I applaud ye for it, but I am afraid we have a healer in residence. One my husband dares not dismiss, for it is I. The woman who serves my husband's parents has taught me all she knows."

Iana felt her heart sink.

Lady Mairi looked fondly at her spouse. "But I daresay we'll find something for ye to do in lieu of tending the ill. Come with me and I shall show ye to a chamber. Ye must be weary of that wee pack upon your back. Are we to know aught of it?"

Iana glanced at Henri, who merely waited for her to answer as she would. She looked the lady straight in the eye. "I found this child and her mother in the woods near my home some two months past. The woman had me pledge to save her daughter before she died. The bairn is Thomasina, called Tam. I have claimed her as mine, for she has none other to care for her."

The look of sympathy on Lady Mairi's face gave Iana hope that the truth had sounded more plausible to her than it had to Henri. At present he wore no look of doubt, no expression at all, but Iana could feel his disbelief as surely as if he had contradicted her aloud.

"Come. Let us go inside now," the lady said, offering her hand. "There's no sense standing about out here. Rain's coming." Again she looked to her husband. "Rob, see to Henri's comfort. I know ye'll wish to speak in private."

A screech of surprise drew all their attention to the hall entrance. Iana watched, openmouthed, as a small, dark-haired woman rushed down the steps and flung herself against Henri. He laughed and embraced her with an enthusiasm that made Iana grit her teeth. She prayed it was his sister.

"Henri! I am so happy you have come at last! You received my letters?" the woman demanded. "Have you come for me?"

He wore a puzzled look, but was still smiling widely. "Letters?"

The woman reared back her head and looked up at him, her eyes shining. "I wrote to you twice! I am so sorry that I missed you the last two times you were here. Rob neglected to tell me you were coming, and I was away with Grandfather. Have you missed me?"

He nodded, glanced at his brother and then returned his puzzled gaze to the girl. "Of course, Jehannie. It is delightful to see you, as always."

Lady Mairi was frowning, Lord Robert biting back laughter and Henri looking distinctly uncomfortable in the woman's clutches. She hugged him again, nuzzling her face against his chest. "How wonderful to have you here at long last. I prayed you would come and here you are."

Lady Mairi took Iana's arm and spoke rather loudly.

"Lady Iana, this is *Lady* Jehan de Brus, sister to our steward, Sir Thomas."

The woman smiled at Iana, but did not relinquish her hold upon Henri. In fact, she shifted even closer, as though claiming possession of him. "Welcome to Baincroft," she said offhandedly, then dismissed Iana completely by closing her eyes, sighing with pleasure and rubbing her face against Henri's tunic.

Lady Mairi huffed. "Come, we'll leave them to their reunion if they've a mind to stand there and get soakin' wet," she muttered.

The mist was growing more substantial. Iana gave the couple one last look before surrendering to good sense and following Lady Mairi up the steps and into the keep.

Apparently Henri had his hands full, though he appeared none too thrilled about it. Mayhaps he was embarrassed by the fact that the woman was so open with her affections. Well he should be. The feelings engendered in Iana by that fervent display deserved to be ignored, and so she did, turning her attention instead to the woman who would, hopefully, become her new employer.

"You have the sound of the Highlands in your voice," Iana ventured as they entered the great hall.

"Aye, I know," she answered with a short laugh, "'tis not easily concealed, so I've ceased to try. My husband couldna fathom a word I said when first we met. We've remedied that, of course," she admitted with a sly chuckle.

"Of course." Iana made no further reply, for she knew not whether it would be polite to comment upon Lord Robert's deafness.

They stopped only a moment in the hall while Lady

Mairi called to one of the maids and ordered water heated and sent up.

It was an impressive hall, with whitewashed walls festooned with painted designs and tapestries. There were stout oaken furnishings waxed to a shine. The pleasant fragrance of bayberry permeated the air. The daylight from the glazed windows was augmented by groups of scented candles illuminating every dark corner. Lord MacBain must be very prosperous, indeed, Iana thought.

She did not like comparing it to the penurious existence she had endured in Duncan's keep, with its dingy, undressed stones and the noisome tallow smell that made her head ache. This reminded her all too much of the way she had lived as a girl, in her relatively comfortable home at Ochney Castle.

Iana tried not to fidget, but she felt a great need to be alone. Her chances of living here did not seem very great at the moment, but she did wish a day or so to recover from her journey and decide what she must do next. One thing she did know, she did not want to hang about and see any further mauling of Henri by that woman outside.

While she was extremely curious about Henri's relationship to that wanton, she knew it would be highly impolitic to ask. What business of it was hers if he was somehow attached to her? Iana had no claim upon Henri and did not wish to have one. Still, the sight of the two embracing would not leave her mind no matter how hard she tried to banish it.

Lady Mairi soon led her through the well-appointed hall and up the stairs to a small chamber on the next floor. Once there, Iana sat upon a bed strewn with rich furs and hung with damask draperies, and wearily shrugged off the sling.

"Ah, look at her!" Lady Mairi cooed, reaching for

Tam. "Poor mite hasna any meat on her bones, does she? 'Tis a full plate this day and hereafter for ye, my lass." She sat beside Iana and cuddled the baby close. Iana saw tears shining in her eyes. "Worse than this when ye found her, was she?" the lady asked.

"Aye," Iana answered, giving Tam's back a pat. "She made no sounds and hardly moved until a few days past. She is improving quickly."

"How is it ye came to be alone?" Lady Mairi asked suddenly. "Why can ye not call upon yer own family to aid ye in this act of charity? Did they refuse to honor yer pledge to th' mother, then?"

Iana sighed. "No." Obviously, Lady Mairi had no compunction about prying and would not be satisfied with evasion. She seemed kind enough and might understand Iana's plight. Then again, she might not. "What do you think about marrying a woman off against her will? Twice?"

Mairi scoffed. "Abominable practice, and illegal I think. But I do know 'tis still done."

"My family knows nothing of Tam. I left them weeks before I found her."

"May I be asking why? It has to do with a marriage, then?"

Iana decided to tell her. There was little to be lost in doing so. In order for Iana to be returned to her brother, she would have to give his name, which she would not do. "I was wed once to a man of my father's choosing. When I was widowed, my father was already dead. My brother would have had me wed again to another just as old, just as wicked, just as driven by greed. Thank heaven my brother's wife warned me in time. When my brother put forth the match, I refused."

"And he threw ye out?" Lady Mairi asked, horrified.

"Banished me to teach me a lesson. I was living in a small village when Everand approached me. I saw a chance to leave with him and Sir Henri, so I took it. He promised to ask your husband if he would allow me to work and live here, so I suppose he did not know you were a healer, too. I'm afraid there is little else I know how to do."

For a few moments, Lady Mairi considered that. Then she laid Tam upon the bed and tickled her under the chin. "Ye are both welcome to stay. If ye had allowed Henri to die, his kin and his friends here would have been inconsolable. We can never reward ye enough for that."

"I will not accept charity," Iana warned her.

"I know. For now, consider this a visit. Later, we shall decide together what ye might do to earn yer way. Aye?"

"Aye," Iana agreed, vastly relieved that the lady understood.

"May I ask where ye hail from and the name of this family who has wronged ye so?"

Iana looked away from the woman's steady blue gaze. "I believe it would be wiser of me not to say."

"Henri knows all of this?"

"Nay, I do not trust men. Even Sir Henri. He would attempt to make matters right, I think, but would only make them worse."

"I see," Lady Mairi said. She rose and handed Tam to Iana. "I'll leave ye to rest a bit and tend the bairn. Come down to the solar in a while. We'll speak more then and see what the menfolk have to say on the matter." When Iana started to protest her telling them, the lady forestalled her. "This has gone too far for ye to handle alone now. Come down soon and let us talk it out."

"I shall be glad to," Iana said, though she lied. She

had no wish at all to share her woes with Henri and perfect strangers, for fear of where that would lead. Probably right back to Newell. And she certainly did not look forward to watching that hoyden throw herself at Henri.

Mairi winked and grinned. "Henri will be glad if ye join us. God's truth, I've never seen him so quiet. And proper? 'Tis not at all like him. As a rule, he's worse behaved than Rob and my lads, all jests and tricks."

"Sir Henri?" Iana stared at her, disbelieving, and watched her nod.

"I can see he's right taken with ye."

"He is not taken!" Iana objected, feeling her face heat with agitation. "Leastways, not with me."

Lady Mairi gave her a wicked grin and ducked out of the chamber, leaving a trail of merry laughter in her wake.

"She is the one who jests," Iana said to the silent Tam, who lay watching her with a small, almost imperceptible smile.

Awhile later, after she had bathed the baby, Iana slid into the tub of warm water to soak away her own travel dust. She slipped down to allow the scented water to close over her head, reveling in the comfort she had not enjoyed since she had left her brother's keep.

"Pardon my intrusion," a soft voice said.

Iana jumped, sloshing water over the edge. "Lady Jehan? What do you here?"

The woman strolled over, peeked at Tam, who lay sleeping, and then settled herself on the trunk at the foot of the bed. "I came to get acquainted," she said sweetly. "And to apologize for my lack of civility when you arrived."

Her soft, slender hands brushed an errant black lock

off her cheek in what appeared to be a practiced gesture. "You see, I was so relieved that Henri had finally arrived, I could think of nothing else."

"So I noticed," Iana replied, busying herself with her bath, hinting to her visitor that she did not wish to converse.

"How well do you know him?" Jehan asked pointedly. "Aside from saving his life, which I must thank you for doing."

"I know him hardly at all," Iana said grudgingly. "We traveled together with his squire. The man promised me employment. That is all."

The woman rose and strolled about aimlessly, stopping to look out through the window at the rain. "Henri and I were children together, did you know? He needs looking after, and I mean to do it."

"As his wife," Iana guessed.

"Yes. He has said he will not wed again, but his reason means little to me. Once I convince him I do not care if I remain childless, I think he will be glad of it."

"Childless?" Iana could have bitten her tongue off for courting this woman's confidence. But she was curious. Henri had not appeared to be very agreeable to the woman's attentions. Could that have been because he wanted Lady Jehan, but could not bring himself to disappoint her?

"Yes, he cannot get an heir," Jehan said sadly. "Henri was wed quite young to a French noblewoman. For six years, she never quickened, and they had resigned themselves that it was not possible for her to conceive. Then suddenly she began to swell. Henri discovered that she had taken a lover and was about to bear the man's child."

"Oh no," Iana gasped, caught up in the awful tale the woman spun. She could only imagine Henri's grief at the betrayal and disappointment that the child was not his own.

"Oh yes," Jehan said, nodding sadly. "And good man that he is, Henri did not toss her out as she deserved, but kept her by him, intending to play out the farce to the end. He would have claimed the child and forgiven her, but both died during the birth."

"How tragic for all of them," Iana whispered, her unseeing gaze trained upon the water.

She looked up when Jehan turned from the window, hands on her hips, wearing a sad frown when she spoke. "So you see, Henri knows that he cannot father an heir or he would have done so during those first years. His wife was not barren. Consequently, he has said he likely will not wed again."

"But you mean to change his mind," Iana guessed. "Do you love Henri?"

"Of course I do. We have always been friends. He needs me." Jehan's eyes narrowed as she studied Iana. "I wanted to see how matters stand with you and him. I saw the glare you gave us below and wondered…"

Iana shook her head. "I am nothing to him, nor he, to me." No point in revealing that she could have been his mistress had she a few less scruples. A prospective wife did not need to hear such a thing, and Iana was certainly not proud of the fact that she had been asked. "I wish you every happiness should you be successful in your quest."

"Thank you," said Lady Jehan, sounding quite sincere now instead of sly. "May you find what you seek, as well."

Iana waited until the woman had departed, then slipped lower into the water, submersing her head and wishing she did not have to come up again and face her new life.

A life without Henri. But that had been a given, even before Lady Jehan's disruption.

Henri felt better than he had in well over a month. Bathed, shaved, combed, and dressed in one of Rob's finest tunics, he sat comfortably ensconced in one of the padded chairs beside the fire, while a driving rain beat relentlessly against the windows.

At least Jehan was not here to plague him. She must be off somewhere upon some errand. Henri hoped it took awhile.

The girl seemed to have set her sights upon *him* now that Rob was wed. He and his brother had discussed it at length before Mairi came down to join them.

From childhood, Jehan had been trained to become Rob's wife. They had all grown up together, Rob, Henri, Jehan and her brother, Thomas de Brus. Then Jehan's grandfather had broken the betrothal, stating Rob's deafness as the cause. When Jehan discovered that the contract had been nulled, it had been too late. Rob had already found himself a wife from the Highlands, one he loved to distraction.

Now Jehan must believe that Henri would fulfill his brother's destiny. The very thought of it gave Henri cold chills. Jehan was a beauty, right enough, but as wild and unpredictable as an untrained kestrel. He shuddered to think what chaos she would cause as his countess.

If he was willing—which he certainly was not—a wedding between them would not be strictly impossible, he supposed. Though she was not French, she was related to Robert the Bruce, which made her kin to royalty, but that was the one point in her favor. The only one, as far as he was concerned. He would have to make the matter clear to her right away.

The solar was pleasantly warm, lulling him nicely while he idly watched the conversation flow between Mairi and Rob. The graceful movements of her hands were almost too swift to allow Henri to grasp the meaning of the signs she made. Rob's were brief and to the point.

Always the way, Henri thought. Women had too much to say and took too long in the saying of it. Men were lucky to get in a word here and there unless they were spouting praise or poetry. He loved Mairi like a sister. Even if he had not liked her, he would have loved her, simply because she made Rob so happy.

But he did like her. She was funny, irreverent and totally unaware of her charm. In that last aspect, she brought to mind Iana, who also seemed not to realize her own appeal. He liked that in a female, especially after suffering the presence of so many great beauties at court who knew well their allure and used it shamelessly. Jehan was certainly not above doing that, he recalled. Hell, she was trying to do it even now. Something had to be done about her.

As he watched, Mairi pressed three fingers to her neck, and that sign for *healer* caught Henri's attention. He began to take more careful note of what she and Rob were saying.

Ye will send someone to find out who she is. Mairi's signs were curt now, demanding. *And soon.*

Rob frowned and dismissed her demand. *This is not our concern. Whatever her name, she saved my brother and she may stay. Give her sewing to do and we will pay her well for it.*

Mairi shook her head vehemently. *Nay! She is no hireling. She is a lady.*

Henri held up a hand to interrupt. They both looked at

him. "Send Thomas if you can spare him," Henri suggested. "Iana is from near Largsmuth, I believe. She might have wed someone near Ayr…if she was wed at all. I would know the details."

Rob's lips tightened. *I watched your face when she spoke outside. You think she lies about the child.*

Henri shrugged. He knew better than to make up an untruth. Rob could not be fooled. Mairi might as well know, too, for Rob would tell her if Henri himself did not.

He abandoned speech and fell to signing, so that Rob would get every word. *She denies the child is her husband's get and now says she found it in the woods. Iana is a noblewoman, yet was living in a hovel with a baby. What do you make of that?*

Rob pursed his lips and paced a few moments, arms akimbo and his head lowered in thought. "Thomas will find out," he said aloud.

"It could be so," Mairi announced, defiantly crossing her arms over her chest. "'Tis entirely possible that she found the bairn. And she told me that her brother would have forced her to a marriage she did not want. I think he has cast her out because she refused."

Henri shook his head. "A noble kinswoman is too valuable to throw to the winds. If she eschewed one alliance, her brother might be angry with her, but would surely propose another more to her liking and to his advantage. It makes no sense he would simply have done with her."

"Maybe he has no sense," Mairi suggested wryly.

Henri did not want to ask, but he did need the truth. *Does she lie, Rob?* He signed. His brother would know. Rob could see into hearts.

Rob shrugged, sighed and then nodded. *She either lies or keeps some truth hidden. I know not which.*

"Same thing," Henri muttered, sadly disappointed that he was right about Iana.

No. Not the same. Rob walked over to him, clapped a hand on his shoulder and gave it a sympathetic shake.

Henri thought it was the same. *She will not tell me who they are, this family of hers. And she is not born of Ayr, of that I'm almost certain.*

Rob smiled and signed emphatically. *Her name is what she hides, then, and she might have good reason not to tell it. The rest of her story may well be true. Why is it so important that you know about her? You wish to wed this woman?*

"Wed her? Heavens, no," Henri declared.

Rob's rueful expression told him his denial was fruitless. Henri might as well admit he wished he could wed Iana. He could not hide that from his brother. "You know it is not possible," he added.

Rob raised a hand and looked as if he were about to object.

"Do I interrupt?" Iana said softly from the doorway.

Henri saw that she wore the same clothing she had arrived in, the simple amber gown he had bought for her. Her face was scrubbed and her hair looked wet. It was now wound in a heavy braid about her head like a crown, glinting gold.

Henri's servants back home dressed better than this, but none of them possessed the regal bearing Iana displayed. No one could ever mistake her for less than the lady she was. How beautiful she looked in her simplicity, he thought, offering her a smile of greeting.

"Come in, come in," Mairi said brightly, gesturing her to a chair. "If ye agree, Iana, I'll be asking young Jonnet to care for the wee'un whilst we eat. She's a good lass. I fear 'tis too near noon meal for us to undertake any planning for yer future. That can wait.''

Iana glanced at Henri, then lowered her gaze to the floor. ''That is very kind of you, Lady Mairi.''

Henri noticed that Mairi's welcoming expression now appeared somewhat strained, when earlier it had looked truly sincere. This worried him. Had Rob's pronouncement of Iana's guilt tainted his wife's goodwill toward Iana? If so, Henri regretted insisting on his brother's honest opinion, an opinion almost everyone who knew Rob believed as true assessment.

Lives had hung in the balance before when Robert MacBain had judged a person's honesty. Henri would need to take Iana elsewhere soon, where no one would know or care whether she'd ever been wed or had born a bastard or had lied.

First, however, he would learn everything he could about her. She would simply have to endure life at Baincroft until Rob's steward and friend, Thomas de Brus, had completed his inquiries. Then they could leave.

Iana would become Henri's mistress and he would treasure her no matter who or what she was. That would have to be enough for the both of them.

Chapter Nine

Iana endured the midday meal. Lady Mairi had convinced her to allow one of the maids to tend Tam above stairs. Though Iana's shoulders still ached from bearing the sling, she wished for the child's company. She felt very alone now despite the crowd gathered in the hall for dinner.

The only bright spot in the entire event was that Lady Jehan, thankfully, was not present. Iana told herself that her dislike of the woman had nothing to do with Henri. It was the calculating gleam in Jehan's eye, the aggressive way in which she planned to go about gaining a husband, as if the poor man would have no say in it at all. That was it, surely.

Lord Robert smiled often and regarded Iana with open curiosity, though he had said nothing more after his earlier greeting. He had a clever look about him and was quite handsome in a very different way than Henri. Though he spoke less, he seemed more open, almost garrulous by comparison, to the dark knight who had brought her here.

Henri kept close by her and shared her trencher. He seemed altogether too quiet, somehow troubled. Lady

Mairi chattered to first one, then another, trying to fill the uneasy silence probably caused by Iana's very presence.

She glanced at Everand, who was not talking at all, since he only spoke French, which no one else here seemed to be using. It worried her that her young friend looked so ill at ease. Since he sat at a lower table, with two other squires and several other castle folk, he was not near enough for her or Henri to include him in any conversation.

"Where is this steward whom you mentioned?" she asked Henri.

He offered the wine cup and she shook her head. Henri set the cup down carefully then, avoiding her eyes. "Why do you ask?"

"Oh, I simply thought Everand might feel more comfortable if there were another with whom he could converse. He appears quite lost."

Henri looked at Ev and shrugged. "He will survive. I wish we could stay long enough that he could learn the language."

She jerked her gaze to his face. "You're not leaving soon?"

"Quite soon," he told her, nodding. "However, I must see my parents and sister before we return to France."

"Oh," she said, her heart sinking at the thought. Though she liked Lady Mairi and Lord Robert, she did not know them well yet. Somehow she had believed Henri and Everand would be here until she became accustomed to her new home. If it was to be her home, she thought with a frown.

What if MacBain could find nothing else for her to do? Suppose he did not really want her here and was only being congenial for Henri's sake?

"Mayhaps there is some kind of work for me at your

father's estate," she suggested. "Do your parents need a healer?"

"No," he said curtly. "They have one who is very proficient. It will not do to take you there."

Precious little she could say to that, Iana thought. His words intimated that she would be less than welcome.

The remainder of the meal passed quickly. She excused herself as soon as she possibly could and went back to her chamber to resume care of Tam. And to think.

What was she to do if these people set her out on her own as soon as Henri left? There was nowhere else to go. She could not simply take up life in a strange village or at some other lord's estate without someone to recommend her.

With horror, she imagined a future of trudging along the byways carrying poor wee Tam on her back and begging alms to survive.

"God save us from that," she muttered. But Iana knew she had gotten herself into this coil because of her willful ways and would probably have to untwist it herself.

Throughout that day and the next, Henri noticed no outward scorn directed toward Iana and her child. The castlefolk were following their lady's lead, of course. Mairi went to great lengths to include her in all the daily activities.

The two women were ever together, one or the other of them carting Tam about on a hip, usually giving her nibbles of bannock or special treats the cook had prepared to please Harry and Ned. Henri was most relieved to see the baby behaving less like a helpless infant just out of the womb.

The surprising urge to hold the child almost overtook him several times when her wide dark eyes would seek him out across a room. Yet he kept his distance, knowing he would be wiser not to form any stronger attachment to her. Or to Iana, whom he would also love to hold, though in a distinctly different way.

It seemed he had worried for nothing regarding Iana's acceptance here. His feeling of disappointment was unworthy of him and he knew it. She would not be forced to leave Baincroft after all, and now he had no excuse to save her by making her his mistress and taking her away. The fact that she was welcomed here should have made him happy for her, and it did. But he also regretted that he would have to leave her soon and return to France to take up his duties there.

Mairi had either given or loaned Iana a gown to befit her rank. She was a vision dressed in dark blue, embroidered with delicate flowers and leaves. The soft wool clung to her supple curves so enticingly that Henri sucked in a deep breath of frustrated appreciation. Though she wore no jewels, she needed none. She was a jewel herself, he thought with a smile.

Her honey-colored locks were loosely caught up beneath a shimmering, transparent veil of palest gold, beautiful against her slightly sun-kissed skin. Seeing Iana so properly attired only made him realize the enormity of what he had asked of her.

He should apologize for that. Even if she had taken a lover in the past, it did not follow that she should embark on a life of sin with him in order to survive. Yes, in one way, he truly was glad she would be welcome here, yet another, darker part of him sorely regretted his own loss. Now he could never have her. His selfishness appalled him.

Go, speak with her. Rob signed to him as they sat at

the chessboard and watched the ladies playing with the children across the hall. *You know you wish to.*

Henri ignored him and moved a pawn, sacrificing his queen. Though there were moves to make yet, he had lost this game as well as the other.

"Hapless Harry," Rob muttered, chuckling as he nudged a knight forward on the board.

"Indeed," Henri admitted, throwing up his hands in defeat. "I am for bed."

Rob laughed and shook his head as he stretched his beefy arms out to the side and leaned back in his chair.

One of the squires came running from the entrance and halted, breathless, before them. "Lord Rob, your father comes," he gasped, his slender hands forming clumsy gestures to accompany his words. "Rode through the gates just now. He's looking mightily...overset."

Rob and Henri stood immediately and hurried for the hall door together. It was full dark outside. Why would their father be arriving at such a late hour?

It was only a few leagues' ride from Trouville's castle, but the road was treacherous in places when traversed at night. It could not be that his mother or sister were ill, for Trouville would never leave their side if that were so. He would have sent someone to tell Rob.

Before they had half crossed the hall, the Comte de Trouville burst in, his handsome face a study in despair, tracks of tears cutting through the travel dust.

"Father!" Henri called out. Suddenly Trouville halted, eyes wide with shock, his hands clutching his chest. Rob and Henri rushed forward to catch him, for he looked sure to collapse. For a long moment, the silence was broken only by a solitary sob. Then Trouville's powerful arms closed around Henri as if bound to crush him.

"What is wrong? Is someone ill?"

"Incroyable!" his father whispered, grasping Henri's
cheeks roughly in his agitation. Henri's heart almost
stopped. He had never seen his sire less than composed,
even in the midst of disaster. "Is it Maman? Alys?"

"You! We heard—" He clenched his eyes shut, took
a deep breath and shuddered before he began again. "The
king sent Duquesne to tell me...your ship went down.
All drowned, he said." Fresh tears trailed down his father's face unchecked. "But you live."

Henri embraced him more fully than he could ever
recall doing. Trouville thrived on control, of himself and
of others. Henri had never once known him to weep or
abandon his reserve in this way. It pained him to see his
father reduced to such distress because of his exploits.
"It is true about the ship. And the men. I could not save
them, Father."

"But you survived. Thanks be to God." Trouville
sniffed, drawing in a deep breath, regained a bit of his
composure and pulled away as if to examine Henri for
damage. "You were not hurt, Son?"

"Yes, but I am recovered. Come and sit down, Father.
You need to collect yourself."

Henri glanced at Rob, who wore an expression of absolute fright. Henri felt it as well. They both feared Trouville would expire of a failed heart right in front of them.
How pale he was. He had been their strength, the one
who never faltered in any instance. At the moment, he
seemed all too human and as like to die as the next man.

A sobering thing, Henri thought, suddenly to realize
the mortality of one's own father. He and Rob held on
to Trouville's arms until they had him seated beside the
fire.

Mairi had rushed over and was now hovering as well.
Henri saw that Iana stood a little apart, holding Tam in

her arms and attempting to keep the twins in check for their mother. Even Ned and Harry frowned to see their beloved grandfather so blanched and disordered.

Rob shoved the tankard of ale he had been drinking before into Trouville's hand. "Drink," he ordered. The *comte* did so and deeply, too, heaving a huge sigh when he had finished.

He ran a hand through his gray-streaked, windblown hair. "God's mercy, what a night this has been." Again he grasped Henri's forearm as if he needed the connection, needed to feel the realness of it.

Then he seemed to remember something and turned to Mairi. "Daughter, send Thomas immediately. Anne and Alys are distraught with grief and should be informed that Henri lives."

She nodded. Thomas was gone, of course, delving into Iana's secrets in the area around Largsmuth, but Mairi would send someone in his stead.

"I feel terrible to have caused such anguish," Henri told his father as he knelt beside him. "I was coming to you tomorrow for a visit. Had I any notion you would suffer this news from France, I would have come sooner. Duquesne came today?"

"*Oui,* some three hours past. It took awhile to calm your mother enough so that I could come to tell Rob and Mairi." He swallowed hard and shook his head as if to clear it. "I had to see Rob." Without looking up, he reached for Rob's hand, then Henri's, and pressed them to his chest. "My sons," he whispered, his head bowed.

Tears formed in Henri's own eyes. He had always known his father loved him, but this evidence of it almost undid him completely.

He glanced at Iana, wondering if she would consider

his tears a weakness. Her face was wet as well, and she was biting her lower lip.

The twins broke away from her then and ran to Trouville. He released Henri and Rob and caught the two young ones, raising them to his lap as one. "Harry, Ned," he said gruffly. "All is well now. Do not fret." He seemed to be speaking to reassure himself as well. In but a few moments' time, he appeared regal and composed.

The stalwart count they knew and loved was himself again, a smile firmly in place. They all breathed a sigh of relief. All was well, as he had assured the twins. Or it would be as soon as Henri's mother and sister were notified.

Mairi was back now, having sent a messenger as Trouville ordered. "Ye'll stay the night, Father," she announced. "I'll have no argument."

He gave a succinct nod, a surprising admission that he was not fit to ride home. "Bring me wine if you will, Mairi, and a bit of food."

She rushed to comply, while Trouville began to notice those gathered around him. His gaze settled upon Iana, and Henri knew he expected introductions.

"My father, the Comte de Trouville," Henri said to her, then beckoned her closer. "This is Lady Iana. She sewed my wound and brought me through the fever, Father. Had she not, I might have succumbed."

Trouville set his grandsons on their feet and stood, bowing to Iana even as she dropped a curtsy. "Anything you wish, you have but to ask and it is yours," he said softly to her. "From whence do you hail, my lady?"

That was the question, Henri thought. Would she lie to his father as she had to him?

"I am from the west, my lord. From a village near the

coast. Your son's squire hired me to tend his master and paid me in silver. You owe me nothing.''

Henri watched his father's eyes narrow in speculation. "How do you come to be here?''

She blushed, darted Henri a quick glance and dropped her gaze to the floor. "Your son was not completely well when we set out. And also, I came to work here. That was a part of the arrangement, my lord.''

"Work? Your family is impoverished? I shall have a fortune sent them,'' he declared, firm in the resolve. "I shall take it personally and give them thanks myself for your great service to my son. Whatever Henri gave you is not enough, and I will certainly not allow you put to any task so long as I have a sou to give you.''

"But work is what I wish, my lord,'' Iana said, visibly trembling. "Nothing more is necessary.''

"I insist on rewarding your kindness. You have no idea how grateful—''

Henri could stand no more. "Father, let it be for now. You and I have much to discuss and the hour grows late.''

His father pinned him with the same stare he had used when Henri had misbehaved as a boy. "You think this is not of import, Son? This woman saved your life. You uprooted her from her family and brought her across the country with you. Look, she even has a child.'' He redirected his attention to Iana. "That is your child, is it not?''

"Yes, my lord, she belongs to me,'' Iana said defiantly.

"Then we must reunite this lady with her family and give them proper compensation for her absence, Henri. It is only right. So, who are they?''

For a long moment, no one said anything. Henri had

no answer for him, and Iana obviously did not have one she wished to offer. Finally, she spoke. "My parents are dead, my lord. And so is my husband."

"Who is your overlord?"

"I recognize none," she answered, her shoulders stiff. Tam had begun to wriggle, sensing Iana's discomfort.

"Then, by all rights, the king should—"

"Father, I implore you, let this matter rest until morning. Can you not see you have upset her with all these questions? We are all overwrought at the moment," Henri said gently. "Tomorrow will be soon enough to honor her efforts."

Trouville studied his face for a moment, then Iana's. "Very well," he finally agreed. "Tomorrow." Iana dipped a swift curtsy and departed so hastily they had no time to wish her good sleep.

His father sat again, his gaze settling on the food Mairi brought as she positioned it upon the chessboard near him. Henri knew he did not see the silver tray or its contents. He was puzzling over Iana's reluctance to name her family. They all were.

"She will not tell you, sir. Thomas has gone to inquire," he explained, knowing his father would not abandon the riddle until it was solved to his satisfaction.

"She is a widow," his father said. He had propped one elbow upon the arm of his chair and was worrying his chin with his forefinger, pondering. "She has other family," Trouville declared. "I saw it in her eyes. For one reason or another, she fears our finding out."

"She confided to Mairi that there was an unwanted marriage in the offing and she was banished by her brother for refusing it," Henri admitted. "She will not say his name or from whence she hails, but I will have the truth about her. We decided Thomas could make discreet inquiries.''

Again, Henri received an assessing look. ''And why must you know the truth? More than curiosity, surely.''

Henri did not avoid the question. ''Because I care what happened to the lady before, and what could occur once I leave her here. Like you, I wish to insure her welfare.''

His father looked around and saw that Rob and Mairi were occupied in calming their children. Voice lowered so that no one else could hear him, Trouville asked, ''You want this woman, do you not?''

''I do.''

''I feared as much.''

Henri looked at the stairs where he had seen Iana disappear only moments before with her child clutched in her arms. Though Trouville had himself wed a Scotswoman, and a widow at that, he had previously wed the French noblewoman who had produced his heir, Henri. Trouville had taken two other French wives who did not survive. He had done his duty to the crown. Henri knew he must do the same.

The wish for marriage to Iana was futile. He was not even certain when the thought had first budded in his mind, but now that he recognized it, it seemed to bloom fully on the instant. Doomed to die just as quickly, of course.

''Do not worry on it, Father. I know what is expected of me as your successor.''

He did not want to see the look of relief upon his father's face at that declaration, so he kept his gaze where it was. He could not help adding, ''I confess I am sorely tempted to fly in the face of expectation and do as I will. But you, of all people, know that I shall not. My next wife will be as French as the last, so if there should, by some miracle, be an heir, he might be included within the line of succession.''

Silence was his answer. He did look at Trouville then, but the smile his father wore might have signified pride in a son's submission to duty or simply relief that his heir lived. If Henri had vaguely hoped for a blessing to do as he pleased in this instance, it was not forthcoming.

Iana hated cowardice in any form, but the next morning she found herself indulging in it. Even after she arose and dressed for the day, she decided she would plead fatigue and remain in her chamber to avoid facing Henri's father.

Merciful God, the man would not be put off. If he interrogated her again as he had last eve, she feared what she might give away.

She could only imagine Newell's response if a French count arrived at his gates bearing gifts to reward him for her deeds. Her brother would accept what was offered, no doubt of that. He would also come for her with all haste in hopes of receiving even more wealth from the man to whom he would wed her. Dorothea had told her how much her brother would profit by the alliance with Sturrock and that he had vowed to force Iana to wed. Iana had made her own vow then. She'd not be sold like a possession again.

Long after they had eaten and the maid had gone out with the leavings of their meal, Tam played beside Iana as she half reclined upon the large, comfortable bed. Bright sun through the open window warmed the chamber. The maid had left the door open, and Iana could hear the distant bustle and laughter from below in the hall. It seemed a pleasant way to spend a day, she thought. They were alone, yet not lonely.

Tiny fingers plucked at the rich embroidery on Iana's sleeve. She smiled down at the child and dropped a kiss upon the wispy hair, so happy that Tam was now showing interest in everything around her.

Much to her surprise, the baby leaned forward and pressed her lips to Iana's wrist in an answering gesture of affection. "Oh, sweeting," she said, cuddling her closer. Tam looked up, her small mouth forming the ghost of a smile. In that all too brief exchange, Iana felt her heart open as wide as any mother's and enfold Tam's promise within it.

"No matter what happens in our none-too-certain future, my love," Iana whispered, "I must consider your welfare first. My own bid for a good life might be past and gone, but you shall not suffer so, my girl. No man will purchase you like a ribbon from a tinker." She brushed Tam's smooth brow with one finger. "You will be strong one day. Stronger than I."

And how would she teach Tam to be so? Iana wondered. By hiding out here in this borrowed bed, wearing borrowed clothing, accepting pity from a family she did not know?

"Certainly not," she said aloud. "I must face what is to be. Make my own decisions. If the MacBains will not employ me, then I will demand that Sir Henri introduce me elsewhere. Surely a man such as he knows many wealthy families. One of them will surely welcome the services of a healer."

On that thought, she propped the baby upon the pillow and got out of the bed to dress. "We shall go downstairs," she told the child, speaking to her as if she were a confidante. "The Comte de Trouville may harry me until he runs out of words," Iana declared with a firm nod in Tam's direction. "I am in no way bound to answer his questions if I do not choose to do so. He is not my overlord and, God willing, will never discover who is.''

"Oo-is," Tam muttered.

Iana froze. Then she whirled toward the bed and leaned over the baby. "You spoke!"

Tam blinked up at her, a steady gaze the only acknowledgment of her feat.

With a laugh, Iana scooped her up and hugged her. "Ah, love, wait until I tell Henri! He will be so—"

"So…what?" said a deep voice from the doorway.

In her excitement over Tam's new skill, Iana ran to him. "She said *words,* Henri! Two of them!"

"Dem," Tam mimicked.

Henri reached for the baby and took her in his arms. His face mirrored Iana's joy as he gently chucked Tam under her delicate chin. "Have you a word for me, *ma petite?* For Henri?"

"Oray," Tam obligingly repeated.

"Unfair!" Iana said, laughing with glee, patting Tam's back with one hand while she clasped Henri's forearm with the other. "She calls you first and I am her mama."

"Mama," the baby repeated.

"Wondrous day!" Iana exclaimed, unable to stand still. "Our Tam can speak!"

Our Tam? Why had she said that? Tam was hers alone. However, Henri had been the cause of Tam's first attempt to crawl. The child had been moved to seek the comfort of his nearness when they were upon their journey here. Iana admitted he had a perfect right to share this great accomplishment.

She did not mind that he wore the same glow of gladness that she must be wearing herself. When their gazes met above Tam's head, Iana smiled without reservation.

"What a good mother you are," Henri avowed. "What a fortunate child is Thomasina."

Iana ducked her head, unable to explore further the powerful bond she felt with Henri in that moment. "Thank you," she whispered.

After a moment of silence, he said, "I came to see if you are rested enough to come below. The hour grows late and we shall soon gather for the noon meal. Have you eaten?"

Iana shook her head and retreated to the side of the bed, where she had left her shoes. "Tam had porridge and milk early this morn. I was not hungry." She slid her feet into the soft slippers Mairi had loaned her for wearing within the keep.

"I would speak privately with you before we descend," Henri told her.

Iana stilled, clutching her palms together firmly in front of her waist to keep from wringing her hands. "You will find me employment elsewhere. Nothing more needs be said."

He sighed and shifted Tam to his shoulder. "I have thought upon it all night. If you will come with me to France, I promise you shall have the position you require."

She scoffed. "And I can well imagine what position that will be, sir. I must decline."

"You misunderstand," he said. "I would wed you if I could, but I am heir to Trouville, with all that implies. We are connected to the throne of France and I am bound to—"

"Nay, 'tis *you* who misunderstand," Iana interrupted, but without the heat of anger. "Even if you were free to wed me, Henri, I would never agree to it. No man will say again what I must or must not do. All I require is that you honor your promise to find me work. Is that so much to ask?"

He frowned. "Obviously more than you realize. Iana, no woman is free to pursue her own course. Every one, from princess to meanest peasant, is subject to the rule of her overlord. Only a queen with no king may have such freedom as you would like. And, regal as you appear, you are no queen."

"I recognize no master."

"Well, you have one," he argued. "Somewhere, you have one."

"It is not you, however," Iana reminded him. "Does it threaten you so that a woman might decide her own path? It is not as if I proclaim that right for all, but I will take it for myself. I have taken it." She straightened her shoulders and raised her chin. "If you refuse to do as you promised, then I shall go my own way."

"We shall see." He held Tam out and Iana came forward to relieve him of the child. Their hands brushed in the exchange. He covered hers when she had Tam firmly in her grasp. "Think on it, Iana. I would not force my will upon you in any way. You have my vow on that."

"Not unless you thought it for my own good," she qualified. "Then you would not hesitate to impose it, would you?"

He looked into her eyes for a long, silent interval before he removed his hands, turned away from her and left the chamber. That was as good as any admission he might have made as far as she was concerned.

Henri might care for her, but he would never allow her the freedom to make her own decisions. His word would be her law if she accepted his protection. Not only would she relinquish control over her life, she would endure a status even lower than that of a wife. Heaven only knew, the role of a woman properly wed had proved almost too humbling to bear.

Her desire for him might well have led her into dependence upon him were he not so honest in his intent. If he had insisted only a bit more, offered her another of those mind-rending kisses he was wont to ply, she feared she would have surrendered despite her resolve. She might yet if she were not careful.

"What a frightening thought that is," she muttered, hugging the baby close.

"Dat is," Tam agreed.

Chapter Ten

Baincroft was a busy keep without much space for privacy unless one remained above stairs in a sleeping chamber. However, Henri needed only a few moments alone to think before he met with his father and Rob, so he had ducked into the wall recess sometimes used as a haven for unimportant visitors to pass a night. There he sat upon the cushioned ledge and leaned back against the wall, out of sight of any who might pass by.

Henri had never believed eavesdropping ignoble. He had indulged in it since he was a small boy, finding the practice highly informative and sometimes lifesaving. The plots and intrigues of the French court had made keen ears imperative.

At times he wished for Rob's capability of reading words on lips from across a room. Henri did not need it now, however, for he could not see them directly.

The speakers stood not six feet away from the alcove where he sat. From the shadows that he saw cast upon the floor, and the scent that reached his nostrils, he knew they were attending the sconces that lighted the darker corners of Baincroft.

"She's not much of a mother, if you ask me," Glenys

the maid was saying now. "Did you see the poor wee bastard? She must have starved it for months, hoping it would die."

Henri almost bolted out of concealment to throttle the little tongue-wagger, but quickly recalled that these were Rob's people, not his, to chastise. He felt like doing bodily harm to the bitch and that would not do.

Besides, he needed to hear the reply to learn if the maid's opinion was isolated.

"Mind your mouth unless you're wishing to become a goose girl or worse," Mistress Aiden warned her. "'Tis naught to you what your betters do."

"She's not *my* better," Glenys argued hotly as they strolled past the place where Henri listened. "The common clothes she wore here marked her for what she is. And the lack of jewels. There's not a ring, even a braided token, on her finger. We were all talking about that last evening."

"Maybe her proof was lost or stolen," Mistress Aiden countered. "I still say it's naught to the likes of us whether she was ever wed."

They stopped then to replace the candles farther down the wall. Through the opening, Henri could no longer see their shadows upon the floor, but could clearly hear their words.

Glenys snorted. "She wants to be a healer, I heard her say. She'll not be giving me no herbs, I can tell you that."

"Nor me," Mistress Aiden agreed. "'Tis one thing to keep quiet and not court Lady Mairi's anger, quite another to allow Sir Henri's harlot to cure one's ills. Betwixt you and me, she's bewitched that one, you mark my words."

A gasp. "Surely not! She does spells, you think?"

"Potions, most likely," Mistress Aiden declared. "She admitted to Lady Mairi she knows her herbs. It ain't like our fine Harry's a man to trip over just any skirt, now is he? You ever known him to?"

"Ain't never showed no interest in mine," Glenys admitted with a rueful chuckle.

Henri leaned back against the wall, his hands fisted to keep from reaching out, grabbing the two tale bearers and shaking them soundly. But that would be futile, he knew. He could not use force to shush every loose tongue within Baincroft.

The servants' voices grew fainter as they moved out of earshot and on into the hall proper.

At least now he knew how the wind blew. It was as he had feared. Rob and Mairi might hold the hearts of their people, but they could not control their thoughts and beliefs. Or their gossip. And, not knowing Iana as Henri did, his brother and sister-in-law might succumb to those beliefs themselves after he was gone.

He recalled with horror the time when his father's new wife, the woman Henri now revered as his mother, had been accused of poisoning Trouville. Saving her had taken a miracle plus a great deal of planning on his part.

Henri could not bear to think Iana might suffer a like accusation, but if he left her here, she could. Sorcery was as serious a charge as murder.

If, in assisting Mairi in the healing one day, she should administer any herb that did not do its work or that caused someone to sicken or act strangely, Iana would bear the consequences. And he would not be here to save her as he had Lady Anne. Somehow he must convince her to leave with him.

With that thought in mind, he left the alcove with the intent of finding her and beginning his persuasion in earnest. He did not need to look far. The moment he stepped from the enclosure, he saw her.

Her hand fisted against her lips, her eyes wide and swimming with tears, she stepped from behind the stone wall that supported the stairs. The women would not have seen her there, he knew. But Iana would have heard every word.

In a way, he supposed that was for the best. She would not need much in the way of convincing after listening to that conversation.

Henri approached her. "You heard," he said.

"Aye," she admitted in a pained whisper.

"Where is Thomasina?" he asked, only because her arms looked so empty. He was used to seeing them together. At the moment, he knew Iana could have used the comfort.

"She is with Lady Mairi and her lads in the solar. I was…exploring."

He watched her carefully. "And discovered more than you wished to."

She straightened, pulling about her the cloak of dignity that fit her so well. "A necessary bit of knowledge, for all that."

"You'll come with me when I leave," he stated, reaching out to touch her, to take her hand.

She stepped back, lifted her gaze to his, and he saw the steel in it. "Nay, I will not."

"Iana, you cannot remain here. There's a danger that—"

"I am well aware of the danger," she informed him, "and I shall move on, go elsewhere."

"Oh? Do tell me where that would be?" he demanded softly. "To a convent? You will not be welcomed without sufficient dowry. Braid a straw ring and pose as some peasant's widow? Hammer one of metal and admit your true station? Either way, you would be expected to serve some man, somewhere. As beautiful as you are—''

"Hush!" she cried, turning away from him, clasping her arms across her chest. "Leave me alone!" Her voice broke.

Henri could not stand to witness her dismay, nor could he leave her there to suffer alone. He embraced her from behind and pressed a kiss upon her bowed head. "Please. Let me care for you, Iana."

She broke away from him and almost ran several steps before whirling around to confront him, shaking a fist as she glanced about to see if anyone had witnessed his embrace.

"You foster their suspicions apurpose, Henri! Would you have me branded whore? Is that your intent? You think if they call me so, I will accept that I am? Well, I am *not* and never have been! And I never will be, so please cease in your attempt to make me one!"

He exhaled and rolled his eyes in exasperation. "I know you are no whore, Iana. Listen to me," he pleaded. "You cannot stay here and you cannot go on alone, just you and Tam. I shall find you a place. I will purchase you a ring and swear you were wed to a friend of mine. If lies it takes to see you settled, I shall tell them in abundance. Will that suffice?''

She sucked in a breath and gave her head a shake, but said nothing more.

Henri held out a hand to her. "Come, we will put the matter before my father. He awaits me now in Rob's accounting chamber. If you do not trust me to see to your future, perhaps you will trust him.''

Iana looked absolutely horrified at that idea and he knew why. Trouville had not yet cornered her again with all his questions about her family. The noon meal had proved a veritable noise fest in celebration of Henri's return, and she had escaped the melee the moment the servants had cleared the tables.

She must have settled Tam with Mairi and the boys immediately in order to arrive where he had found her so quickly. She had been hiding, or at least seeking a moment's peace to think, just as he had been doing inside the alcove.

Reluctantly, she did take the hand he offered. He closed his around hers, engulfing the delicate shape with a profound urge to shelter all of her that completely. If only she would allow him to surround her with his strength and wealth and rank. None would dare insult or threaten her.

But she did have a point. Whether she shared his bed or not, Iana would be branded his leman unless he wed her. And that he could not do. Helpless at the moment to resolve her plight, Henri simply held her worried gaze with a look of sympathy and frustration.

She wanted him, too. There was no mistaking it and never had been. He could feel the trembling in her hand, see the yearning in her eyes and hear the shallow, unsteady breathing so like his own. Her lips parted to speak, but no words emerged. Henri leaned forward to kiss away her fears.

"There you are," said the deep voice he had almost been expecting. Trouville had tired of waiting and had come to seek him out. Henri did not miss the pointed look that he focused upon their joined hands.

Iana pulled away and clasped her hands together, her knuckles dead white with the force of her grip.

"Ah, and you have located Lady Iana. My dear, I am preparing your rewards even now," he assured her. "I have sent home for a veritible caravan of gifts to bestow on your family, and we shall set out whenever you are rested from your journey with Henri. How fares your child? We shall bring a nurse to tend her along the way, of course.''

Iana dropped a belated and somewhat clumsy curtsy before she whirled and ran up the stairs without uttering a single word.

His father sighed and quirked a dark brow. "No success in discovering her origins, I presume."

"Father, will you leave her be? She's so overset by her circumstance she cannot think straight. I must go after her."

Before Henri took two steps, Trouville grasped his arm. "No, you shall not."

"She will be weeping, distressed beyond bearing. I might convince her—"

"No!" he thundered, then took a deep breath and lowered his voice. "She will not fall apart, Henri. She means to flee. I could see her intent as clearly as if she had told us her plan outright."

Henri forcibly relaxed his muscles and remained still. "Surely you do not wish for that to happen, Father. I certainly cannot allow it."

Trouville frowned. "There is a reason she refuses to give us her true name, Henri, and I would know what it is. Once she confesses why, we will be able to help her resolve it. If she runs, either with you to France or into the wilds to escape, we shall never know what threatens her so. It may only be as she says, that she thinks her brother will make her marry if we return her to him. Surely you know that I can dissuade him from forcing her. Do you not believe we owe her peace of mind and a reconciliation with her family?"

"I do not think even you can manage the last," Henri

said. "Thomasina is not the legitimate issue of her husband. That she has admitted. I believe she has been cast out in shame, Father."

Trouville leaned against the stone wall and crossed his feet at the ankles, a study in composure. "Even after what she confided to Mairi? You do not believe her?"

Henri shrugged and propped one hand against the stones, rubbing the back of his neck with the other. God's truth, his head ached from lack of sleep and worry. "It could be that she bore the child out of wedlock and her kin consider her dishonored."

His father smiled. "Then why has she not accepted your *kind* offer? If what you say is true, what would she have to lose?"

Henri straightened and pinched the bridge of his nose. "She wants freedom to do as she chooses, to answer to no man."

Trouville laughed uproariously at that. When he calmed, he said ruefully, "They all want that, Son. And bless God, a few of them have it. I suspect she will, too, no matter what the outcome of all this. She must have a stronger will than most to have survived thus far."

"Tell me what to do, Father."

"Bide your time. Keep her here until Thomas returns. On the chance that he finds out nothing about her, I would suggest that we not let up in our bid for the truth from her own lips."

"You underestimate her. She will never tell us."

His father shook his head. "She is cornered, with nowhere to turn, Henri. I hate to pressure her so, but it is the only way to get at the heart of the matter so we can correct it for her."

"What if it cannot be made right? Do you suggest we simply toss her to the four winds as did that brother of hers?"

Trouville regarded him for a long moment. "Of course not. We shall give her the freedom she wishes and the wealth to maintain it wherever she chooses."

"She would see that boon as charity and not accept it from us. I already offered."

"Just as well she would not, Henri, for I believe she deserves more."

"And what more is it that you think she needs, Father?"

"Someone to love her, of course. A family. A husband. A father for her daughter. She needs that whether she believes it or not. We *all* need that." Trouville looked at him with eyes narrowed. "Do you not agree?"

Henri could not bear to think of Iana wed to another man, even one who would treasure her above anyone, even one who would accept Tam as his own and glory in her small triumphs as Henri had done earlier when Tam spoke his name.

He could not answer his father, either to agree to or argue the matter. What his father said was true. Iana certainly merited the happiness and safety that marriage and a family could bring. But Henri was also quite sure that neither he nor Iana wanted her married to someone else. If only...

"Henri?" Trouville prodded.

"Excuse me, sir. I need to notify the guards on the gates that Iana is not to pass unaccompanied under any circumstances."

"Very well." There was a long pause before Trouville added, "You are excused."

The moment she reached her chamber, Iana's first impulse was to stuff her meager belongings into a tote, collect Tam from the solar and depart with all haste. That father of Henri's and Henri himself were like to drive her mad if she stayed.

As it was, she had nearly blurted out that not only would Newell delight in the extra wealth that she herself had earned, he would be overjoyed to have her back, to barter off again like some prize mare for breeding.

She longed to demand if they considered that a just reward for her saving Henri's life. But she realized before she spoke that those two men would not find that an offensive fate at all for her. Aye, they would consider it quite just indeed, the very thing a woman should desire.

If only she had the remainder of the silver links, she might set out on her own, but Henri had forgotten to return them. Would he surrender them if she asked? Not likely, she decided. He would remind her yet again that she would be no better off in a new place than she was here. The awful thing was, he was right.

It seemed two choices remained. She could run and risk falling prey to some man unknown to her as yet, or she could accept Henri's offer and become his mistress.

Iana sank into the chair in her chamber, leaned forward and cradled her head in her hands. Good heavens, she had been better off in the village, poor as dirt and free to come and go at will. Yet she could not have remained there for long. Newell would have come soon and employed stronger force to change her mind once he had seen that her pitiful exile had not weakened her resolve at all.

She straightened in the chair and rested her head against the back of it. *What to do, what to do?*

"My lady?" called a soft voice from the open doorway. Everand.

"Come in, Ev," she invited. Why not? she thought. Everyone else had had their say. Was he here on Henri's behalf? "Do sit down and feel free to advise me," she invited with a rueful grimace.

"Advise you?" he repeated. "On what?"

"Whatever you like, Ev. It seems a woman has no mind of her own and must be led about like an unsteady weanling. I expect no less of you than any other man."

He laughed as he ambled in and plopped into the chair facing her. "A jest, surely. I am not yet a man," he admitted. "Nor are you mindless."

Iana sighed and closed her eyes. "They will surely banish you from their ranks forever for spouting that heresy, my lad. Have a care where you deliver such drops of wisdom."

"I came to share my news. Father intends to adopt me in a legal court. And the *comte* acknowledged me as a grandson this morn," he said, changing the subject. "It is but a token honor, since I am not of Trouville blood and cannot be titled, but grand all the same that he accepts me. He seems a kind man and very like my lord Henri."

"Oh, very like," Iana agreed. "In all ways, more's the pity."

Ev cleared his throat and stared into the empty fireplace. His fingers danced nervously on the arms of the chair.

"There is another reason I came," he said, his voice dropping almost to a whisper and sounding woeful. "Something you should know."

Iana blew out a sharp breath. "I have heard."

His head jerked toward her and his worried gaze fastened on hers. "That they think I am your son. And my lord's?"

"What!" Iana bolted upright.

"I know," he said wearily. "You are too young to have borne me, but they do not know our ages, my lady. I look quite young for mine and you, well, it would be hard to tell how old you are by your appearance. Many women seem much younger than they are if they lead a life without toil." He added, "And they believe you have. As Sir Henri's leman."

Iana began to pace, her anger doubling with every step. "How dare they—"

"They do not dare, not in MacBain's or his lady's hearing. I had it from Jean-Louis, one of the pages who traveled from court with the lady Jehan. He and I seem to be the only inhabitants in this place, save you, Sir Henri and his father, who speak French."

"Lady Jehan told the lad this lie?" Iana demanded, aghast that the woman would fabricate such a falsehood. She needed her eyes scratched out for it.

"I do not know that she made it up," Ev admitted. "I believe he might have heard it from some of the other boys. He can understand them well enough, he says. In any case, it is no secret now. The entire castle is abuzz with the news, at least among the servants. They say my lord fathered me on you years ago, and Tam more recently, of course. It is believed he means to ship us all to France. They resent his bringing his light-o'-love and bastards to live among them, even for a short while. They think it shows disrespect for Lord Rob and Lady Mairi."

"This is absurd!" Iana buried her face in her hands. "God's truth, Ev, I wish to be quit of this place. Now, *today!*"

He shook his head and picked at the fabric of his cap. "Impossible. I overheard Sir Henri tell his father that he would not allow you to leave. I fear you are captive here, my lady. I wish I could help.''

''Captive?'' Iana gasped. How could this be? How could Henri do this to her? She had brought this on herself by saving him. But even now she had to admit that she would have done no differently had she known what would occur as a result.

She would have saved Henri's life. But she would not have come here with him had she known. She would have stayed and faced her brother. With Newell, she might have stood at least a small chance of retaining her honor and the respect she deserved.

''Ev, would you go and fetch Tam from the solar for me?'' she asked. ''Then tell your lord I would speak with him.''

''Will you accept his offer now?'' Everand asked her.

A hardness enveloped her. She felt as brittle as the ice that settled upon the edges of the lochs in midwinter. ''Not for the promise of heaven would I accept anything from that man!''

''Then accept me,'' he pleaded. ''I will wed you. I offered before, but you thought it a jest. My real father willed me what he had, so I am not dependent upon Sir Henri. Marry me and I—''

''Oh, Ev.'' Iana softened at the sympathy and true caring in his earnest eyes. She reached out and brushed a lock of hair off his brow, then cradled his rounded cheek in her hand. ''Dear lad.''

''Do not say me nay. I will love you,'' he declared. ''I *do* love you.''

''My dear, I love you, too,'' she said sincerely. ''But this is no solution. We have spoken of this before and both know it would never do. Still, I thank you from my heart for being the kind soul you are and wishing to save me grief.''

He gave her a strange look, one she could not interpret, then nodded and left to do her bidding.

If Iana had ever experienced a lower moment in her life, she could not recall it. Even the beatings she had endured during her marriage had not left her feeling so defeated and completely without hope.

Even Everand realized how dire was her predicament.

Chapter Eleven

"**O**h, there you are, *Father*," Everand said as he approached the stables. Henri noted how the boy emphasized the last word, with a thread of near sarcasm in his voice. Surely not, for he had seemed quite pleased to be considered Henri's son.

"Here I am," he replied.

"I thought perhaps you had departed without me."

"Hardly," Henri answered, smiling. "Who would scrub my new mail and shine the plates? I only came out to see how the mounts fare. You were searching for me?"

"To bring a message. Lady Iana awaits you in her chamber."

Henri silently debated whether it would be wise to answer her summons. "What is her mood?"

Ev looked away and rocked heel to toe, his hands clasped behind his back. "Troubled."

Henri wondered how much of the gossip Everand had divined, since he did not speak the language of the servants here. However, there was that one lad Rob told him about who knew some French, the page who had arrived with Jehan. Rob had even sent the boy to keep Ev company after supper last eve.

"You seem bothered by something yourself. Do you wish to discuss it?" Henri asked.

"I think not," Ev said. "There has been enough said about it already."

So he *had* heard. "Just so. Well, see what you can do about the mare, would you? She seems fretful. I will go and try to soothe the other female."

Ev's sound of disgust made him turn to see what the matter was. The boy looked outraged. "You would compare the lady to a beast, sir? I would not have thought it of you!"

Henri laughed and clapped him on the shoulder. "Hold your temper, Son! I meant naught by it. Only that the gentler sex often make something out of nothing."

"Nothing?" Ev questioned, his jaw clenched hard.

"Truth told, I grant she has a right to be trammeled, but it is not the end of the world, Ev. We shall put everything right for her, do not worry."

Ev stepped closer, head tilted, eyes narrowed. "How much did my father bequeath me?"

Taken aback by the seemingly unrelated question, Henri frowned. "I would have to examine the documents and figure the worth of some of the investments to give you a precise figure. Why?"

"A thousand pounds?"

Henri nodded, unsure what Ev had in mind. "Several times that. Have you need of coin, Ev? Have you been wagering?"

"The largest wager of all, sir. I plan to use a thousand of it as a bride price."

Henri laughed. "Are you not rushing a bit? You've not even had your first woman yet and you're planning to marry? Tell me, what young minx has caught your eye?"

Everand looked deadly serious. "I am of age and shall wed Lady Iana. I have already asked her."

Henri sobered on the instant. "You did what?"

"She did not refuse me."

"Then she is mad!" Henri exclaimed. "You cannot marry her and she knows it. Aside from the matter of your disparate ages, she is a lady and you are the son of a merchant."

"Wrong. I am now a son of the house of Trouville," Everand reminded him.

The sly pup! The wily, conniving little dog. "I will not allow it, Everand."

"Why not?" Ev demanded, then gave a very adult smirk. "Of course, I know the answer to that. You want her for yourself. Not enough to wed her, but certainly enough to besmirch her even further than these low-minded serfs who gobble your brother's meat and spit out lies with the bones."

Henri shuddered with the urge to crack a hand across Ev's face. How dare the little ingrate speak thusly to him, the man who had offered him everything. "What of your loyalty to me, Everand?"

"Steadfast, sir. I seek to save your honor as well as hers."

Henri struggled to speak without shouting. He sucked in a harsh breath and demanded in a grating voice, "To whom would you pay this bride price of yours? Has she named her kin?"

Ev smiled. "No, but we shall know it soon enough when your brother's spy returns, shall we not? And I do not care what news he brings, what she has done or what the results of it were. It will not affect my decision at all."

Henri knew he had best leave the vicinity before he

did something his newly acquired *son* would never forgive. Without another word, he stalked across the bailey and up the steps to the hall door. "She wishes to speak with me, does she?" he muttered through gritted teeth. "I have a few choice words for her as well!"

He entered the keep and was about to mount the stairs when Jehan called out to him from across the hall. Not in a mood to suffer delay, Henri simply lifted a hand in greeting and continued on his way.

She caught up with him on the third stair tread, snaked her arms around his elbow and apparently planned to accompany him to the upper floor.

Henri could readily see how Iana would greet him if he arrived with Jehannie in tow, so he stopped. "What do you want of me? And hurry, if you will. I have matters to attend that cannot wait."

Her cat eyes rounded and her reddened lips drew down in a mock frown. "Ooh, who hid a burr in your braies, laddie?"

"Leave off," he told her, trying to disentangle her arms. "Go and bother Rob."

Instantly, he regretted his words, for she looked hurt by them. Without another word, she backed away, turned and would have left him alone as he had demanded.

He reached out, touching her shoulder. "Jehannie, wait. I did not mean that."

"Yes, you did," she said in a small, sad voice.

Contrite, Henri grasped her shoulders. What had gotten into him, treating her so? Jehan had been a friend since the day he first came to Baincroft as a boy. True, she had spent most of that time bedeviling him, but it had only been her notion of fun. She had done that to everyone.

Now she had grown up and was not that wicked child

any longer. Beautiful as she had turned out to be, however, Henri still had trouble seeing her as a woman.

"Look, I was worried about something else," he admitted. "You are not crying, are you?"

She was. Huge, fat droplets rolled down both cheeks. "Why do you do this to me?" he asked with a huge sigh of defeat. "You know I could never abide tears."

She sniffled. "First Robbie, now you desert me."

Henri put his arms around her and pulled her close, patting her back. "Hush now. Rob has not deserted you. In the event you've not noticed, you *are* living in his house at present. And my return to France can hardly be termed desertion. That was ordained the day I was born and you've always known it. Besides, Rob and I are not your only friends."

She pounded his shoulder lightly with one small fist, a halfhearted blow more like a gesture of affection than a protest of his words. Her tearful gaze connected with his. "I had hoped you might seek me out after Rob wed Mairi, and at least offer me some comfort."

"Ye Gods, tell me you're not jealous of Rob's wife, Jehannie! If so, what the devil are you doing here?" He frowned down at her. "You do not mean to cause him trouble after all this time? They have been wed for years now."

She lowered her head so that her brow rested upon his chest. Henri had to strain to hear her muffled words. "Of course not. I love Mairi like a sister and she makes him a better wife than I would have done. Still, I find I cannot marry any of the strangers my grandfather puts before me at court. I need a man I can trust. Someone strong, honorable and good." Her palm flattened upon his body and moved in a slight caress. "Someone like you."

Oh no. A thousand times no. "Jehannie, my dear, that

man will not be me, much as I care for you," Henri said firmly as he held her arms and set her away from him.

She touched his face. "Because you are not free to marry for love?"

He grasped her hands gently to keep them from roaming. "You do not love me, little cat."

"I could," she argued. Her small teeth caught her bottom lip as she looked deeply into his eyes. "I might not be French, but my connection to Robert the Bruce is royal enough, closer to a crown than even your own. We would suit each other."

"We would *kill* each other," he declared ruefully, not exaggerating by much. Henri remembered their arguments and all the times he, Rob and her brother Thomas had been obliged to extricate the little adventuress from one scrape or another. So willful and audacious, she had been. And still was, it seemed. Daring, even now, trying to secure her own future before her old grandfather forced the issue.

He felt her hands slide from his and was glad to release her.

Suddenly she raised up on her toes, slipped her arms around his neck and kissed him fully on the mouth. Not the kiss of a childhood friend, but of a determined seductress.

The move shocked him so soundly he simply stood there, breathless, arms outstretched. Then he almost shoved her away from him, remembering only at the last instant why she was doing this. Gently, he put his hands on her shoulders, broke the kiss and stepped back.

"Jehannie—"

"Do not let me interrupt," said a soft voice above them on the stairs.

Iana. Damn.

Henri did not even attempt to explain why he was standing on the stairs with Jehan, accepting a kiss. Iana's bland expression was devoid of any emotion, but he knew what she was thinking. He had so recently asked her to accept his protection and come away with him, and now it looked as if he were courting Jehan's favor immediately after.

Jehan was wearing her cat's smile. Anything he said to Iana at this point would sound blatantly false, even ridiculous. Henri moved past Jehan and descended the few steps that led back into the hall, leaving the scene as unhurriedly and with as much dignity as he could muster.

Only when he was outside again did he recall why he had entered the keep in the first place.

Iana was contemplating marriage to Everand. And Jehan seemed to be implementing her own guileful scheme. How had life become such a mockery? And how could he set matters right?

Lady Jehan appeared rather satisfied with herself, Iana thought. If the woman only knew how free Henri was with his kisses, she might not be quite so elated. "You had best run after him," she advised Jehan, "for he might be seeking out the nearest maid to finish what you began."

A trill of delighted laughter greeted the advice. "Henri? Do not believe it. A man such as he will be as constant as the day is long."

"Only if you count the hours in that day as moments," Iana snapped.

Jehan shrugged and reached up to grasp Iana's hand, though that took some doing. Iana had rarely felt such reluctance to allow another's touch. Still, the woman insisted. "Come, let us join Mairi in the solar. She sent me to find you."

Iana went with her, suspecting that Lady Mairi now wished her to come and take over Tam's care. The baby had been there for nigh on an hour. Though there were maids aplenty, none would be eager to mind the *bastard* of Henri's *whore,* she thought darkly. A plague on them all for their twisted imaginings.

Jehan snaked her arm through Iana's and smiled at her. "I wish you to know I do not believe what they are saying."

Iana gasped. Did the woman read minds?

"Oh yes, the entire place is humming with rumors. Yet I know Henri fathered no lad upon you in his youth. Nor is he responsible for your babe."

"And how would you know this for certain?" Iana countered. At the moment, she almost wished it were true so that she could fling it in the trollop's face.

"Simple," Jehan declared, hugging Iana's arm to her. "You are not the sort of woman he would have tupped, and even if you were," she added sagely, "I've told you that he cannot father a child on anyone or else he would have done so on that wife of his. I had the entire tale from Rob and Mairi long ago."

"They told you?" Iana could not feature the MacBains telling anyone of Henri's private marriage matters. She was amazed Henri had told *them.* It was not a thing a man would boast of, surely, or even admit to unless necessary.

"Of course they would not tell me! But sometimes they forget that I can read their hand signs. It is very convenient when it comes to gathering secrets, I can tell you. You should learn if you are to stay here for any length of time."

"That's abominable! You should not!"

Again, the woman laughed. "I rarely do what I should. It makes for such a dull existence." She sighed and released Iana as they neared the door to the solar. "You must not fret so, you know. When my brother returns and tells us exactly who you are, we shall best know how to help you out of this quandary."

Iana halted midstep and grabbled the lady's arm. "What do you mean?"

Lady Jehan wore a look of utter innocence. "Thomas has gone to Largsmuth to inquire about your family. He should return within a day or so."

Iana almost fainted. She, who rarely quailed at anything, felt ill and undone. Newell would arrive either with or upon the heels of this man sent to discover who she was. And she would not be allowed to flee Baincroft before that happened. Henri had seen to that.

Suddenly outraged, she gathered up her fractured wits and marched into the solar. "Lady Mairi, I insist you tell me why I am being held prisoner here in your home when I have done no one any wrong!"

The lady looked up from where she sat, her mouth rounded in surprise. Iana fumed, awaiting her answer.

"Prisoner? Whatever are you talking about and why are you so angry?"

"Because I am not permitted to depart." Iana flung out an arm toward Jehan. "*Her* brother has gone to inform mine of my whereabouts, that is what I mean! Do you know what will happen?" she demanded. "My brother will haul me away to face that marriage about which I confided. The one I abhor. And he will not allow me to keep this child, you may stake your life upon that fact! I shall lose Thomasina due to simple curiosity. And you wonder why I am angry?"

She darted a look at Lady Jehan, who also appeared guilt-stricken by her announcement. Mayhaps she could play upon that guilt. "Will you help me get away? For the child's sake? Please?"

They looked almost ready to comply. Surely they would be happy to be rid of her. Lady Mairi had already opened her mouth to answer when men's voices and footsteps resounded from the hall and distracted her. She rose quickly, handed Tam to Iana and rushed to the door. "What commotion is this?"

Jehan joined her in the doorway and gasped, "*Who* is that with Rob, Henri and Trouville? Oh, would you *look* at him!"

Iana peered over their shoulders at the stranger, a tall, handsome man who looked rather imperious in full mail and a bright red emblazoned tunic.

"Far be it from me to deny him the hospitality of your keep, Mairi," Jehan said with a short laugh of pure excitement. "Allow me to provide him welcome." Without further ado she strode into the hall with a definite spring in her step.

Mairi followed, with only a bit less enthusiasm than Jehan. Iana brought up the rear, clutching Tam in her arms. Whoever he was, at least the imposing visitor was not Newell, she thought with relief.

When they approached, Henri undertook introductions. "Sir Ambrose, may I present to you Lady Mairi, wife to Lord Robert, Lady Jehan de Brus and Lady Iana of Ayr." For the first time in introducing her that way, Henri had not included that mocking hesitation before her place name. He studied Iana so intently during the entire exchange, she felt like backing away from the group. Instead, she tried to ignore him, and bent her knee in a half curtsy to honor the knight.

"My ladies," Sir Ambrose acknowledged, bowing politely. He had also trained his blue gaze upon Iana and kept it there, which she thought strange, since Jehan stood nearest, was quite richly garbed and certainly more beautiful than she. Courtesy should have demanded he give his full attention to his hostess, yet he hardly noticed either of the other women.

"Ayr? That is on the coast, is it not?" the knight demanded.

"It is, sir," she replied.

"Near Whitethistle, if I am not mistaken," he added.

Iana remained silent. He *knew* about her. But mayhaps not, she thought, unwilling to entertain the thought that Newell might have sent him here. Yet why else would he mention that village? She looked even more closely at the knight. Something about him seemed familiar, but she could not think what it was.

"Welladay, what brings ye to Baincroft, good sir?" Lady Mairi asked, as if in attempt to engage a different topic of conversation.

"I am searching for someone, a lady," he replied in a deep, commanding voice.

Iana's heart skipped a beat, then began thundering in her chest. He was here for her. She just knew it.

"And you have found three!" Jehan announced gleefully as she slipped her arm through his. "Come and take your ease, sir. Have some wine. When you have rested, we shall see you to a chamber and prepare a bath. 'Tis *my* duty to see you comfortable," she said suggestively.

As if noticing Jehan for the first time, the knight peered down at her from his much greater height. "Your duty?"

She dimpled and batted her lashes like the veriest bawd, Iana thought, thanking the woman with all her heart for providing distraction.

At that moment, Iana would have stolen away from the company and made herself scarce. Henri aborted that move by taking her arm firmly in his hand and guiding her toward the table, where the others were headed.

"I must go," she whispered insistently, tugging with renewed effort.

"You will stay," he declared firmly, tightening his hold on her. "This man has come for you and I will know why."

"Do not let him take me," Iana pleaded before she could stop herself. "Please, Henri!"

"You wish my protection?" he asked, though it sounded more statement than question.

"Aye," she answered readily, willing to do most anything rather than be returned to Newell. At least Henri would allow her to keep Tam.

"Then be honest with me for once. Are you a runaway wife?" he asked through gritted teeth.

"Nay, I swear not. I have told you my husband is long dead. That is the truth!"

They continued on their way across the hall, lagging behind the others far enough so they could not be overheard.

"It is obvious you do not know this chevalier," he remarked in a hurried whisper.

"True, he is a stranger, but I fear he has come for me in another's stead," she answered in kind.

"The man who would wed you?" he asked. She nodded. His frowned deepened. "Is there a contract?"

"I refused to sign. I shall not wed again. Not ever."

"What of Everand? You led him to think—"

"Spare me jests, would you? I am sore afraid at the moment." To no avail, Iana tried once more to extract her arm from his grasp.

"Do not fear," he said. "You are mine."

"I am not *yours!*" she insisted, her words hurried, desperate and nearly inaudible, since she and Henri were drawing near the others. "I belong to no man. I but wish your help in this matter, is all. Give it and you are quit of any promises to me. Keep what is left of your silver and I shall disappear the moment you let me out these gates."

"And go to ground again like a frightened hare and starve to death? I think not."

"Please!" Iana implored, the last word she could afford without a large audience.

"For your sake, I must say no." He smiled down at her, baring his straight white teeth in such a savage look that she gave up. For the moment.

Later she would convince him to let her go her own way. For now, it might be best to allow him apparent victory. She was, after all, dependent upon his goodwill.

When all were seated informally about the hastily prepared table, they partook of wine, cheese and broken meats provided by the maids and two pages.

Lady Jehan, who had appointed herself chief entertainer, regaled their guest with bright and amusing tales of the French and English courts where she had spent most of the last six years with her grandfather.

Iana had to admit the woman knew how to engage attention. Hers should have seemed a self-centered recitation, yet somehow did not. Sir Ambrose's regard for Lady Jehan changed from politely disinterested to enthralled in the space of half an hour, though he did spare several curious and guilt-filled glances in Iana's direction.

Whenever he did look her way, Henri would lean nearer, chuck Tam under her chin and smile at Iana so sweetly she almost wished he were not acting a part.

Soon their repast was over and Jehan was leading the knight up the stairs to his appointed chamber, cooing over him as if he were an exhausted child too long at play.

"She has him eating from her hand," Henri said. "The poor sod has likely forgotten why he came here."

"I devoutly hope so. By the by, your eyes are turning green," Iana observed.

He laughed, regarding her with astonishment. "You think me jealous?"

"Aye, given how you were kissing her earlier yourself. I would not take you for a man who shares so readily, but then I am no great judge of men." Her words had a biting quality to them, despite her effort to make them sound casual.

Henri shook his head. "I do not share at all. Jehan is not and never has been my lover."

"She plans to wed you," Iana declared, instantly sorry, for she feared she might have betrayed a confidence. Lady Jehan had stated the intent to her, but mayhaps not yet to Henri himself. "Or it seems that way. She must love you," she added quickly.

"So she does," he admitted without surprise. "And I love her." He hesitated, as if he would add more to the confession, then looked away and remained silent.

The faraway look in his eyes struck Iana with a small wave of pity. She reached out and touched his forearm. "How sad for you both. Jehan is not suitable either, is she?"

Either? Why the devil had she said that? It sounded as if she regretted the fact that she was not a candidate for marriage to him herself.

He smiled knowingly. "She is related to Scottish royalty and would make a truly fine match for almost any nobleman. But not for me."

"Oh." Iana understood instantly. He considered *him-self* the problem, then. Jehan had intimated that Henri could not father a child. How noble of him not to take the woman he loved to wife, knowing he could provide her no sons or daughters.

God help her, Iana could not make herself say she was sorry again. Though she felt terrible for thinking it, she did not want to see the two of them wed, no matter how much they loved.

She told herself it was simply that they were not right for each other, but in her heart of hearts, Iana greatly feared that was not the real reason at all.

Henri took Tam from her and cradled the sleeping child against his chest. "I shall carry her up for you. I do swear you could use a bit of rest yourself."

"Doubtless," she replied softly, weary to her bones with all the worry over Sir Ambrose's arrival. She would not be able to rest, however. Not when she knew there would soon be a confrontation of some kind with regard to the knight's mission for Newell.

At least she need worry no longer about the steward's return with information about her former life. What did it matter now? As soon as Sir Ambrose had rested and gathered his wits about him, he would impart everything about her to Lord MacBain, Henri and Lord Trouville.

Thanks be to God she had not argued any further about coming under Henri's protection. He would claim her and not allow this Sir Ambrose to take her back to Newell. Indeed, with her honor in such shreds, it would hardly take much convincing to get the knight to leave her where she was. Newell would be furious, but would not want her back after he heard the knight's report.

But Henri obviously would expect something in return

for his appropriation of her, and Iana knew exactly what that something was.

She stole a quick look at his profile as he accompanied her up the stairs. How strong and formidable he appeared, yet how gentle he could be at times. Like now, as he held Tam.

The idea of becoming Henri's mistress should have upset her far more than it did, but what difference did it make now? Everyone thought she was already his. And she supposed being his light-o'-love for a short time would afford her more freedom in the future than becoming a wife.

Chapter Twelve

Henri placed the sleeping child upon the bed in Iana's chamber. "How frail she still appears, though her limbs have begun to flesh out a bit since first we met," he whispered.

"You believe so?" Iana asked hopefully. "I feared it was only my wishing that made it seem so. It is hard to judge, since I am ever with her. She does seem heavier."

He turned and smiled at her motherly concern. "I agree. Has she spoken again since she said my name?"

"A few words, and she makes more sounds than before. I worry so about her health."

Henri watched Iana as she trailed a finger across the child's soft dark hair, her love apparent in the small gesture.

"We shall see she has the best physician France has to offer," he promised. "Perhaps even the king's own. In no time at all, she will be as fat and noisy as any child."

"You would do this for her?" Iana asked. "Why?" Then she grimaced. "How ungracious of me to ask such a thing. I know you have a natural kindness in you, Henri.

But I also know you must expect something in return for such generosity.''

''Oh, Iana.'' He sighed as he brushed his palm along her arm and took her hand in his. What he was doing seemed more wrong than ever. Wanting her so fiercely was one thing, having her become his in order to gain refuge for herself and her child was quite another. No matter what she might have done before, this path he would have her take should be freely traveled or not traveled at all.

However, if she did not align herself with him, what would she do? Go back to some mean hovel and dig in the woods for plants? Yes. Either that or accept some other man to her bed. Most likely the suitor she did not want and would do most anything to avoid taking as a husband. Or else the earnest Everand, who would have no idea what to do with such a woman. Or any woman, for that matter. None of those alternatives bore thinking about.

''Rest now while Tam sleeps,'' he suggested as he released her and turned to leave. ''We will speak of it later.''

''Henri?'' she said, stopping him at the doorway.

''Yes?''

''Thank you.'' She paused. ''For what you did, for making Sir Ambrose think…well, you know, that you had claim to Tam and me.''

''I do have claim,'' he said, warring with his conscience even as he reaffirmed his resolve. ''And God help any man who tries to alter that.''

He supposed he could set her up somewhere and see that she wanted for nothing, if she would accept that from him outright. Somehow, he knew Iana would not. She would insist on some sort of exchange rather than charity, even if it meant sharing his bed. That was, after all, the only thing she had to offer him.

Something in his heart would not allow him to leave her standing there, looking as if he were driving a stake through her heart.

He crossed the room again and stood before her. "Iana, I cannot bear that you feel bereft of your honor in this matter."

She smiled sadly and nodded. "But you will do what you must. For my own benefit, of course."

"And mine," he said softly, cradling her face in his hands. With all care, he lowered his mouth to hers and kissed her. Her lips softened against his, but did not open with invitation when he touched that softness with his tongue. Henri tried to content himself with what she gave, knowing it was unwise to bestir what could not be placated in the midst of the day with a child present.

But she stirred him all the same, tasting of the spiced wine they had shared in the hall, bringing to mind the way she had accepted his gestures of possession then as if she welcomed and found them perfectly natural. Her sweet scent invaded, insidiously beckoning him to draw more upon it, as if her essence, and not the air that bore it, were necessary to his life.

"Henri." She breathed his name upon his lips, and the very word coalesced his senses so perfectly he knew he would never forget the instant should he live forever.

His hands drifted slowly down from her face, following the graceful curve of her neck until his palms rested lightly upon her breasts. The rightness of it flooded through him as surely as did the desire to touch more.

The laces at the sides of her overgown tangled in his fingers as he loosened them. Henri kissed her deeply to prevent any protest she might make, and she accepted his invasion with surprising eagerness. The exquisite taste of her robbed his mind of reason, but he did not care.

He groaned with absolute pleasure as he slipped his hands inside the gown's opening, which reached to her hips. Small wonder priests called this fashion the gates of hell. He felt himself going straight for the fire. Through the thin fabric of her chemise, he gloried in the heat of her skin, the slenderness of her waist, the gently rounded curve of her nether cheeks. So perfectly they fit there in his palms! He squeezed.

She pressed even closer, her body flush with his own, her arms around him, her small fingers clutching restlessly at his back. The enticing sounds she made in her throat as they kissed fueled the crimson haze of need that enveloped them both.

Unable to wait a moment longer to test her readiness, to feel proof of her desire, he moved one hand between their bodies and touched her intimately through the gossamer cloth.

Suddenly she pushed back, breaking the spell that had engulfed them. "We cannot," she gasped, holding him at arm's length, one hand flat against his chest, the other at her throat. "I cannot." Her gaze moved past him to settle upon the sleeping Tam.

Henri covered the hand that held him away from her and brought it to his lips. Fervently he kissed her palm, his eyes closed, his heart thundering in his chest.

Had he misread her response? Did his lust for her create in him the fantasy that her own wants equaled his? For a long moment Henri stood thus, fighting against his overpowering need to have her that instant. Never in his life had a woman moved him so that he forgot where he was and what the result of a coupling might be.

When he spoke, his voice rasped with disappointment

and regret, despite his attempt to sound enticing. "Would you come to me this night if I ask it?"

For an instant, she seemed to waver, then took in a deep breath and let it out haltingly. Frustrated desire or dismay? He could not tell. A bit of both, he suspected.

"Do not ask," she told him. It was almost a plea. "Not here in your brother's home. It seems...somehow worse than in any other place."

"Worse?" Well, that said it all, did it not? Their loving would be bad anywhere, but here it would be *worse?* Anger rose to displace his frustration, though it did not succeed completely. He wished it had. Wanting anything or anyone this keenly, this mindlessly, endangered a man.

He released her hand abruptly and made a short, very formal bow. "Very well. I shall see you this eve. Do not be alarmed if I fawn upon you at that time as I did earlier. Consider the consequences if I seem to have done with you before our guest departs."

"I have considered," she assured him, steadier now, her eyes flashing with sparks of indignation, "and I have thanked you prettily enough, I think. If you wish me to come to your bed, *I* shall choose the time and place. Allow me that decision if you possess any fairness at all."

He snatched up one of her fists, roughly kissed the back of it and summarily dropped it. "I am ever fair, yet how can I know whether *you* will choose a time when I am too old to perform. It could be years from now!"

"Thus speaks a bairn unused to *nay!*" she accused.

Henri bit back a curse. As much as he hated to admit it, she was right. How long had it been since anyone had refused him anything he was set on having? Was that why he wanted her so much?

With a shrug he conceded. "You win. I cannot argue that."

She bit her lips together, trying to hide her smile. Her eyes sparkled with sudden mirth and her shoulders trembled.

Henri suddenly laughed aloud at his own pique, and she joined him. Unable to help himself, he threw his arms around her and hugged her. "You are like to drive me mad. Have a care you do not, for a madman will not dance to your every tune."

She leaned her head back and looked up at him, her expression almost coy. "Somehow, I cannot envision your doing that for anyone."

He caught her by surprise, ravishing her with a kiss as thorough as if he were still bent upon immediate seduction. Her defenses down, she responded with an alacrity that astounded. The heady sensation of it almost overwhelmed Henri's true purpose before he deliberately tore himself away and left the room. He had only wanted to leave her wishing for more.

Another moment and she would have had no choice left about either the time or the place.

Henri attempted to quell his desire for her by training his mind upon qualities in her that had nothing to do with bedding. She was a wonderful mother, a delightful companion when her worry abated, and she possessed a loving nature.

The way she had tended him, a stranger she had no call to trust, spoke very well of her. He remembered the gentleness of her fingers, the sympathetic hiss of her breath when she had removed the stitches she had set to close his wound. Caring.

Iana had gained Everand's trust so completely, the boy

leapt to her defense even when she did not need defending.

Yes, she had all of the qualities a man should seek in a wife. And here he was, about to waste all of those honorable attributes of hers by making her his mistress. That was wrong and he knew it well.

Sir Ambrose must have made short work of his bath, Henri thought, for the knight rejoined the company within the hall soon after Henri returned from Iana's chamber.

Jehan appeared subdued, as calm and serene as Mairi. That was unlike her, unless she was plotting something. Ah, yes, Henri recognized that sly gleam in her eye.

"I shall come straight to the heart of the matter," Sir Ambrose announced, "for I have little time to waste."

"Do so," Rob advised, wearing what Henri thought of as his lord-of-the-manor face. "We are busy also."

Henri knew his brother to be as playful as a pup when it suited him. Or every bit as imposing as their father when the occasion called for it. He chose appropriately now to mirror the mood of the visitor, which was somewhat pompous and haughty.

Henri misliked the knight for reasons other than the fact that he obviously had come to take Iana away. That would not happen in any event. But Ambrose acted almost rude in his haste to complete his purpose.

A guest who did not see fit to observe the common civility inherent in visits between nobles deserved no quarter, in Henri's opinion. He could not abide discourtesy in one who should know better.

If Sir Ambrose was so hot to have matters concluded briefly for him, then so be it. It was not as if they enjoyed his company. Henri intervened. "You search for a lady, you say. What makes you think to look here?"

"Lady Iana is the one I seek," he stated bluntly. "She is not of Ayr, as you say, but of Ochney and later of Dunsmor, where she was widowed of James Duncan, lord of that place. Lord Newell has promised her to me, so I have come to take her."

At last the mystery was solved. Henri leaned back in his chair, laced his hands across his midsection and inclined his head, studying the knight for a moment before he spoke. "While it is true that Iana is no common name, *our* Lady Iana does not seem to know you at all. Perhaps you search in the wrong place."

Sir Ambrose shook his head. "We were never introduced by her brother, but she is the one. I followed her to a place just south of here. The people there assured me she was bound for Baincroft."

"Indeed?" Henri asked with a cold smile.

"Aye. Her brother, Laird Newell Hamilton, gave me leave to fetch the widowed lady from the village of Whitethistle. She was not where she should have been when I arrived to collect her."

"Ah. And where were you to find her, Sir Ambrose?" Henri asked politely. "Was she a guest of some noble thereabout? Or still residing with her dead husband's family?"

The knight shook his head and appeared somewhat embarrassed by the question. As well he should, Henri thought, if that thrice-damned brother of Iana's had sent him to find the lady in a hovel unfit for habitation.

Instead of answering, Sir Ambrose went on with his tale. "As I said, she was gone when I arrived. Somehow she came into possession of a silver chain and paid her way across Scotland with the links of it, which left a clear trail to follow. In Largsmuth I discovered that she was accompanied by a foreigner and his two children. The local constable declared that these travelers had slain a man at one of the inns and thereby called attention to themselves.''

"The authorities are still seeking these travelers?" Henri asked with an air of studied nonchalance.

Ambrose paused and regarded Henri with a sly look. "The victim was a known thief, not one whose death caused much of a stir. The innkeep merely noted that the man likely to have knifed the wretch was foreign. French, I believe he said.''

"There are many Frenchmen in Scotland these days," Mairi declared.

Ambrose nodded in agreement. "Aye, but it seems this one and the Lady Iana stopped in a village not far from here, and he was recognized. He paid for supplies with links of that same silver.'' The knight leaned forward and cocked his head. "That man, sir, I believe, is you. Unless you have another here by the name of Henri Gillet, heir of Trouville and stepbrother to the lord of Baincroft?''

"There is only one of me," Henri admitted.

He noted that the others were observing the exchange so quietly one could hear a hound's tail thumping against the flagstones beneath a nearby table. Therefore he could hardly proclaim Iana to be his as he might have done were this interview private.

Henri continued. "I repeat, the lady does not know you. You would have us release a woman into the care of a stranger, sir?''

"She is to be my wife, and has taken it upon herself to run from her duty. What care you who takes charge of her? What is she to you?''

This was damned difficult, Henri thought, allowing

none of his emotion to show. "The lady and her child are—"

"*Her* child?" Ambrose interrupted. "What child?"

Henri kept his voice pleasant in response to the knight's abrupt bark. "Her daughter, sir. The one she was holding when you first met. Today was your first meeting, was it not?"

Sir Ambrose snapped his mouth shut, glanced around, then dropped his gaze to the floor between his feet for a moment. When he looked up, Henri saw confusion and a flicker of anger in his eyes. "Lord Newell mentioned no child. How old is this lass?"

"Near two years of age, I believe."

"Impossible! She had no child of James Duncan. This much I do know."

"No one has said she did," Henri said evenly. He could see the realization dawn on the knight's face. If the babe was not her husband's, then whose? Ambrose turned a choleric shade of crimson and remained speechless.

"Welladay!" Jehan exclaimed, startling the entire audience. "That settles that. Our Iana is the wrong woman for you, Sir Ambrose. The one you seek has no child and ours does."

The knight looked over at her, frowning, his fists still clenched.

Jehan's smile did not falter in the least. "So you must stay for a few days and console yourself. Your intended has flown like a frightened bird and has no wish to be found."

"Oh, I will have her, make no mistake." Ambrose ground out the words one by one.

Jehan reached over and lay her hand on his fist, a sweet, if highly inappropriate gesture of consolation.

"Oh, sir, do not tell me you would welcome a wife who spurns the married state. How awful for you to endure such a match! Surely you would prefer a willing bride?"

He grunted what could have been his assent or speechless frustration.

Jehan rose quickly from her bench, reached down and took his elbow in her hands, urging him to rise, as well. "Oh, sir, your disappointment breaks my heart. Come, walk in the pleasance with me where all is quiet. You need time to think on this and recover."

"I need a drink," he muttered.

"And have it you shall," Jehan crooned, shooting a pointed look at Mairi, who snatched up and handed her the half-filled chalice Trouville had been cradling. Jehan shoved it into the knight's hand. He downed it on the instant and went with Jehan like an obedient babe in leading strings.

Everyone stared at the couple as they walked unhurriedly toward the door and disappeared through it.

Mairi laughed. Rob and Trouville grinned at each other and Henri whooshed out a breath of relief. It was not over. Sir Ambrose clearly was no fool, though he might be feeling like one at the moment.

He knew well and true that Iana was the woman he sought, but her having a child certainly had made the fellow less than enthusiastic about making her acquaintance for the purpose of a betrothal. And Jehan, bless her fickle heart, would see that he was consoled right out of the idea altogether. Why she seemed so determined to aid Iana's cause, Henri could not figure, but he would not question it.

"He could salvage his pride if he declared Iana was the wrong lady and left immediately," Trouville said, motioning for one of the maids to fetch him another cup.

"He might be a dour sort," Henri observed, "but I do not believe Ambrose will lie to us or to himself to save face. You saw how forthcoming he was in relating the circumstances. When he leaves here, I think he will go and confront this Lord Newell. That will be the real contretemps."

Rob nodded his agreement. "Ambrose is honest. I like him."

They all stared at him in disbelief.

"I do," Rob affirmed, as though they had argued the matter, which none would do, of course. Rob was the authority on a man's goodness. "As does Jehannie," he added.

Mairi elbowed Rob to get his attention, gave him a sly look and made a small flourish with her fingers, the sign for *handsome*. Rob wrinkled his nose and laughed.

They were all thinking the same thing. No signs or words were needed in this case. Jehan seemed to have set her cap for the knight. If that were so, unless he had a will of forged steel, she would have him.

It would solve several problems neatly enough if that happened. Ambrose would have Jehan. And Iana would be free to do as she pleased. Provided her brother approved whatever she decided to do. There was the real complication. She did have an overlord and he must be obeyed.

"Newell Hamilton. Do you know him, Father?" Henri asked.

"Hamilton..." He thought for a moment. "I did meet a laird called Malcolm Hamilton. You might have encountered him as well. Remember the contingent of Scots who traveled to Paris with young David Bruce?"

"Vaguely," Henri replied. "That was years ago. So this Newell must be his heir." If so, it was possible that

Lady Iana was very well connected indeed. Most of the men who accompanied young Bruce when he went into exile were somehow related to the family.

The implications of that caused mixed feelings. He could not have Iana for a mistress if she were a relation of a Scots king. Even his own birth was not high enough to excuse that breach of propriety. But he might marry her.

One look at his father doused that hope. Trouville slowly shook his head, as if he had already entertained the thought and discarded it. Damn.

The depth of Henri's disappointment astounded him. He grieved, not only for the dashed possibility of having Iana in his bed, but also because he wished devoutly to have her in his life, all aspects of it.

In that instant, Henri realized there was no use denying that he loved her. Quite profoundly and without any reservation whatsoever. He no longer cared about her past, what she had done or not done. It mattered not a whit whether she had found Tam as she avowed or had borne her of a peasant oaf. He wanted both her and the child with a yearning that nearly stole his breath away.

Aware of the futility of voicing all of this to his father, he shoved out of his chair and stalked away to be alone with his anguish. The only place he could find any solitude was outside Baincroft. He would ride.

Iana spread the bed's coverlet upon the floor, smoothed it flat and then set Tam upon it. For a while, the two engaged in a game of roll and fetch with a ball of bright yarn.

Tam could creep about on all fours quite swiftly when she wished, now that her legs were growing stronger. Iana stood her upright from time to time and watched her balance, ready to catch her if she toppled. Crooning words of praise, she reveled in the progress the baby was making.

A soft knock upon the door distracted her from her efforts. "Come," she called, fully expecting one of the pair of young maids Lady Mairi had sent earlier to offer their services in tending Tam. She liked the sweet nature of the girls, who seemed to dote on babies. Apparently the child's origin did not matter to those two.

"*Madame,* would you grant me a few moments of your time?"

Iana's attention jerked from Tam to the doorway. She quickly scrambled up from the floor and made a deep curtsy. "Lord Trouville," she gasped, breathless with surprise.

He calmly walked over, stood for a moment, then sat down cross-legged on the coverlet, indicating with a gesture that she should join him. Iana all but collapsed.

"Would you not be more comfortable in...the chair, my lord?"

He smiled a slow, lazy smile. "Doubtless, but this will do." He regarded the wide-eyed Tam for some time before speaking. "She has not the look of you, *madame.*"

Iana felt like slumping with defeat. Would no one believe her? "With all due respect, my lord, she is not of my body, so why should she resemble me?"

He reached out and took Tam, his large palms cradling her delicate frame, and put her on his lap. "I love children," he said, apropos of nothing. "I only have two living, Henri and a daughter, Alys. Two sons were lost in the borning. I grieve for them still."

"How sad. You must be doubly proud of Henri. He seems a fine man," she commented, noting all the while how Trouville handled Tam with all the expertise of a nurse.

"The physicians warned me Henri would not live to see his second day," he confided, "yet he has seen three decades and more. Your daughter has been ill?" he asked gently.

"She was starving when I found her. I thank God she did not take on her mother's illness or I could not have saved her, either." Iana raised her chin and narrowed her eyes, daring him to question her word.

"I believe you, so do not ruffle up your feathers." He picked up the ball of yarn and placed it in Tam's hands as he spoke.

When he raised his warm, dark gaze to hers, Iana believed him. "Why are you here, my lord?" she asked softly.

"I have come to question you, of course. You must tell me what it is that you wish. What will make you happiest? I have a debt to discharge here and would like to be about it."

Iana sighed. "I want the power to choose what happens to me and to Thomasina."

"Granted," he said simply.

"What?" Iana laughed at the simplicity of his response. "How can you possibly offer me such a thing when you know nothing at all about me?"

"*Au contraire,* I know everything about you."

"You could not!"

"But I do. And you have complete freedom to state whatever you want and I shall make it happen for you. This knight who has come for you? I shall banish him." He smiled and snapped his fingers. "Your brother demands to settle your future? I shall buy him off." Again, a snap. He leaned closer as if imparting a secret. "You wish to be rid of my Henri's company forever? Consider him gone to the nether reaches of France.''

Iana laughed. ''Aha, now it comes clear, my lord. You fear I shall entangle Henri somehow.''

Ignoring that as if she had not spoken, he insisted, ''If you were quit of all these men who mean to play with your future, what would you do, Iana?'' He looked very serious now.

''I told you! I want—''

''Do not spout again all this obscure nonsense about freedom to choose your own path and go where you will. Be specific. Tell me exactly where you want to go and precisely what you wish to do with your life once you get there. And your reasons for it.''

His question astounded her, mostly because she could think of no answer to it. ''You presume much, my lord,'' she said, to put him off.

''I would have your answer, and do not prevaricate,'' he warned.

''I never—''

''Your answer. Now!'' he insisted, his dark eyes flashing with determination.

Iana wanted to shrink away from his demand. Somehow he would not release her, though he was not touching her at all. While staring into those deep brown eyes of his, eyes that seemed to see within her soul, she received the real message he meant for her to absorb.

''I do not know,'' she admitted softly. She felt tears trail down her cheeks. She truly did not know.

''A revelation, is it not?'' he asked gently. ''My dear child, if you do not know what it is that you want, chances are slim that you will ever obtain it. Even should it fall at your feet, you would not recognize its worth.''

He reached out then and brushed away a tear with his thumb. "Do you love my son?"

Iana covered her mouth with her hand, her blurry gaze still locked upon his. She dared not admit or deny it, for she was unsure.

She cared for Henri so much, admired him beyond all, recognized her jealousy of him when she had seen him with Lady Jehan, and desired him with a ferocity she had not thought possible for her to feel. And yet he threatened to swallow her up in his great strength, to make her what she would not be, and trap her within his will.

Trouville nodded, as if he had gleaned a truth one way or another. "Do not give yourself to him," he advised. "Do *not*."

Iana nodded in turn, certain she could keep that particular promise if nothing else. She so greatly feared Henri would bind her to him if she gave way to her desire. She would lose herself and be nothing but a part of him.

Trouville set Tam down and got to his feet with a nimbleness that belied his age. Iana accepted his hand and rose as well. He looked worried. "You have much to think on, *ma petite*. I shall leave you now."

Iana squeezed the hand that held hers and thanked him. *"Je vous remercie, monsieur le comte."*

He beamed. *"Bien dit. Votre accent est parfait."*

"Thank you." Iana shrugged away his compliment. "My mother was from Avignon. I spoke little other than her language before she died."

The strangest look appeared upon his face and his hand tightened upon hers. "Your mother was French? Her sire?"

"Eustace de Ribemont," Iana answered, not certain

why that mattered. She certainly had never met her grandfather and knew nothing of him save his name.

"Les dieux sourient," Trouville whispered to himself as he hastily kissed her hand and left the chamber as if he had urgent business elsewhere.

The gods smile. What on earth had he meant by that? Iana wondered.

Chapter Thirteen

Trouville could strike fear in a stone without lifting his voice. Yet that was not the reason Henri dreaded the planned confrontation with his father. The only thing he feared was the disappointment he would cause his sire by the decision he had made.

He knew the look. There would be that slight shift of the strong shoulders he had leaned upon as a boy, the sadness in the dark eyes so like his own, the tightening of the lips that usually formed the smile of approval everyone sought.

The dashing of a father's expectations was no easy thing, but in this instance, quite necessary. Issuing a harsh sigh of resignation, Henri set out to look for him.

"Ho, Harry!" Rob hailed from the doorway of the armory the moment Henri stepped out of the keep. His brother was propped idly against the door frame while their father sat upon a bench in front of the building.

He was examining a crossbow, Henri noted as he approached. "I will wager you have never used one of those," Henri remarked.

Trouville looked up and smiled. "It is no weapon for a knight, as you well know. Fine workmanship, however, and might prove quite useful should Baincroft come under siege or attack. Unlike the sword, anyone could ply one of these."

Henri looked at Rob. Baincroft had suffered only two attacks in his memory. Neither had proved a serious threat. "You anticipate trouble?"

Rob shook his head. "Always ready."

Trouville turned so that Rob could see his face fully. He rarely used the signs to help Rob understand what he was saying, for he never allowed either of his sons to take the easier path. Henri thought him hard in this instance, but Rob never seemed to mind.

"Leave us, Rob. Your brother has come with a problem," Trouville said.

Rob pushed away from where he leaned and grimaced at Henri as if to tease him that his face was so easily read. He bumped Henri playfully with his arm as he passed by, and Henri's fist shot out with a halfhearted blow to Rob's back. In years past, they would have scuffled right there in the dirt, happily testing their prowess at the least provocation. He had missed Rob sorely since taking up his duties in France.

"That is a wistful frown you wear, Son," his father remarked.

Henri sat down beside him on the bench and leaned forward, his elbows resting on his knees. "I am going to marry Iana, Father. Nothing you can say will change my mind."

There came a long moment of silence, then Trouville spoke as if he had not heard Henri's declaration. "This crossbow is crafted so expertly I could never consider it inferior to a noble blade. Though its employment by one of our rank in warfare is not sanctioned, I do plan to test its worth…unofficially, of course." He pulled the string taut and locked it into the fittings.

Henri looked at him squarely, but his father's attention remained on the weapon he held. "I will not test Iana's worth by making her my leman if that is what you suggest. She is worth more to me."

The dark eyes raised slowly to meet his. "Indeed? Worth the future title of *comte* if the king disapproves your choice? Worth forfeiting the possibility of one day wearing the crown?"

"There are what, only sixteen in line before me?" Henri scoffed. "To include the King of England and all his get?"

"Fifteen," his father corrected. "Not counting myself. A mere twelve years ago there were forty-two under the Capetians. If Salic law continues to be upheld by the Valois, that eliminates the females and reduces the present number to nine." He shrugged. "A mere Scots baron's daughter will never make a queen of France, nor any of her sons a king."

"You overestimate my ambition to rule, Father. I'd sooner move to Ireland and breed sheep." He cleared his throat and squared his shoulders. "I will marry her."

"She might have other plans."

"Then I shall change them. Will you give us your blessing?"

His father carefully laid the crossbow down on the bench between them and stood.

He walked a few steps away, then turned to Henri and pointed to the bow. "If you lost your sword in the midst of a battle and happened upon one of these, would you take it up and use it? Even if your noble comrades all around you might later sneer that you had broken with long-held tradition and wielded a weapon unworthy of you?"

Henri ran a finger over the smoothly carved oak. "Would you have me grind it underfoot if it might be the very thing that saves my life?"

"I would hope if you were caught in such a plight, you would not leave the field to come to me and ask."

"You mistake me, Father. I am not asking your permission. I am informing you of what I intend to do."

"You are a man. Do what you must, Henri, and answer only to yourself." With that, Trouville pivoted swiftly and strode away.

Henri stood, took up the crossbow and started to return it to the storage with the others. "No, by God," he said aloud as he tucked it beneath one arm. "I shall keep it." He would learn to use it as well, better than any other man could do, and be damned to any who looked askance at his choice.

"Lesson on weapons?" Rob tapped a finger on the crossbow and fell into step with him as Henri entered the hall.

"You watched?" No surprise there, Henri thought. Rob was the world's worst in minding his own affairs. "Yes. A lesson."

Wed her. Rob signed the words emphatically. *Mairi likes her.*

"Oh well, there is excellent reason," Henri muttered darkly. He would add that to the list when he proposed.

"He was smiling," Rob said aloud, cutting his gaze sidewise and giving Henri a sly wink.

Henri halted suddenly and grasped Rob's arm. "Smiling? You are certain? Just now?"

"All the way," his brother assured him. "He approves."

"Then why…? Of course! He wished *me* to be certain. To know whether I was wedding Iana out of some misguided need to protect her or to reward her for saving my life." Henri laughed and slapped Rob on the back. "What would I do without your keen eyes, Robbie?"

Not waiting for an answer, he hurried toward the stairs to share the news with Iana. They could be wed in three weeks, as soon as the banns were called and the celebration prepared. She would be so happy.

He stopped on the third step. Or would she?

So caught up in his own delight, he had almost forgotten her emphatic avowel that she would never wed any man. How was it she would agree to share his bed, yet would not become a wife? Her blasted freedom from a man's rule, he decided.

As if she thought she could do as she pleased when serving as a mistress. He knew no man who would countenance that, nor would he. Iana must simply accept his word that he would allow her more say in her doings than would most husbands.

He continued up the stairs, mentally rehearsing how he would put his suit to her. Once she had accepted, then he would approach her brother, as was proper. That should not prove a problem at all if the man wished helpful allies here and in France. And if it was wealth the man wanted, Henri meant to make him a bride price he could not afford to refuse.

Iana had washed her face and combed out her hair. Margery, the youngest of the maids, had come to fetch Tam, promising to feed her in the nursery with the MacBain twins and their nurse. Iana had just begun to plait her braids again when there came a soft knock. "Come."

Henri entered, his cap clutched in one hand and a smile upon his face. "I have come to speak with you," he said.

Iana gestured toward the remaining chair, then continued what she was doing. He sat and simply watched her, making her fingers clumsy as she wound one thick strand of hair over another. "Well, what have you to say?" she asked, despising the breathlessness he fostered in her. She could think of nothing but that kiss.

"I have decided we shall wed," he told her.

She kept her gaze on the braid until she came to the end of it, then looked up at him. "*You* have decided," she repeated.

His smile faltered a bit and he seemed to consider his words carefully before he spoke. "Let me put it a different way, then. I have decided to ask you if you would consent to wed me."

"Better, but I still must say no." She sectioned off the remaining hair and began to plait furiously despite her trembling hands.

"You must say yes," he argued, but did so kindly. "The pious Sir Ambrose Sturrock will not mind. Though I could see he found you more beautiful than expected, he will have changed his mind about the betrothal."

"Betrothal? What do you mean?" she asked. "I thought he had only come because my brother hired him. *Douglas* Sturrock, the man Newell wished me to wed, is as old as my first husband. Newell's wife described him to me time and again, for she knew him well. She said naught of a Sir Ambrose!"

"This knight must be his son. Perhaps you misunderstood. But you'll not wed this man now that you have seen him, no matter how young and handsome he is. I warn you, I will not allow it even if you—"

"No, I will not consider him, Henri." Not in a hundred years.

"Just as well. He will be quite taken with Jehan by this time, if I know her at all. As for our marriage, my father will not protest. I have spoken to him already. And I am certain your brother will not prevent it. So there is no one who will object."

"I object," she said baldly.

He drew in a deep breath. Iana suspected it was to calm his temper, for his face had gone quite red. A vein pulsed in his temple and his jaw clenched rather tightly.

Even so, once he unclenched it, his voice remained smooth as new cream. "I understand your reasons," he said, "but let me set your mind at rest. You will never find another man to wed who will grant you more license than I shall. This I promise on my honor."

She felt terrible for dealing his pride such a blow, but she must be truthful. "I shall never find another man to wed at all. Believe me when I say that marriage is not for me, Henri."

"Did your husband treat you so foully that you do not trust anyone? Can you not see that I would never offer you hurt or insult?" He shifted sidewise in the chair and stared out the window. "You insult me now, lumping me with the likes of him. What was he like?"

"Very different from you in most ways," she admitted. "Though his looks were fair enough, Duncan was old, at least twice your age. He was mean, rarely smiled, and no one liked him, least of all me."

Henri threw out his hands as if to present himself. "Well then, here am I, quite young, smooth tempered, bearing all my teeth and the darling of this household. What more could you ask?"

Iana almost laughed, but the sadness inside her overcame the mirth. "Henri, I do care for you very much. I will even admit that I desire you, for you already know that. But you are like James Duncan in the very way that is of most import. You *will* take full charge over everything and everyone around you. You cannot help it, for it is your nature to do so. Think, now. How would you like it if someone called your every move and punished you severely when you acted upon your own, thought for yourself and spoke those thoughts?"

Ah, she had truly angered him now. His nostrils flared and he forwent all speech for a time. To his credit, he mastered his feelings and the tone of his words more quickly than she would have reckoned. "I should not like it at all, of course. Within reason, you may do what you will as my wife. But whatever you do, I would never punish you, Iana, you must believe that."

She slanted him a sly look. "Why must I believe it? For I am not going to marry you, Henri Gillet. Not under any circumstance." She added, "This is for your own good as well as for mine."

"I would wager you have always wanted to say *those* words, have you not?" He leaned his elbow on the arm of the chair and propped his chin upon his hand. The fingers of his other hand tapped rhythmically upon his knee as he regarded her intently.

He seemed altogether too calm now, past the flush of anger and well into dogged determination. She could see the purpose glowing in those deep, dark eyes of his.

Iana tried to ignore him while she wound her braids around her head into a coronet and wove the bone hairpins in to hold it firmly in place.

"I shall wear you down. I am good at it," he warned with a calculating smile. Ah, he would become playful now and tease her. The man had so many tricks to ply.

More than Duncan had ever thought about when he was courting.

Well, she was much wiser now than the stupid girl she had been. Wear her down, would he?

She treated him to a quelling look. "I am already *worn*, Henri. You have declared as much yourself, accusing me of bearing a child outside of marriage. I do deny that yet again, but, God knows the marriage itself was wearing enough. Let us not treat one another to a battle of wills. My answer to you is no and ever shall be."

"Suppose I beg?" he asked, unfazed by her continued refusal. "I have never gone on my knee to a woman. You would be the first. Think how you could brag of it! The entire family—no, the whole of France and all who know me—will be astounded at the power you hold."

Iana could not contain her own smile in the face of his. She shook her head. "I beg *you*. Leave off!"

"My answer is no and ever shall be," he assured her, using her own words against her. "We are destined to go back and forth upon this issue until you relent."

"Then escort me to the hall so I may fortify myself, for I am starving." She rose and offered him her hand.

He stood up and took it in his, closing his strong fingers around hers. She let herself enjoy the warmth of the contact. No harm in that.

"I could withhold your food," he said lightly, even as he led her from the chamber to the stair.

"That has been tried. It availed him nothing."

Henri's hand tightened upon hers. "I swear that was only a thoughtless jest. You know I could not—"

"I know it well, you scapegrace. Now will you cease, if only for the duration of the evening meal?"

He nodded. "Granted, but I take this to mean you will allow me to continue after we have eaten."

And he would, she knew. There would be a game of it until he finally took her at her word. Then, she hoped that somehow he would remain her friend. She must make certain Henri knew that this was no personal affront to him, but merely a decision she had made and meant to keep.

She could not forget Dorothea's tale of woe and how Iana's own brother had changed since their marriage. The absolute power a man held over a woman must distort his mind, somehow. There had been the formerly sweet-tempered Newell abusing poor Dorothea all the years Iana was enduring James Duncan's cruelty. Who would have thought it?

Thank goodness her sister-by-law had been kind enough to confide in her and warn her to expect more of the same at the hands of old Douglas Sturrock. Once Dorothea told Iana of Newell's plans, Iana had refused to speak or listen to him except to object vociferously the instant he brought up the subject. There would be no wedding in her future, no matter what happened.

As much as she wanted him, marriage to Henri would be even more disastrous than one to Sturrock. Henri had the power to break her heart once he turned on her. Even a liaison would be too much. She knew that now. His father had made her promise to deny Henri her body, and she knew full well it was the best thing for her to do.

Henri must soon see that what he was attempting was precisely what she fought so hard to avoid. He meant to bend her will to his in the issue of a marriage between them, and that would be only the first step in exerting his mastery over her. It would hardly stop there if she acquiesced.

It would go on forever and grow worse as time went by.

Henri concealed his worry and kept an untroubled countenance during the evening meal, though the urgency he felt to settle things between Iana and himself grew apace. He smiled at those present as if he had met with complete success.

"More wine, my dear?" he asked, offering her the chalice they shared. Henri placed it in her hand, brushing his fingers over hers as she accepted. With a heated gaze, he followed the cup's path to her inviting lips.

While she blushed at that, Iana gave no real indication that she suffered under his close attention. That he had applied in generous measure, touching her at every opportunity, feeding her the choicest morsels from their shared trencher. He hoped they gave the outward appearance of a couple in complete accord.

"Finish it, for I dare not have more," she said quietly, setting the wine cup near his hand. "I would keep my wits about me. Especially now."

"As would I," Henri replied, "since there are important arrangements to be made."

"A plague on your schemes," she whispered fiercely through a smile. It seemed she was no more willing than he to open their disagreement to the scrutiny of all.

He smiled back. "Schemes? You wrong me severely. I speak of planning festivities."

Rob would have already told Mairi of those plans. She would have told Jehan, who likely had been eager to tell Sir Ambrose. The fact that Henri received many nods and looks of approval from the servants indicated that word had spread of his proposal. They would be glad Henri meant to do right by this Scotswoman upon whom they thought he had fathered two children. The very idea of that was ridiculous, yet it was obviously a widely held belief.

With that uncanny ability of his, Rob would observe the disquiet in Henri, of course. He had already done so, judging by his current expression.

Henri only hoped his brother would not offer any conclusions aloud. Thus far he had refrained from that, and this last course of the meal gave Henri hope they would get through it without comment on his failure to persuade Iana. He needed time to do that and had no wish to publicly restate their opposing views on marriage to all and sundry.

Sir Ambrose still appeared under Jehan's spell, and had little or nothing to say. Truth told, the vixen gave the man little chance to speak. She doted on him, while carefully projecting a winsome gentleness that seemed foreign to those who knew her well. Jehan was naturally rather tempestuous by nature and outspoken to a fault. Not so this night.

At the moment Ambrose truly was eating from her hand, bites of the *emeles,* the small almond cakes that accompanied the sweet cherries provided for the last course. She laughed softly as he nipped her fingers with his lips. If they were not lovers yet, they soon would be, Henri thought.

He did wonder whether Jehan was sincerely taken by the man, or merely indulging in this diversion for her own amusement. In either instance, he could but thank her for what she was doing.

If the knight had continued to insist on the rights granted by Iana's brother, Henri would have been obliged to challenge him. He still might, but it no longer seemed very likely to be necessary. Ambrose had ignored Iana's presence rather pointedly since he'd discovered she had a child.

"I see that Lord Trouville has gone," Iana said, directing her observation to Mairi instead of Henri.

"Aye, but he assured Rob that he would return with Lady Anne and our sister, Alys, in a few days time," Mairi replied.

"I am eager for them to meet you and Tam," Henri added, determined to reclaim her attention. "They will find you both delightful, I am certain."

Iana merely shook her head slightly as if to negate his optimism.

Trouville had not said farewell or any other thing to Henri since they had spoken by the armory. Henri devoutly hoped Rob had read the matter rightly and that his father did approve the marriage with Iana. In the past he had frequently taken a reverse stance on matters to force Rob and Henri to defend their own views and come to trust their decisions. If this was not such an occurrence, however, Henri still meant to proceed as planned.

Mairi carried most of the conversation after that, regaling everyone with tales of the twins' latest derring-do. The boys themselves were not in attendance as they usually were, because there was a guest. Mindful that not all adults enjoyed the presence of clangorous four-year-olds, she'd had them fed in their nursery chamber along with little Thomasina.

The sounds of greetings near the doorway drew everyone's attention from the meal. "Who comes, Henri?" Iana asked, laying her hand upon his sleeve. Her agitated fingers pinched the fabric.

He frowned at the slender figure now approaching the table. "Sir Thomas, the steward, my old friend and playfellow. Come from discovering your past, I expect."

To her credit, she stifled her groan and kept a pleasant expression upon her face. Henri could see she was upset.

"Do not be afraid," he said as they watched Thomas bow before Rob and Mairi. "There is little he can tell us that we do not already know. Thomas's news will not alter a thing."

"I am not concerned about what he will say," she whispered. "Only the trouble he might have brought back with him."

Rob motioned Thomas toward the solar. Then he stood, offered his hand to Mairi and thereby dismissed those assembled for the meal. He beckoned to Iana and Henri and led the way into the solar from the hall, away from the prying eyes and ears of the servants.

Unfortunately, Sir Ambrose and Jehan also accompanied them. Henri supposed it was only right that the knight should attend, since this did concern him to some extent, but Henri had wished they might do without his presence until Thomas's report had been heard and evaluated.

Thomas made short work of what he had to say. "The lady is sister and subject to Baron Hamilton of Ochney, who will present himself early in the morn," he announced.

Henri started at the sharp intake of breath at his side and the sudden clutch of her fingers on his arm. Iana feared her brother.

Perhaps her fear was appropriate, he thought, dwelling for the first time on just how vulnerable she was to her kinsman's whims. Her brother had law on his side and could do practically anything he wanted with Iana. Though the law might state clearly that she could not be wed without her consent, such marriages did happen all too frequently, forced by one means or another.

Suppose Hamilton would not give his approval for her marriage to Henri for any amount of wealth? What if his reasons for betrothing her to Sir Ambrose went deeper than greed or a need for an alliance?

Rob motioned for everyone to sit, and most obeyed, appropriating the benches, stools and chairs grouped around the chamber and arranging themselves to face Rob. Henri seated Iana on an armless chair and then stood behind her, one hand upon her shoulder.

"Continue," Rob ordered Thomas.

The steward cleared his throat, glanced once at Iana and then back to Rob. "I began asking questions of her in Largsmuth, as ordered," he said, making rapid signs as he spoke so that Rob would not miss anything. "Within hours, two men approached me at my inn and had me accompany them to Ochney Castle. They had also been waiting thereabout for more news of Lady Iana. These two had been sent by Sir Ambrose Sturrock to inform her brother that she was gone from the village of Whitethistle and was found to have traveled through Largsmuth."

"So Hamilton is here," Rob said with a nod.

"We traveled together," Thomas affirmed. "He was most concerned for his sister's whereabouts and well-being."

Henri made a sound of disgust, recalling where he had found her. "Well-being, indeed."

Thomas shrugged and continued. "Once satisfied that the lady was in no danger, he was most relieved. He insisted upon coming with me, but did not wish to impose upon you at this late hour of the evening. He and his men are camped in the meadow this side of the burn and will approach the keep when day breaks. If that is not agreeable, I am to ride back and inform them."

"And if we do not intend to receive them or to release Lady Iana?" Mairi asked, appearing a bit petulant. Henri knew she had already sided with Iana in the matter of preventing a forced marriage.

Thomas sighed and inclined his head, as if thinking what might happen as a result of that refusal. "I believe he might try to take her by force. He seems that determined."

Rob grunted and smiled, probably looking forward to a fight. "How many men?"

"Fifteen," Thomas said, "but there are no knights who ride with him."

"There is one who will, because he must," Sir Ambrose declared calmly.

No one needed to ask who that one was, even if he did not looked pleased about it. Henri shot him a dark look. "You would uphold Hamilton in this debacle when you have no wish to wed Iana? Why?"

Ambrose regarded them with all innocence. "Because I gave my word that I would have her. And a great deal of my wealth for the privilege."

"I will repay you," Henri offered, "several times over if you will cry off."

"He has my hand on it," Ambrose argued. "A man's word is his bond and I have given mine. I cannot retract it, even if she is not the honorable lady he vowed she was."

Iana's hand stayed Henri's when he would have planted it in the man's face. She was surprisingly strong, he noted. Besides her objection, there was the fact that Henri had purposely allowed, even encouraged, Ambrose to assume what he had about Iana. That was the only thing that stilled his rage.

"It was not *you* my brother had in mind when he spoke

with me of this betrothal, sir,'' she said. ''The husband he proposed for me was Douglas Sturrock.''

''That was considered at first, but my father is not likely to live for long. Since no formal contract had been signed as yet, your brother approached me about assuming my sire's intention to wed you, since I will eventually gain the title. It seemed only right I should do so, for I have need of a wife, and you of a husband.''

''But you have no wish to wed me,'' Iana declared. ''Not any more than I wish to marry you.''

He looked away and bit his bottom lip, apparently unwilling to admit aloud the truth she offered.

Henri noticed that Jehan appeared dumbstruck for once in her life. Obviously she had counted heavily on Ambrose changing his mind because of her. She was pale and silent, trembling, and certainly not feigning her discomposure.

Chapter Fourteen

"**R**ide out," Rob ordered Thomas. "Have them come."

"Rob!" Mairi objected. "Not now!"

"No." He patted the hand that rested upon his knee. "In the morning."

Henri knew they had little choice. A battle would serve nothing and might cost lives. They must try to reason with Newell Hamilton. If that failed, Henri would think of something else.

"Rob is right, Mairi," he said.

Then he addressed Iana. "He must have your consent to betroth you. If you have signed nothing and have not given your verbal assent, there is no cause to worry. It is the law."

"Newell is a law unto himself," she muttered. "You will see. There is not a more uncompromising man alive than he."

"I would wager that trait is inherited," Henri said with feeling.

He turned to Ambrose. "Tell me of Hamilton. Everything you know of him."

The knight shifted closer to Jehan on the bench they

shared, obviously trying to comfort her without an open show of it. She shied away, still wringing her hands and refusing to look at anyone. Ambrose reluctantly gave way then and surrounded her with one arm, drawing her to him in a right platonic fashion.

"He seems hard, Newell does," the knight said. "We knew one another as lads, though he was a bit older. At that time he was nearly too softhearted. You know, misliked the kill when hunting, cringed when someone kicked a hound, that sort of thing."

Henri nodded. "But now he has conquered that in himself?"

"Mayhaps, though he did urge me to gentleness when he sent me for Lady Iana. More than once he warned me to be patient with his sister."

"Patient?" The lady in question huffed and rolled her eyes.

"What did he do to you, Iana?" Henri asked her. "Exactly."

She blew out a breath and looked around the chamber. All eyes were on her now and it seemed she hated to recount what he had asked.

"A plan is forming here. Humor me," Henri encouraged her.

"He kept me locked in my chamber when I declined the betrothal. Then he denied me anything to eat or drink, save bread and water." She thought for a moment. "When that did not sway me after several days, it became a true contest of wills between us. He threatened to beat me."

"But he did not make good the threat, did he?"

"No," she admitted. "He never struck me. Instead, he and four of his men escorted me to Whitethistle and set me down there in the cottage to live awhile. I was to learn the trials of a woman alone.'' She sighed and shrugged. ''However, Newell did leave a man to guard me so that I would not run away. To be fair, I also heard him say I was not to go hungry. He gave him coins. That man disappeared the day after Newell left, and I never saw him again. I suspect he took my brother's pay for the onerous task of nursemaid and departed to spend it.''

''So you were truly left alone with no protection,'' Henri said, struggling to contain his fury.

Iana did not seem to notice, and continued. ''I had planned to take Tam and leave there to make my way as best I could. Then Everand arrived with the silver chain. It seemed fate had taken a hand. There was a way to escape and I took it.''

Henri sighed. ''So you did. How long were you there in that village, living like a pauper?''

''A bit over a month. Newell was due to come back soon and see whether living on my own had shown me the folly of my ways. It was what I had demanded of him, to go my own way.''

''And so he allowed it,'' Henri said, beginning to understand. Hamilton might have meant to teach her a harsh lesson, but he had left a man to keep watch. So he did care for his sister. ''You were to realize how needful it is for a woman to have a husband to look after her.''

''Aye, and I managed well enough. Yet Newell will never grant that I did so or ever allow it again.''

And neither would any man with any wits or compassion, Henri decided. He shuddered to think what would have happened come winter. She might have frozen or starved in that cottage if left to fend for herself. Yet as strange as Iana's idea of freedom seemed, he did understand her longing for it.

Surrounded by such strong women in his own life,

Henri had never given much thought to females who were continually subjected to the absolute rule of their men. It was the natural way and order of things, but most of the men he knew used reason when dealing with their women.

Any man of good sense knew how important it was to his own happiness to keep his woman content. Aside from preventing a wronged female's deadly wrath, treating a woman fairly and with respect was simply the right thing for a man to do. Only Henri knew all men did not do right.

He did understand Newell Hamilton's reluctance to give Iana complete control of her life. Unaccustomed as she was to that, and the discipline and strength it required, she might have put herself in danger. But marrying her off to a stranger when she hated the very thought was not the answer.

Henri asked Thomas, "Did you see any evidence of Hamilton's mistreatment among the inhabitants of his keep? Any outright cruelty?"

"None," Thomas said, "though I was only there for a half day and one night."

"Is it possible, Iana, that your brother really does have your best interests at heart and is only attempting to overcome your unnatural dislike of marriage?"

"*Unnatural?*" she demanded, suddenly incensed, rounding on him as if he had insulted her highly. "You think it unnatural for me to avoid being beaten and held up to ridicule?"

"Now, now, you said your brother never—"

"He mistreats his own wife! Dorothea told me as much. Just as my husband mistreated me! Just as he forced—" She broke off when she realized everyone was listening, and her voice suddenly became calm, quiet and without inflection. She smacked one fist into her other palm. "I tell you I will not marry again. I shall die first."

Mairi rushed to Iana's side and wrapped her arms around her. "Hush now, dearling. Ye shall not have to wed, or yet say more of it. By my troth, ye have suffered enough. Damn that man—"

"Did you tell your brother of your treatment at James Duncan's hand?" Henri insisted.

"He would listen to none of it," she whispered. "He did not want to hear. I believe he thought I lied. Duncan always was the soul of kindness whenever Newell was with us." In a very small voice, she added, "Once I thought my brother loved me. And before the wedding, I thought my husband might. I was so wrong."

"And wronged, as well," Henri added. So Newell Hamilton must regard her as merely a willful and obstinate sister, one who needed the strong guidance of a husband to set her to rights.

Iana saw her brother as a greedy ogre who had seen her sold once and wished to do so again, with no regard to her safety or happiness. Both their opinions might hold a grain of truth, Henri decided. It was time to find out.

"All right, hear me." He held up his hands, pushing his own anger at the dead James Duncan to the back of his mind. He could not afford to indulge in that at the moment if this plan was to work. "Are we all here in accord that Lady Iana should not be forced to wed, nor Sir Ambrose held to the agreement with Hamilton?"

Everyone nodded except Ambrose. His frown deepened as he shook his head. "I told you I have given my word. I cannot honorably recant. I will not."

Henri considered. "Suppose Hamilton releases you of his own accord, even insists on your not wedding her? Would that satisfy your honor?"

Ambrose looked at Jehan, then placed his hand over both of hers. He nodded once, reluctantly but emphatically.

"Very well, then. We are agreed on our purpose." Henri smiled at each in turn. "Then listen, each of you." Hoping against hope that he had the key to unlock Newell Hamilton's hardened heart, he began to lay out his scheme. "We shall become players...."

Two hours later, they left the solar, each eager to set his plan in motion. Henri regretted that he'd had no time to continue persuading Iana to marry him tonight, but knew he must postpone that until after the current problem was solved.

Even then, he was uncertain whether he would meet with success. The trouble was he truly had begun to see Iana's side of this issue. She had no reason at all to trust that once any man married her, he would treat her better than her first husband had done.

"What a devious mind you have," she commented as he walked with her to the stairs. "A pity Ambrose would not take part in this, but I cannot see that one approving any form of deception."

Henri laughed. "Ambrose is a self-righteous prude. At least he gave his word not to betray our purpose. He'll keep it."

Henri wondered if by employing deviousness, he might be putting an end to any hope of ever gaining Iana's trust.

He turned her so that she faced him, and grasped both her hands. "I have never told you an untruth, Iana, and I never shall. Not by word or deed will I ever seek to deceive you in any way. Please believe this of me."

She smiled up at him and squeezed his hands, but she did not answer.

* * *

The morning dawned fair without the sign of a cloud. When Lord Newell Hamilton rode through the gates, he shone bright as a newly buffed helm. Henri, Rob and Sir Ambrose awaited him upon the steps.

The man resembled Iana, Henri noted, as Newell drew nearer. He had the same light hair, shape of eyes and fair skin, though the baron was a man of sturdy build and much taller than his sister. Henri noted a hardness around the eyes and mouth that appeared somewhat forced, as if he were determined to appear more fierce than he actually was. This boded well indeed.

"Ready?" Henri asked the others. Rob nodded. Ambrose looked away.

Thomas had ridden out to meet their guest and now dismounted to make the introductions.

Newell's comrades had gone as far as the barracks and would remain there, to be made welcome by Rob's men. Quite welcome, Henri knew for certain. The ale would flow like the water in the burn, plentiful and cold. And intoxicating. Unless Newell meant to make the trip home alone, he would not be leaving before tomorrow.

Once he had been introduced, Newell quickly stated his business. "I have come for my sister."

"We know," Henri said offhandedly. "Sir Ambrose tells us there's to be a wedding soon. Come inside and allow us to celebrate with you."

Newell looked from one to the other. "I thank you, but that will not be necessary."

"Nonsense!" Henri exclaimed. "We are men of like mind, Hamilton. Come and have a drink. There is no use hurrying away from here," he said, dropping his voice as he slung an arm around the baron. "The wine is French, the best to be had in Scotland, take my word."

"Stay the night," Rob invited, at his most gregarious, smiling with apparent pleasure at having a new drinking companion. "Meet my *lady,*" he added with a wink.

Henri and Rob laughed uproariously. Ambrose did not.

The newcomer frowned, but agreed to join them. With Henri's firm grip on his shoulders, Newell really had little choice in the matter unless he fought his way out.

The hall was fairly cold despite the fact that it was summer. It took a fire to banish the chill even in the milder months, and none had been laid this day. The fire hole had spilled a heavy layer of cold ash across the hearth.

"Damn your hide! Woman?" Rob shouted, causing Newell to jump.

Mairi came running from the solar, sniffling and cowering like a terrified bitch before the master of the hounds. "Aye, milord?" she cried.

The poor thing had almost overdone her part, Henri thought. Her lovely hair was a tangled mess, trailing down on one side from the untidy coil atop her head. Though of rich fabric, as befitting her station, her gown looked as if she had been sewn into it sometime last year and had outgrown it in the interim.

Rob raised a hand to point toward the fire hole. Mairi cried out and cringed back as if to avoid a blow. "Light a bloody *fire!*" he ordered, growling the words between his teeth as if in foul threat.

She scurried to obey.

"Highland wife," Henri explained in an aside to Newell. "He says she requires more instruction than most."

Newell glanced at Mairi. "His wife? But I thought—"

"Yes, I know. She looks a trull. But you should have seen her when she first came here. Sad that the lady scarcely has time to fret about her appearance these days, but she brought it on herself. Not to say Robbie's un-happy with her, not at all. But she did take some tam-ing.''

"Taming?" Newell repeated, his eyes narrowing on Mairi. "She looks...bruised."

Indeed she did, Henri thought, nodding with satisfac-tion. A bit of ash, saffron and berry juice had worked very effectively on one cheek, her chin and both her arms.

Jehan sidled up to Ambrose with a flagon in one hand and four cups in the other. "Look what I have for you, my fine strong knight," she cooed.

To Henri's surprise, Ambrose lowered his hand to Je-han's backside, and she scooted away giggling, sloshing wine over the table near Rob's arm. Rob lashed a hand out behind him and she screamed, though his blow had missed connecting.

"Here now, Rob!" Henri chided. "You gave that one to Ambrose. Don't do her damage!"

Rob snorted while a laughing Jehan ventured close enough to set down the cups and fill them.

"Ambrose?" Newell asked, one eyebrow raised at his former friend.

Henri grabbed a cup and plunked it down in front of Newell. "The poor man will need something to keep him occupied once your sister's breeding."

Ambrose quaffed his drink and let out a prolonged belch. "Umm, fine as any I've ever had, Newell."

"The woman or the wine?" Henri asked, laughing wickedly as he sipped his own. "Both, I daresay."

The baron rose and stood back, glaring at the knight. "Ambrose, you are to wed my sister! I had your word!"

"Well, he *knows* that, Hamilton," Henri declared. "But give a thought to his comfort, will you? A man cannot forever plant the same field without wearing out the soil.''

With a snort of disgust, Ambrose pushed away from the table and got up. He slammed down his empty cup and headed out of the hall. Jehan ran to catch up, grasping his arm and clinging as she chattered merrily up at him.

''Where is Iana?'' Newell demanded.

''Mairi!'' Rob shouted.

Again, she rushed toward him, stopping just out of arm's reach and sketching a stiff curtsy. The fire was burning sluggishly now, Henri noted. Mairi was unused to building one.

Rob demanded, ''Where's the wench?''

''Locked away, my lord,'' she assured him in a small voice. ''Sir Ambrose ordered it.''

Newell seemed shocked. ''What is the meaning of this? How dare he treat Iana thus! She is to be his wife!''

Henri shrugged. ''You told him to go and fetch her, so he did. But she's not one for staying where you put her, as you should know. So he was to keep chasing her around the countryside or lock her up.'' Henri paused a second, then added, ''Just as you once did yourself.''

Newell glared at him. ''How would you know that?''

''Well, she screamed it to the heavens, man. I could hardly avoid hearing. Your sister will take some minding, that one. Putting her on bread and water might have weakened her some, but if I were Ambrose, I would think twice about leaving her untethered up there. Suppose she jumps from the window?''

Wearing a look of horror, Newell demanded, ''I would see her. Take me to her!'' He clenched his fists and looked ready to attack if denied. ''And I had best not find her ill from this!''

Henri nodded sympathetically. "Any man worth his salt hates to see a female in distress. I know *I* do. However," he admitted grudgingly, "like a good mare, she must learn who is the master. Once she admits that and means it, Ambrose will be able to go a bit easier, I should think. Rob has been able to give his wife run of the keep now. She's fairly well broken, I believe. Lady Iana will take to the rein soon enough."

"God's blood! Are you all mad, letting him treat her so?" Newell shouted, throwing hands up in the air. "This is my sister you speak of! Take me to her! If Ambrose has caused her hurt, I will kill him!"

As if unworried, bored even, Rob sighed loudly and made a small shooing motion with his hand. "Mairi, take him."

She bobbed a curtsy and backed away, shifting from one foot to the other, dashing worried glances back and forth. The instant Newell turned in her direction, she hurried toward the stairs, leading the way.

"Her brother's furious. Shouldn't we go up with him?" Jehannie had drifted back into the hall and rested an arm on Henri's shoulder. Ambrose was nowhere to be seen.

"No, we decided not. I believe she can manage without us. His sympathy is stirred and he might listen to her now. Mairi will call out if she needs us."

"The plan appears to be working," Jehannie said, meeting his and Rob's gaze in turn, then glancing up the stairs. "Don't you think?"

Henri hoped so, but it remained to be seen whether Newell Hamilton would recognize his own behavior when he saw it manifested in others. He could very well attempt to drag Iana from the keep and take her away the instant he saw evidence of her mistreatment. That was certainly what Henri would do in his place.

The trick was to keep them here until Newell realized and admitted the error of his ways. Once he did that, Henri hoped for a reconciliation between brother and sister. And finally, after confessions were made and Newell understood why they had done what they'd done, Henri could offer for Iana.

So much could go wrong, he did not want to dwell on it, Henri thought to himself. If only he had something that would sway Iana and make her more amenable to the notion of marrying him once the other problems had been settled. Some small thing. But what would that be?

Iana heard voices and footsteps approaching the small chamber in which she lay. Could she do this? Would she be able to appeal to Newell's sympathy? It ran against her nature, that was for certain, and she was more inclined to lash out at him than to cozen. However, if the deception would solve this matter to everyone's satisfaction, she supposed she could manage.

The key rattled in the lock and the heavy door swung open.

"Iana?" Newell said, rushing to kneel beside her, taking her hands in his. "I cannot credit this treatment of you! Obviously Ambrose is not the man I thought him to be." He brushed a tendril of hair from her brow.

"I am not hurt," she admitted weakly. "He only had me locked away." She closed her eyes and sighed. "No more than you have done yourself. At least neither of you beat me first, as Duncan did. And my cell is not below the kitchens, where there is no light. Mayhaps this marriage you command will not be so bad as the last."

She raised her lashes and saw the guilt in his eyes. For

that moment at least, he seemed the brother she had known in her youth, the one who had loved and protected her. How long had it been since she had seen that side of him? Years, she reflected. Not since their father died and Newell became laird.

"Did he truly hurt you? Duncan, I mean?" His voice was a near whisper.

"Aye. I told you this before. That is why I sought to avoid another marriage, Newell."

"But Dorothea said—"

"I know what you thought. Duncan was always kind when you were near. Go now." She interrupted him and withdrew her hand from his, turning her face to the wall. "I know there is no escape."

He leaned over her, his fingers beneath her chin, bringing her gaze back to his. "Wee Ana, do not despair," he pleaded, using the pet name for her that he had not uttered since she had become a woman. "I promise I'll not let him have you. I shall go now, immediately, and tell him so."

"Never mind," she muttered, testing good fortune when she probably should leave well enough alone. But she could not risk his agreeing to a match with Henri later. "You will only find another for me to wed. Men are all the same, so it might as well be this one."

"Nay, now that is not so," he argued gently, carefully adjusting the blanket that covered her, tucking it beneath her chin as if she were a child. "And who says you must wed at all?"

"*You* do!" she exclaimed heatedly, almost forgetting her resolve to remain docile and obedient and suffering. Quickly, she masked her anger with a heaving sigh and a sniff. "You have said so."

"But Dorothea told me you needed to wed." He raked

a hand through his hair and sat back as if he meant to stay awhile. "After Duncan died and you returned home to us, she told me I must be firm with you. She pointed out that Sturrock was old enough to settle your flighty ways and—"

"Dorothea? *She* suggested Sturrock?" Iana stared at him. Was he lying?

"Aye," he admitted. "In truth, I thought him too old, but she assured me he was a fine and gentle lord, one who would treat you well, as Father once had done." His voice hardened then. "But you were angry just because I chose for you."

"I did not wish to marry at all," she corrected. "I told you that!"

He scoffed. "You made that quite clear. I regret that I allowed you to rouse my temper so. I never should have locked you in your chamber, but you were acting the child, Iana. And Dorothea assured me—"

"Forget Dorothea!" she declared, a hairsbreadth away from striking him. "You used to applaud my spirit when I *was* a child, Newell," she reminded him tartly. "Why should that change just because I became a woman? I am still the same person I was all those years ago when you encouraged me to learn all that I could and to think for myself. What changed you, Newell? When did you become so hard and unyielding instead of the person I most admired? Now you strike your wife and threaten me, as well."

"Don't be absurd," he said distractedly. "If I hit her, she would poison my food."

Iana could scarcely believe what she was hearing. Yet Newell had answered all too readily to have just made that up. In fact, she could more easily picture his wife ladling out poison than Newell plying a fist.

He continued as if she had never mentioned Dorothea. "You were my responsibility, Iana. Father made me vow I would see to your welfare if you were ever widowed. Yet you crossed me at every turn and would not listen to what was best for you. Dorothea and I thought a few weeks at Whitethistle might bring you to your senses. That was a foolhardy notion on my part."

"So that was another of her ideas," Iana guessed.

"Yes, you have been foolish, Brother," she agreed. "You still are. Though I doubt you will ever realize the true extent of it. You are still determined that I marry Sir Ambrose?"

For a long moment he stared down at her intently. "Dorothea argued when I decided that, but he is a much better choice than his father would have been. Aye, I believe you should," he said. "However, if you still refuse to wed, then you should consider the church. I will dower you if you would go to the sisters."

Iana had no desire to immure herself within a convent, and grasped at the only excuse at hand. "I cannot. They will not take my child. And even if they would—"

"Child?" he demanded, his body tensing. "You have no child. You are increasing? Whose is it? I demand to know—"

She lay her hand upon his arm, as if doing so could calm him. "She is a foundling, Newell. Her mother died and I have taken her as my own. Please do not—"

"A foundling. Thank God," he gasped, too engrossed in his relief to hear the rest. Iana realized then that she had broached the matter of Tam too suddenly and at the wrong time, but it was too late to retract it.

"Please heed me, Newell. I love this child. She will be my family. However, a convent is no place for either of us."

"The sisters will welcome you if I offer them enough—"

Iana sat up, throwing the coverlet aside. "Newell, hear me! I will not go!"

He stared at her as if she had spouted heresy.

"You cannot make me! Have you learned nothing? I will not be forced!" she cried.

Slowly he rose to his feet and stood over her, his hands braced on his hips. "What game do you play here, Iana?"

She got up, too, casting aside all pretense of being weak and in need of sympathy. "I see it is of no use! Your head is as thick as an oak stump, Newell. I swear—"

"Cease!" he ordered, holding up one hand. "They have not starved you at all, have they?"

Her shoulders squared. "Nay. Not even with bread and water as *you* once did."

Slowly he nodded. "I see. All of this," he said, gesturing around the room and then at her, "was meant to stoke my compassion. Make me feel guilt and give in to you. Tell me, how did you persuade the men to take up your cause? Dorothea told me you were a schemer. What did you promise them?"

"Nothing!" she declared heatedly. "And damn your precious Dorothea! My friends here only wished to show you by example how wrongly you have done your sister!"

He pressed his lips together and shook his head. Iana could tell he fought hard to hold anger at bay, and knew she should do the same. Else they would be at each other's throats ere this was done. "Lord MacBain arranged this mockery?"

"Nay, he did not."

"Ambrose?"

Iana felt cornered. "Nay, not him."

"The French knight, then? Aye, he did have the most to say. What has he to do with you?"

Iana turned away, refusing to answer.

"Are you lovers?" Newell pressed, fists clenched and eyes narrowed.

"Sir Henri brought me here from Whitethistle."

Her brother's fierce growl told her exactly what he thought, that she had sold herself for the privilege of leaving that village.

Why bother to explain how it had happened? No denial of hers would change his opinion. Still, she supposed she had to try. There was little to be gained by Newell challenging Henri over her honor.

"Sir Henri and I are not lovers," she stated emphatically. Not quite lovers, but at least she had not been forced to lie outright.

How had it come to this—her brother thinking her dishonored, with Henri the cause of it? Not moments ago, she'd had Newell near to apologizing for past treatment and believing every word she said.

Iana noticed how he held his peace now, pacing a few steps in one direction, then another. She had to admit he was not behaving as impulsively as he usually did.

His voice was not kind when he did speak, nor was it the shout of anger she expected. "This Frenchman, is he in love with you?"

Iana remained silent. In truth, she was uncertain how to reply. Henri had decided to marry her, but she was not at all sure that it had anything to do with love. He acted very possessive of her, but that did not mean love. That signaled ownership. She had tolerated it from Newell once, and also from her husband, because she had no choice. But no more.

"Answer me!" Newell thundered.

An overwhelming urge to wound him overtook her. "Henri is protective of me, Newell," she snapped. "I am no judge of whether he considers that love, but there is danger that I might misconstrue it as such. So few men have *bothered* to care for my safety. Most especially *you!*"

He blanched. "I do care for you," he insisted, "else I would not care whether you remained unwed, or where you went or what you did with your life." His voice and his demeanor softened. "Please understand, Iana. I want you settled, content."

She turned her back on him. "So take the bride price, as you did before, and do not grant me another thought. Go home."

After a short pause, he asked, "You will accept Ambrose then?"

"I accept nothing. I shall see to my own fate," she declared.

"We have spoken of all this before," he said, his voice flat. "I see no point in continuing."

She listened to his footsteps as he left the room. He was right. They would never agree on this issue.

However, this time he had allowed her more say than he ever had before. Did she dare hope he would think on her words awhile and come to some other decision?

The door closed gently. Then she heard the key turn in the lock.

"Damn you, Newell!" she cried, rushing to the door and pounding upon it with her fists.

She knew very well that Mairi would return in a few moments and let her out. But it hurt terribly that her own brother had treated her this way. Why could he not see how betrayed she felt?

Chapter Fifteen

More time had passed than Iana anticipated when she finally heard the rasp of the key and her cell door opened. It was not Mairi as she expected. It was Henri.

Before he spoke, he fitted the large key into the lock on the inside. Iana smiled at the gesture. He was granting her the power to lock out the world if she wanted, even though she had no intention of staying in this chamber longer than it took to finish this conversation.

"Our ruse did not play out," he said, frowning as he turned to her.

Iana shook her head. "I know. It was my fault that it did not. For a while things were going well." She released a sigh. "Then my brother and I fell into the same old argument. My temper overrode good sense, I fear."

"Yes, well, he came below just now and commended Ambrose for being so firm with you. I knew from the wry way he said it that he had guessed at our deception. If it consoles you at all, I believe he secretly feels terrible that you are so unhappy."

Iana nodded and plopped down upon the straw-filled bed, her hands cradled in her lap. "A lot of good that does. Now we are found out and there is no hope he will relent, is there? He will insist I wed and that Ambrose keep his word about the betrothal.''

''Ambrose will not need his insistence. The fool feels bound to go through with it, though everyone can see it goes against his heart. He shocked me with that one concession he made to our deception of Newell.''

''A concession? From Sir Ambrose?''

Henri grinned. ''He fondled Jehannie's hindquarters. Not a planned gesture. I think the impulse simply overcame him.''

Iana smiled in spite of herself, then felt her humor fade. ''I shall have to give in to Newell's wishes or else leave here without his knowing.''

Henri crossed from the doorway and sat upon the floor next to her pallet before he said anything. When he did, he spoke softly. ''You have one other choice.''

Iana rolled her eyes heavenward and expelled a harsh breath. ''Do allow me a guess. I could marry *you*.''

He smiled. ''*Oui*. There is that.''

She laughed bitterly. ''And Newell will permit it, you think, after you made him look the idiot?''

''I have ceased to care what Newell thinks, Iana,'' he said softly. She looked up to meet his gaze. The astounding need there held her captive. For what seemed an endless time, she peered directly into his heart through those dark brown eyes and saw how deeply he felt. The fervor of his feelings frightened her, but she could not look away.

His mouth drew nearer and nearer until she could feel his breath upon hers. When their lips touched, Iana could think of nothing save the heat coursing through her body. Strong arms slid gently around her, pulling her close so that she could feel his hard chest against her breasts and his large hands splayed across her back.

When he turned his head slightly, her mouth fit perfectly with his, their lips opened to draw from one another the taste of forbidden pleasure she remembered so well. Iana found she not only recalled, but craved the heady, enervating sweetness, and sought more.

She slipped her hands up to his face and reveled in the feel of his skin beneath her fingers, the movement of the muscles there as he deepened their kisses, the soft caress of his hair as it fell forward and brushed across the back of her hands. Only then did she dimly realize they were no longer sitting, but lying upon the pallet.

Henri lay half over her, his hands now stroking her shoulders and her arms, deftly baring them so that he could touch. His fingertips grazed the curve of her neck, the curve of her shoulder, the swell of her breasts.

She ached for more and he gave it, adding the insistent persuasion of his mouth where his hands had strayed. Lips closed over the tingling bud of one breast and she cried out, uncaring who heard, oblivious to anything but sheer sensation. He drew deeply of her and she reveled in the mind-rending pleasure.

Again that magic mouth of his engulfed hers, while his left thigh pressed between her lower limbs. Iana rose against him, drawing him closer, but still not close enough.

The cool air of the chamber did nothing to chill her ardor, for all her senses were filled by his heat. She knew nothing but the deep rumble of his wordless praise, the exotic scent of his skin, the salt-sweet taste of it as she drew her open lips along the curve of his neck. His pulse beat against her tongue.

She gazed up at him through half-closed eyes when he pushed away from her upper body. His lips firmed with purpose and passion as he reached down to his waist and began to tug at the hem of his tunic. Iana added her efforts, and together they pulled the garment from him. His shirt followed in a billow of soft, white linen.

Her singlemost desire at that moment was to see, to watch the dense play of his muscles beneath the hot, sleek surface of his skin.

Her own clothing had bunched around her waist in a twist of blue and saffron. She pushed her gown and chemise down over her hips the instant Henri moved off her to shed his breeks and shoes. At last her eager eyes feasted upon his naked strength. The beauty of him stole her breath away in a sigh of awe.

She had seen him before, but not without the screen of apprehension. Now she had none of that. He would be hers for this small space of time caught betwixt near freedom and forced duty. Hers to hold.

She reached up to him in invitation. In demand. He answered her slowly, his motion bestirring itself within a confounding thickness of the air that would not permit hurry. Iana could but devour him with a hungry gaze as he lowered himself to meet her.

His dark eyes narrowed upon her own, his lips slightly opened in anticipation of hers. His nostrils were flared as though drawing in the scent of her like life's breath....

She could hear the sound of his breathing and matched hers to it. *One with you,* she might have whispered, but somehow knew the words remained a swell of need within her mind.

Light from the high window limned his wide shoulders and heavily muscled arms, outlining their brawn and crowning their contours. Her lashes lowered, drawing her gaze to that part of him that would be part of her. She ceased to think at all when it sought purchase within her and wrought a swirl of sensation so overpowering she cried out. Her body rippled and shuddered within and without even as he sank into her, completing her so fully she could but weep at the wonder.

He moved then, drawing back as if he would deny, then giving forth as though in surrender. Desire redoubled inside her and she knew he willed it, made it happen and was glad of it. Iana took and gave, suddenly discovering a power of her own to wrench from him unwitting sounds and the ability to control his patience. At a sinuous upward curl of her body, he came undone.

With a harsh catch of breath, he abandoned himself as she had seen no one do before. Fascinated, she watched his face—head thrown back, eyes clenched and teeth bared as he poured himself into her. The force of it stirred within her a swift gathering, then a flowering of pure, raw feeling that left her stunned and helpless.

He carefully shifted to his side, holding her fast so that they remained together. Softly his lips touched her forehead, her cheek, her lips. Mere hints of kisses. Murmurs of passion.

Iana clung to him in delight and in desolation, both a result of the truth that now dawned. She loved Henri. All along she had loved him. And she knew he loved her, too.

Matters were far worse than she had ever thought.

"Iana, my love…" he said, and would have said more.

"Please." She placed her fingertips over his lips and sought forgiveness with her eyes. "This changes nothing."

"It must," he insisted vehemently, holding her tighter.

She sighed. "For years on end I was not even a person, Henri. I was a thing to be cast about, this way and that, chattel to my father and my husband, then my brother. Now I have found my courage and I would be *me*, whatever the cost. I know you do not understand this and I'll not ask it of you again.''

Silently, he released her, sat up and began to don his clothes. He did not hurry, nor did he seem angry. Iana watched, holding fast the memory of the golden hour now past. Whatever came afterward, this would never dim.

How she wished she could touch him now, tell him that she loved him and how much she regretted that they could not go through life together. But he would latch on to her words and take hope from them, which they were not meant to convey.

Today in this chamber Henri had made her feel not owned, but treasured. He had behaved so apurpose, she knew, in order to change her mind about marriage.

If only he could understand how much she needed to be her own person, not someone else's creature, they might dwell together in some way or another as equals. But alas, he was a man, so must make claims. Must rule. Must possess. If she demanded he alter his very nature, she would be no better than the men who had strived so to change her.

Before he left, he looked down at her once, a long assessing stare. Then he calmly walked out of the chamber and silently closed the door behind him. Iana felt bereft, but also relieved. Somehow she knew that he would no longer push her to do what she would not. And still she wept.

Henri had done all that he could to change Iana's mind about wedding him, and yet she held firm. The only hope he had left to make her happy was removing her from her brother's wardship. Ambrose would follow through on the betrothal unless Hamilton called it off. And Hamilton would not be so disposed, certainly not to hand Iana over to Henri.

His mind full to bursting with problems and no solutions, Henri clattered down the stairs and across the hall, looking for Rob.

"God's truth, you look fit to groove daggers with your teeth!" Jehannie said. "What's amiss?"

"What is *not* amiss?" he countered with a frown. "Where is Robbie?"

"With the guests in the solar," she said, nodding that way and matching her steps to his. "I do swear Rob must be ready to toss you all out the gates and bar them."

"No doubt."

"Did you bed her, then?" she asked.

Henri halted midstride. *"Merde!"*

She rolled her eyes. "Oh, for heaven's sake, do not go all French and haughty. Her scent is on you, so do not bother to deny it."

She yelped when he grasped her shoulder. "Stay out of this, Jehan! I warn you!"

Instead of dashing away frightened, as he'd meant for her to do, she held her ground and shook a slender finger under his nose. "Harry, I want Ambrose, so this is my muddle, too. There's no point in our dueling over it, when we could—"

"Hold a moment! What did you say?" He shook her shoulder. "Dueling?" He pounded his forehead with his other hand. "Of course! *C'est parfait!* A duel with Hamilton." He kissed her soundly on top of her head, delighted with the idea she'd given him.

"Harry, *no!*" she argued.

He blinked and caught his lip between his teeth, thinking. "You are right. Not with her brother. With *Ambrose. Oui,* there is the solution."

He left her standing there and rushed to find the man. A deal could be worked, an honorable way out of the knight's promise. Newell could not argue with that.

Jehan followed and grabbed at his arm. He shook her off.

"Do not do this, I beg you!" she pleaded.

Henri hated to distress her any more than she already was, so he stopped. "I will not hurt him. I give you my word. Have you ever known me to lie?"

One of her dark brows kicked up and her lips quirked to one side.

"I mean about anything of import. Surely you do not question my honor, Jehan. If I say the man will be safe, he will be safe."

"You promise? You vow?"

"I do," he assured her. "I have no real quarrel with Ambrose. I quite like him, even if he is more than a bit—"

"Careful, Harry," she warned.

He laughed. "Do not worry."

She seemed to accept that, for she gave a half shrug and left off haranguing him.

"Go see to Iana for me, would you, Jehan? Do not speak of what you suspected of us, however. Also, no mention of the duel. Talk only of mundane things, things to soothe her, eh? Be my friend?"

She nodded and turned reluctantly toward the stairs. "All will be well, Jehannie," he called after her. "I promise."

This could solve everything, he thought as he strode toward the solar to present his challenge. Already he was thinking of how he and Ambrose might enact this. No doubt the knight was well trained with a blade. One could always tell by the way a man stood, his confidence and, of course, the slightly larger muscles in his sword arm.

Oh, he and Ambrose would make this a show never to be forgotten. The public defeat might sting the knight's overweening pride, Henri knew, but gaining the right to court Jehan openly would soothe that readily enough. They would each have what they wanted in the end.

If Iana would accept him. But that was a problem for another day. For now, he must free her from her brother's plans.

He pushed open the door, stalked inside and, wearing his fiercest, most determined expression, addressed Newell. "Hamilton, I would wed your sister."

The eyes, so like Iana's, hardened. "I think not, Gillet," he replied. "She is promised." He glanced lazily at Ambrose. "Is that not so?"

"Aye, you have had my word," Ambrose answered firmly.

"There you have it," Newell said, raising one hand, palm up as if he could not change a thing.

Henri had expected as much. He turned to Ambrose. "Then I will fight you for the honor of her hand, for I love the lady. Since you are all that stands in my way, I must remove you."

"Harry!" Rob shouted as he leapt to his feet. "Do not!"

"Be still, brother. This is my concern, not yours. What say you, Ambrose?"

The knight looked crestfallen, not at all eager to engage in a contest. How could he not see this was his only chance to have Jehan?

Henri gritted his teeth and widened his eyes slightly, trying to impart his intent silently. Ambrose stared back as if Henri had lost his senses.

"I have reasons for betrothing Iana to Sir Ambrose," Newell said calmly. "Yet none in aligning my name with a French knight of no account. Aside from that, I do not like you, Gillet. I believe you can guess why."

Yes, he could guess. Newell had figured out that Henri was behind the earlier deception. Ambrose must have apologized for his part of that in the interim, for he seemed back in Newell's good graces.

As for being of no account, Henri abruptly realized Newell did not know that he was heir to the Comte de Trouville. Likely no one had told the laird of the vast wealth and four estates in France owned by Trouville. Henri had more property, as well as gold he had acquired on his own, in addition to that. Such news might sway Newell's decision right enough.

However, boasting of it would appear as if he were trying to buy Iana's hand, which in essence he would be doing. True, that was the way brides were usually acquired, but he knew she would never forgive him if he did so in this instance. She had been sold before and he would not stoop to making a purchase of her again.

He would simply have to go as he'd begun and make it an outright challenge for her, borne of love. Hopefully, that would prove to her that he truly cared and that she need never question his reason for wanting her as his wife.

In his experience, there was no greater compliment to a woman than for a man to fight for her. Again he applauded himself for thinking of this. How could she refuse him when he put his life at risk to have her? She need never know the outcome was a foregone conclusion.

Henri repeated his challenge. "I shall win her, Hamilton. When I have done with Ambrose and you betroth her to another, I will remove him as well. On and on, until there is no one left standing but myself for you to consider.''

He realized he meant every word of that speech, if it came to that. But it would not. Her brother would give his word, Henri would best Ambrose, then the way would be clear. At least, clear of Ambrose and her brother. Iana herself would probably present a much greater challenge, but Henri felt hopeful. She had allowed him to make love to her. She was his now no matter what happened. He loved her and would never let her go.

Newell Hamilton smiled craftily. ''Ambrose is not one to tolerate defeat so easily, Gillet. I have seen him fight. You might find him more capable than you expect.''

''If he should win, you would be rid of me, would you not?'' Henri asked, returning the forced smile with one of his own.

But Ambrose would not win, Henri knew. If he did, he would have to go through with the betrothal and wedding, and thereby lose Jehan. Any fool could see those two were smitten with one another. As besotted as he himself was with Iana.

The only problem might be in arranging the battle so that it lasted long enough for Ambrose to lay down his sword and cry mercy without appearing cowardly.

Rob was signing surreptitiously, warning Henri emphatically to withdraw, to cease this. It was unlike Rob not to catch on to a trick such as this at the outset. Surely his own brother did not think Ambrose could defeat him.

Anger at that notion spurred Henri on. ''Sanction this, Hamilton. You shall have the bride price, come what may. And I'll wager Sir Ambrose will not withdraw his friendship from you when he loses. You could still count on his support in matters politic. What say you?''

Ambrose nodded to indicate he agreed with that. His

lips were drawn tight and he frowned. A good guise of unwillingness to risk forfeiting Iana, Henri thought. He would have to commend Ambrose later for that pretense.

Dead silence reigned for a while as Newell considered. He looked from Henri to Ambrose several times, as though judging them. "Ambrose, are you certain of your willingness to reaffirm your right to claim my sister? Is she worth that to you?"

The knight closed his eyes and sighed. "I have given my word to you that I will have her. My conscience demands I do whatever I am able in order to keep it. If you say we fight for her, then I shall fight, and will abide by the will of God."

Newell grinned. "Then show this *parvenu français* how an able Scotsman wields a sword. I want him on his back in the dirt with your blade at his neck."

"Nay!" Rob thundered. "I'll not permit."

"You *will* permit!" Henri declared, signing with his hands the intent to pretend the entire thing.

Rob kept shaking his head, worry apparent in his frown. No matter, Henri thought to himself. He would explain to his brother later what he meant to do.

Sometimes Rob perceived things wrongly. *But rarely did he do so*, a small voice in Henri's head warned him. *Very rarely did Rob mistake a man's intentions.*

Iana had finished her fit of weeping, put on her clothes and returned to her own chamber. She had been glad to leave that improvised cell where Newell had visited her and she had later made love with Henri.

It was not yet midday and so much had happened to her. More than anything, she wished she could simply forget it all.

Foolish to think that possible. She would never be able

to banish the feelings Henri had stirred within her. She pressed her palm to her heart and felt it racing still.

Oh, that man would ensorcell her if she let him. Mayhaps he already had, for she certainly could dwell on little else at the moment.

She was still standing in the middle of the floor, her mind fixed on him and their loving, when the door opened.

Alerted by the dour expression she wore, Iana knew Jehan was upset the moment she entered the room. Immediately the woman began to pace, wringing her hands and casting frequent accusing glances at Iana.

Had Henri confessed so soon that they had made love? He must have done. What else would bother Jehan so?

The thought had occurred to Iana that Henri might have seduced her in order to gain her acceptance of his proposal. If so, he had troubled himself for no cause. She did not intend to wed anyone at all. She must tell him she would not stand for this sort of trickery.

A pity that learning of their intimacy angered Jehan when she and Iana were on the brink of becoming friends. "Jehan, mayhaps I should explain. Henri and I did not plan—"

"*You* did not plan," Jehan snapped. "No, *Henri* is the one with all of the grandiose schemes!" She whipped her skirts aside with an angry swat as she whirled. "Tup you and trap you, he thought. Then taunt your brother into agreeing."

"I cannot believe this!" Iana gasped, mortified beyond bearing. "He has told Newell?"

"No, not about *that,* you goose! I am not supposed to tell you this, but I will. That brother of yours actually gave his assent that Henri and Ambrose could fight one another for your hand," Jehan announced. "To the winner goes the spoils.'' She winced at her own words, touching her fingers to her lips. ''Oh, I did not mean that the way it sounded.''

Iana waved away the token apology as unnecessary. ''I am spoiled, why not say so? But I cannot credit Newell's sanction of a contest! First he offers me up to Ambrose like a mare at auction, and next I'm to be a tourney trinket? Och, that is ten times worse!''

Jehan had tears in her eyes now and was hurriedly wiping them away before they fell. ''One or both of them could be hurt, you know. It's that damnable honor of his,'' she cried. ''A plague on knights and their nonsense!''

Iana felt moved to comfort her. There was the worry about injury, of course, but she suspected Jehan's fears went a bit deeper than that. Ambrose would be fighting for the hand of another woman if this farce took place. All because he had given his word to Newell that he would enter into the betrothal. Nothing official had been signed yet, and still Ambrose felt obliged.

She took Jehan by the hand and led her to the chair beside the fireplace. ''Sit. Let us think this through and see what we might do about it.''

''There is nothing to be done!'' Jehan said, sniffling.

''What do you mean?''

''I listened outside the solar door. They have set their minds to it. Eager as lads. I think it is the competition, French against Scot, as much as for the prize at the end of it.'' Again she pressed her fingers to her unruly lips. ''Oh, not that you are no worthy prize, Iana. You *are!*''

Iana blew out her breath in a rude sound and glanced heavenward. ''If you ask me, I think all three of them have had one too many blows to the head. I shall put a stop to this, never you fear.''

"Too late, I think," Jehan said with a sigh.

"Well, I'll not wed either man," Iana assured her. "So you need not fret that Ambrose will be forbidden to you when it's done. You love him, do you not?"

Jehan chewed the corner of her bottom lip and let her gaze wander around the room, avoiding Iana's eyes.

"Well, do you?" She waited until Jehan nodded, a little reluctantly. "Or do you not?"

"I think so," Jehan admitted, plucking at a thread on her sleeve, "though I have never really loved before. What is it like?"

Iana leaned forward, bracing her elbows on her knees and clasping her hands beneath her chin. She thought for a moment. "Let me see…first, you admire him. You know, how he behaves toward you and others."

"Yes, I do that. What else?" Jehan demanded, intent on every word. How flattering it was to be asked advice of this nature. Iana could not recall anyone ever giving full attention to her words of wisdom.

"Well, you feel a certain protectiveness, I think. That should go both ways, of course. He ought to care for your safety and well-being." Iana smiled at her. "You have exhibited that by objecting to this contest, so it is a given."

"So it is. There's more?"

"Ah, yes. You should feel shivery whenever he touches or kisses you. A good sort of trembling, not fright or such. Do you wonder what it would be like…" She hesitated to speak of it, that wicked inner questioning. The memory of her satisfying her own questions about Henri was simply too recent.

"To share his bed?" Jehan supplied. "Oh yes, I do! I dream of it. In truth, I would have offered already if I did not know his cursed honor would hold him back."

She colored. "Uh, I did not mean that Henri was lacking honor. It's simply that Ambrose…"

Iana laughed. "I know what you mean about Ambrose. He could do with a bit less honor and a lot more wit, I should think!"

Jehan began to protest in Ambrose's defense, then stopped and wrinkled her nose. "He could at that. The poor fellow is all too unbending and high-flown. He needs my common sense to put him right."

"Then you do love him," Iana said with a firm nod.

"As you love Henri," Jehan declared.

Iana shook her head. "Nay, I—"

"You do so!" Jehan insisted. "If you did not, how would you know what love entails and be able to advise me of it? Lie to yourself if you must, but there is no need to lie to me. I can see that you love him, and I think you should marry him. Elope. Secret marriages are as valid as those sanctioned. All you need is a priest somewhere about. He need not even participate in the ceremony for it to be legal. My father is a priest, you know, and I'm certain if I asked—"

"Oh nay!" Iana exclaimed, "I do not wish to marry! Not Henri, not Ambrose, not any man alive." She threw up her hands and glared at the ceiling. "Why can no one understand this?"

"'Tis not natural," Jehan said primly, smoothing her skirts over her knees and tapping the toes of her slippers on the floor. "Not at all natural."

"There speaks one who has yet to endure it, my girl. Just you wait until some man has total rule of you!"

Jehan reached out, her face a study in compassion. "Oh, Iana, was it so terrible for you? Was he brutal, your husband?"

Iana nodded, then smiled. "But now I am free. Now I need never bow to any man, nor will I. You will see."

"Then you had best go down there and advise them of that fact before they draw their blades for the privilege of proving you wrong," Jehan advised.

"I shall go on the instant," Iana assured her, "and they will have the sharp side of my tongue, I promise you that!"

Jehan grinned. "But first, were I you, I believe I would right the laces on that gown and comb your hair. Else that brother of yours will be demanding to know the cause of your dishevelment. He might decide he has reason to get you wed right quick."

Chapter Sixteen

Iana found Lady Mairi, Lord Robert, Everand and the twins gathered round the fireplace. One of the little maids sat upon the floor nearby with wee Tam in her lap, playing slap-handy.

"Where is Sir Henri?" Iana demanded.

"Gone to Trouville," the baron told her, then stared into the low-burning fire.

He looked nigh as trammeled as she felt, so distracted he did not even seem to notice that his sons were practicing their knot tying upon the loosened leg-lacings of his soft leather boots.

He would have a surprise when he stood and tried to walk, she thought. No matter, she had more important things to do than warn him of his twins' transgressions. If Lord Robert had participated in plans for this travesty of combat, she almost hoped he would take a headlong trip into the rushes. It would serve him right.

"When will he be back?" she asked of Mairi, who was not her usual smiling self.

"Tonight, mayhaps tomorrow morn," the lady answered. "He goes to inform his father of the *contest.*" She said it with a certain amount of asperity.

Iana squared her shoulders even though she felt like slumping in defeat. "I had naught to do with this foolish design of Henri's, and I mean to stop it if I can. My brother is still here?"

"Aye," Mairi said. "He and Sir Ambrose have gone out to the practice yard. Strategy to plan, I suppose."

Everand scrambled up from his place on the hearth. "I should not interrupt them if I were you, my lady. Uncle Newell would not appreciate—"

"*Uncle* Newell?" Iana exclaimed with a bitter laugh of disbelief.

"*Oui. Father* said your brother is to be my uncle once you are wed." He shook his head and smiled sweetly. "We have had a talk, Father and I. An understanding, we call it."

"I should like one of those talks myself," she muttered, incensed that Henri would enlist this lad in his devious machinations.

Ev patted her sleeve as though to offer her consolation. "Even though I should have liked you very much as a wife, I must admit he is right. You will make a fine mother for me. So I have decided to withdraw my offer in favor of Father's suit. Believe me, it will be the best for all concerned. So, may I call you *Maman?*"

Iana clasped her hands to her head to stop its reeling. "God save us, how young do they learn this plotting? I cannot abide more of it!" With a growl of frustration, she left them and stomped away to locate Newell.

When she arrived outside, a full-scale melee appeared to be taking place in the bailey. Ambrose, her brother, all of Newell's men and most of Lord Robert's had stripped to their waists and were having at one another with a vengeance. Swords clanged while shouted challenges, laughter and jolly whoops of warning rent the air.

She sat on the steps leading down from the hall, waiting for the practice to cease. Surely they would weary of it soon.

After half an hour, she grew tired of sitting there, watching the great gaggle of foolish drakes flap their wings, peck at each other and honk.

Men. Iana could not imagine what dwelt inside their cavernous heads that would prompt them to such outright madness. The entire male contingent within Baincroft looked to be preparing for an imminent war, not a simple sword fight betwixt two of them.

She tried to banish the fear that the fight would not be all that simple. That it could seriously damage one or the other of the combatants or see one of them dead. Even though that would not be their intent at the outset, an accident could so easily happen if they became overly zealous.

How many horrendous tales had she heard of such goings-on? Knights died all too frequently in friendly tournaments where the only purpose was to entertain and compete for the sport of it. Her father once had told her how even the famous Sir William Marshal of England had lost his son to this sort of chance-taking, and that young knight must have had the very best of training.

Iana shuddered and pushed back the awful thought. She would have to make Newell see how pointless this was and have him stop it.

It began to rain, just a soft drizzle. The men fought on, unfazed by the change in weather. She abandoned her place upon the steps and returned to the hall so that she would not get soaked through like the simpletons outside.

Obviously, the fight could not take place until Henri returned, and he would not be back until this night or the morrow. She would have time to speak with Newell later.

Iana rejoined the group within the hall. Lady Mairi now busied herself with a small piece of embroidery. "Did you speak with him?"

"Nay," Iana admitted. "Rather than wend my way through the blades, I decided to wait."

Lord Rob appeared even more disgruntled than before, while the twins, Harry and Ned, sat wriggling at either end of a long stool facing the wall. Iana regretted that she had missed the incident for which they were being punished. No doubt it had to do with those knotted lacings.

She sat down beside the maid upon the floor and reached for Tam. The baby grinned up at her and cooed. "How happy you are, my wee love," Iana remarked.

"Wuv," Tam replied.

The smiles of her new daughter were likely the only thing that could distract her from her present quandary, Iana thought, and she truly needed a diversion at that moment.

Truth be told, Tam had improved considerably in the time they had been here. She was happy and active now. Her eyes had brightened and lost their haunted look. She ate well and grew heavier by the day, though Iana suspected she would never be round and rosy as some bairns were.

The fond attention from everyone was so good for her, Iana wished mightily she could stay on in some capacity other than that of wife to Henri. Yet even if, by some quirk of fate, he trapped her into that, or even if she agreed to become his mistress, they would not remain at Baincroft. He would hie them off to France.

She then remembered Henri's offer of the best physician in that land to see to Tam. Wouldn't it be selfish not to go? Or was she simply grasping at an excuse to bow to Henri's wishes?

The fact that she considered doing so for even an instant made her angry with herself. So he had proved an excellent lover. God only knew he must have had more than enough practice to become proficient at seduction. She had heard the French always *were*. He would likely discard that giving of pleasure as unnecessary as soon as she was his to take at will.

Duncan had. Though they had not been precisely intimate before the wedding, he had used all his powers of persuasion right up to the day of the ceremony. He had promised all sorts of earthly delights, plied her with flowers and such sweet words that she had almost forgotten she had been sold like a sack of meal. Then had come the rude awakening in her marriage bed. And Newell had not even stayed until the following morning to see how she had fared.

Her quest for freedom from the rule of any man did not arise from that one night's incident, however. She could have forgiven Duncan his haste. She could have understood his lack of gentleness. But she could not absolve him of his deception, or for fostering her hope for happiness. Not when he had then cruelly and deliberately crushed that hope to nothingness.

She would never again tolerate that loss of dignity, or assume the abject subservience required of a wife.

Iana had seen no happy marriages in all her life. Even her father had been no easy man for her mother to live with. Though he had not been cruel to Iana, other than to wed her to Duncan, she knew he had been opinionated, sometimes coarse and often violent with others.

Then Dorothea had admitted that Newell made her life a hell.

But was that true? The more Iana thought on it, the more she doubted Dorothea had been honest about that. Newell would have lost nothing by admitting to it when Iana had accused him, and yet he had brushed it aside as ridiculous. If she ever had occasion to see Dorothea again, Iana meant to have a few words with that woman. At any rate, it did not seem that Newell's marriage was one of contentment, whether he beat his wife or not.

No marriage was, Iana believed. Mayhaps with one exception. She regarded her host and hostess.

There was Lady Mairi, humming softly as she stitched upon a sleeve cuff for Lord Robert. Judging by the age of their sons, they had been wed some four or five years, Iana guessed. About the same number of years she had been wed to Duncan before his death. So how was it that this woman had escaped drudgery, servitude and humiliation? What magic did she employ against that man of hers?

Did her lord's lack of hearing give Mairi more power over him than other wives possessed? 'Twas possible he needed her so much he was forced to remain kind and keep her happy. That must be it.

Iana continued to observe the couple, while Tam tried to unravel the fringe at the ends of her woven belt. Though Lord Robert must be worried for his brother and still vexed over the twins' caper, his temper now seemed calm enough. He smiled fondly at his wife and watched her with a singularly devoted expression.

When at last Lady Mairi set aside her embroidery and returned her husband's gaze, some unspoken message seemed to pass betwixt the two. In a few moments, they rose in unison, bade the twins' young nursemaid to mind them well and politely excused themselves from Iana's company.

She could only guess why they were retiring to their chamber at this time of day. Before Henri had shown her the pleasures to be had in a bedding, Iana would have had naught but sympathy for the lady. Now she knew better than to waste a moment's pity on Lady Mairi. Truth told, she felt a bit of envy.

Everand moved closer to her and plucked Tam from her lap. "I shall mind my sister if you have other matters to attend."

"Sister?" she repeated. "Ev, I do swear you have entirely too much faith in Sir Henri's plans. I tell you I am not about to wed him."

The lad merely shrugged, leaned down nose-to-nose with the bairn and began making silly noises with his lips to entertain her.

Another fool in the making, Iana thought as she got to her feet. "As you will, Ev. Bring her to my chamber when she tires or you tire of her. Also, keep an eye out for Sir Henri. If he should by chance return today, I would speak with him immediately."

Iana trudged up the stairs, intending to lie down in an effort to banish the mounting ache in her head. It was likely neither Newell nor Sir Ambrose would give her protests any credence whatsoever, even when she did manage to speak with them. The one was too stubborn and the other too stupid. Still she would try.

God's truth, she could not understand what Jehan saw in Ambrose other than his powerful body and handsome face. Mayhaps for Jehan, that was enough.

However, Duncan, despite his age, had been a strong and attractive man when Iana had married him. In the years that followed, that had accounted for nothing at all.

She reached her chamber, still lost in thought as she turned back the coverlet and lay down, fully clothed.

Round and round in her head raced the memories of all that had gone on.

In the remembering of it all, Iana suddenly realized the truth. Nothing Duncan had ever done to her physically, no matter how unpleasant or painful, had come near to hurting her as foully as his betrayal of her trust.

Her father had betrayed her with the promise of a good life with the husband he chose for her. Then Duncan had revealed his true nature once he'd had her trapped. And Newell, whom she had idolized as a child, had turned ogre.

Now Henri planned to subjugate her, using any manner of cunning available. She hated how much she still longed to trust him, how her mind worked so hard to conjure reasons why she might.

Why had God seen fit to make her a witness to Lord Rob and Lady Mairi's contented union at this crucial time? There was hope, sprouting where it should never have taken root again. Nay, she would not give in to it this time. She had learned her lesson well.

Though Iana admitted to herself that she loved Henri, she must not give in to it, lest he betray her, too.

Henri did not return that day or night. Iana spent much of the time alone, with Tam, attempting to decide how she must handle the matter. Each and every time she went downstairs, Newell was nowhere to be found. He was avoiding her.

She found him the next morn as he stood in the hall, quaffing a tankard of ale. He was alone, save for some servants milling about, arranging trays of freshly baked breads, cold meats and fruits on the cloth-draped tables. They were setting out a veritable feast. She did not have to wonder at the reason for that. The duel would take place today.

Her wakefulness last night had caused her to oversleep and miss Mass. The only person she had spoken with thus far was Jehan. Iana supposed most of the people were still out in the chapel. That was where she should have been, praying for a deluge that would prevent or at least delay the day's grand plans.

She perched Tam on one hip as she prepared to confront Newell.

He treated her to a curious look as she approached. "My, my, the bright red does you justice, Sister. A bride's color, I believe. We must find flowers for your hair once we have a groom secured. The clinging bairn detracts from your appeal, of course, but I suppose she is part of the bargain." Belying his insult to the babe, he chucked Tam under her chin with his finger, making her smile.

Iana stepped back smartly, breaking the contact. She had no wish to see a gentle side of her brother at the moment. Tam's calm acceptance of his touch with a decided lack of her usual shyness made Iana curse inwardly. She was so angry with Newell, she thought it only right that everyone should be.

She also cursed the folly of wearing the gown Jehan had sent up. The amber one Henri had bought her was soiled, her old one too threadbare, and the blue surcoat Mairi had loaned her was wrinkled beyond help, thanks to Henri. The boldness of the red sendal Jehan provided had boosted Iana's courage, so she had worn it.

"Your color is high this morn," Newell taunted.

She suspected it matched well the hue of her borrowed garment.

Intently, he studied her, as if he could not fathom why

two men would do battle to have her. She could have told him clearly enough: Ambrose because he would rather die than break his word, and Henri because she had refused him. He wanted most what he was told he could not have. And mayhaps because he loved her just a little, or thought that he did.

They were misguided fools, the both of them. She wished she could knock their empty heads together and have done with it.

"I see no purpose in small talk to pass the time," she told Newell. "As it happens, we do not have much time left. Lady Jehan tells me that the bout is planned for this very day."

"So it is."

Iana sighed and shifted Tam to a more comfortable position. There was nothing to be gained by displaying her anger. It made better sense to use reason.

She schooled her face into an imploring expression. "Newell, please listen to me. You must reconsider and ban this foolish combat betwixt Henri and Ambrose. It will serve nothing other than to cause hard feelings and possible injury."

"You will accept Ambrose's suit, then?" he asked amiably.

"Nay, I have told you time and again that I shall not. Be warned. Nothing you can do will force me to it."

"I know. So you need not wed." He shrugged, tipped his cup of ale and drained it.

"Oh, Newell! How can I thank—"

"I shall simply *give* you to the one who wins, as a ward. Then he may do as he will with you. All the profits from your lands will go to him, recompense for his bother."

"Lands? What lands?" As far as she knew, she owned

nothing but what she had brought with her from the village.

"Your dower estate, such as it is," he informed her. "Ambrose took some of my men and helped secure it against Duncan's spawn the day he went to fetch you from Whitethistle. You might be a bit more grateful to him for that."

"Why?" she demanded. "He was serving himself if he thought he was to have the profit!"

Newell dismissed that with a negligent wave of his hand. "I am heartily sick of wasting my time trying to arrange your life when you show no appreciation for it. If I relent and allow you to come home with me unwed, then Dorothea will set in on me again."

"What do you mean, set in on you?"

He had the grace to redden. "Well, she resents you, I think. You encroach upon her duties as Lady of Ochney."

"I do not!" Iana argued. "I never have done. She lies, Newell!"

He pressed his forehead with thumb and forefinger as if to pinch away pain. "Nevertheless, she is my wife and I must keep the peace between us somehow." He sighed. "These men are both adequate matches for you, and to my mind, either will do. He who wins the day shall have your wardship, in lieu of your hand. Then you will be *his* problem, not mine."

Fury stole her speech. Iana found she could scarcely breathe, she was so angry. It mattered little, for she could see he had made up his mind, and nothing she could say would change it.

As much as she hated to give in, she knew there was only one thing she could do to halt this travesty. "I had as soon be a wife as a ward," she muttered. Taking a deep breath, she released it again. "Very well, I surrender."

"What?" her brother asked with a look of astonishment.

She nodded. "I choose Henri. Call off the contest and I shall wed him. Anything to stop this madness before someone is harmed."

There came a long silence. "Well?" she asked.

"Nay," he said succinctly, frowning. "That will not do."

"Why ever not?" Iana demanded. "'Tis what you want!"

He braced his hands on his hips and shook his head. "If you had chosen Ambrose, I might have agreed. He has the right to you, for he and I had it all arranged. The only reason I am allowing Gillet this challenge is because I thought you might have come to care for him and he for you. He says he loves you. Ambrose very graciously affords him this opportunity. Gillet is the interloper, so I cannot in all good conscience simply give you to him."

"You are daft, Newell," she told him flatly, in the event that he was not yet aware of it. "And I have no inkling what you mean by that."

He looked around to judge whether anyone was listening, saw they were not and continued in a lowered voice. "Iana, this is a matter of honor here. It is the one way out of our agreement for a man such as Ambrose, don't you see? Gillet will defeat him, if only because Ambrose's heart will not be in the fight. But I suspect, after a good show of strength, he will lose apurpose." He laid a hand on her shoulder and squeezed it. "Besides, if I call it off now, everyone here would be disappointed."

"Not *everyone!*" she assured him.

It was no use.

She left him standing there and stalked off to the kitchens, where she might avoid conversation with anyone else. There she would feed Tam and gather her own thoughts. Mayhaps she would have better luck pleading with Henri.

Her wardship. Iana shook her head. By law, a widow could own her own land and oversee it herself. But to be perfectly honest, Iana knew as well as her brother did that she stood no chance of keeping it without the protection a man would provide.

Her dead husband's sons would only take it from her again, just as they had at Duncan's death, the lawless wretches. And with Newell so many leagues distant and as uncaring as he was now, she would have no one who would trouble to oust them. Unless she were someone's ward. Or wife. Damn them all, every last man of them.

She set Tam upon one of the tables used for preparing the food and plucked up a warm bannock to feed her. Pinching off a bite for Tam and one for herself, she chewed thoughtfully.

"Are you coming out to watch?" Jehan asked from behind her.

"Rob says Henri has just arrived, and they will begin within the hour. He is most anxious about this."

"Lord Robert? Aye, I did notice that yesterday. Why do you think he's troubled?"

Jehan leaned against the table, her arms crossed over her chest and an anxious look in her eye. "He would not say. This worries me, Iana. Rob should not mind a bit of swordplay. He loves a challenge."

"Then what could upset him?" Iana poured a bit of goat's milk from the flagon near the bread bowl and put it to Tam's eager lips. "Have you asked Lady Mairi?"

Jehan shook her head. "She has not yet come in from

Mass. Shall we go and await her in the hall?'' She turned and started that way, then beckoned from the doorway. ''Oh, there she is now. Mairi?''

''They are ready to begin,'' Mairi announced.

''So soon?'' Jehan asked.

''Aye, and ye must come out,'' she told them.

''I suppose *I* must, at any rate,'' Iana said, lifting Tam and brushing away the crumbs from her mouth. ''They will want the expected trophy available, I should think.''

''What will you do, Iana?'' Jehan asked as they left the kitchens and made their way across the hall. ''When it is over, I mean?''

''Laud the winner and wish him good crops. My brother has made it clear that wardship is the real prize,'' she replied, still furious with Newell. ''My lands are *all* he shall have of me.''

''A man cannot have yer dower lands unless ye wed him,'' Mairi assured her.

''The profits from them, then. The selfsame thing.''

When they reached the outdoors, Iana saw the crowd gathered around the clearing used for training. A loud buzz of excitement permeated the air. Lord Robert broke away from the others and came across the bailey. True to Jehan's word, he did appear distraught.

Even before he reached them, he began to make signs with his hands. Lady Mairi gasped and Jehan cried, ''No!''

''What? What has happened?'' Iana demanded, clutching Tam to her chest.

Mairi turned and grasped Iana's forearm. ''Sir Ambrose means to make a real fight of it! Henri is convinced he will feign a loss because of Jehan, but he will not do that! Rob feared this before, but now he is certain.''

''Surely Ambrose will not make it a fight to the death.

That would be absurd!'' Iana argued. "Even *he* is not that thick-witted!''

Mairi made a sound of exasperation. "Nay, but think ye how unprepared Henri will be for it! He could be severely injured if he does not ken this is combat in earnest!''

"Then *tell* him!'' Iana ordered. "Have Lord Robert warn him!'' She hurried her steps to a near run, urging the others to do likewise. "Quickly, before they begin!''

"He *did* give warning,'' Mairi said, "but Henri will not believe it. He is convinced that Rob is wrong, that Ambrose will fight only for show.''

"Then how do you know he will not?'' Iana asked, breathless from rushing. "Did he say as much?''

"No, but Rob knows,'' Jehan moaned. "He always knows.''

Iana stared at her as they reached the crowd and came to a stop. "Ridiculous! No one can read what is in another's mind and heart.''

"Rob can,'' Mairi declared. "He always could.''

Disbelieving, Iana looked again at Jehan, who was now weeping openly and nodding her emphatic agreement.

Newell's voice thundered over the sounds of men and lads wagering and choosing favorites. "Lady Iana, come forward!''

"Lord Newell, go to the devil!'' Iana shouted in answer.

Lord Robert gently took her arm to escort her.

Mairi relieved her of Tam and nodded her encouragement.

Iana decided it would be better if she were closer and could see what was happening. Mayhaps she could prevent disaster if it seemed apparent.

The crowd parted for her, whispered comments on her

attributes assaulting her ears all the way. They were not vulgar words, of course, but she felt cheapened nonetheless. The castlefolk might as well be checking her teeth and feeling the muscles of her legs to see how worthy a prize she was.

Soon she stood beside her brother and was able to see Henri and Sir Ambrose in all their finery. Aye, they meant to make a display of this. She only hoped Lord Robert had not read Ambrose's mind aright and that the knight would give only a token account of himself.

Dressed for the occasion, Henri wore silver and black, with a silver lion rampant upon his chest—Trouville's striking colors and device, and most likely Trouville's own garments. She much doubted Henri kept spare clothing at his father's home. Beneath the fitted, hip-length surcoat, he wore silvered chain mail and chausses. Those, as well as the shining shin and arm guards, appeared quite new.

Ambrose also wore mail beneath his crimson surcoat emblazoned with a white hawk. He had arrived at Baincroft wearing his best, and wore it now as well. His matching shield, which she had not seen before, looked quite impressive.

Henri's protection was smaller by a hand span and appeared to have suffered more use. She worried also at the inadequate helm he wore, a conical basinet that reached just below his ears and exposed his face entirely. It was laced to a chain mail aventail that might save his head from a slicing blow, but would do naught to prevent a broken neck.

However, Ambrose need not worry for his neck, she thought, cursing the difference. It was snugly covered. He was wearing a great helm with eye slits barely the width of her largest finger, and breathing holes cast into the nose and mouth area.

At least their swords were of equal length, both highly polished blades catching the meager light of the morning sun.

"Henri, have a care!" she called before she could stop herself. "Beware!"

He turned to her and raised his weapon so that the cross-guard touched his lips as his gaze met hers. A salute. Then he bowed gracefully, garnering the applause and approval of the assembly. He smiled winningly, obviously looking forward to the entire debacle.

After his brief acknowledgment of her and those watching, Henri immediately returned his attention to the huge, older knight who must be acting as marshal of the event.

In a deep, sonorous voice, the man began imparting a list of conditions. The noise around the circle gradually abated, but all Iana heard were the last two rules.

"Victory is declared only by spoken concession of the vanquished or by the death of one opponent. The victor is charged to grant mercy to the vanquished, or he shall suffer the fine of fifty marks prescribed by law."

Death? At the word, Iana's breath stuck in her throat and her knees suddenly went weak. One of them would have to admit defeat aloud—or die! The hardheaded Ambrose would never cry mercy. And, God's own truth, Henri would never give up so long as he could breathe.

Newell's hand caught her beneath one elbow. "Do not think they will kill one another, Sister," he muttered. "This is but a test of swordsmanship, and the usual warning is given for such at tourneys. The fine will keep them careful."

"You are certain?" she gasped.

He glanced down at her. "Now you flatter yourself."

"Newell, stop them," she pleaded.

His smile was wry. He nudged her arm and inclined his head toward the combatants. "Too late."

And she saw that it was.

"Go to," the marshal cried.

The sudden clang of steel was deafening.

Chapter Seventeen

As the demandant, Henri struck first. He easily absorbed the flat smack of Ambrose's parry. Quick as that, he leapt handily backward to avoid a blow to the knees. Good move, he thought, admiring Ambrose's speed and dexterity.

They circled, each gauging the other's intent. Henri tried not to grin. God, how he loved this! How he had missed it. He stepped in, hefted the sword with its blunted edges and swung a cutting blow to midbody. Ambrose's shield caught it, even as his blade struck Henri's shoulder. Steel bounced against mail.

Henri frowned. Had not that sword been dulled, the edge would have taken off his arm. Had Ambrose struck a more powerful blow than that riposte allowed, it would have broken the bone. As he flexed the numbed muscles, Ambrose lunged again.

Henri blocked with a hanging parry, not all that expertly done, either, he thought, instantly whipping his blade around to block yet another downward stroke.

Damn his eyes, Ambrose was serious about this. And bloody quick. Either he meant to provide a true exhibition on rapid aggression or he meant to win!

Henri pivoted, throwing his entire weight into a swing that caught the edge of the opposing blade. Steel rang, screeched and threw sparks.

"Points off for that, *mon ami,*" Henri muttered. "Fouled your edge!" Such as the edge was on tournament weapons. These were rebated, dulled apurpose and with flat, almost rounded points so as to limit injury.

Ambrose replied with an audacious backhand slice that almost split Henri's shield. He readjusted his stance and met the overhead blow with alacrity. *Saints, the man never paused!*

"You want a lesson," Henri growled through bared teeth, which he almost lost as the tip of Ambrose's sword came within a hairsbreadth of his face. *"Merde!"* He jumped sidewise, dropped to his haunches and swung, catching Ambrose's legs at the shins.

"Oho!" Henri crowed when the knight landed with a thunk directly upon the curve of his gaudy blue shield. It cracked neatly in half. Shouts of encouragement and hoots of derision swelled around them.

Henri tossed his own shield aside, a gesture of fair play he would never have indulged in during true combat. Too late, he wondered whether the courtesy was wise here.

Gamely he waited for Ambrose to rise and make certain no bones had been broken. Perhaps another mistake, Henri thought, reading the tense set of his opponent's body. Still, he did not wish to make such a quick end to this or all would guess it was a mock match. If indeed it was.

He sucked in a deep breath and released it slowly, preparing himself. As one they raised their blades to signify that they would continue.

"Nay!" he heard Iana cry. "No more!" Henri risked a glance in her direction.

Suddenly, Ambrose came at him like a berserker, a mad Viking bent upon total destruction, with no thought to prudence. Henri dodged, parried and caught the sliding blade on his cross-guard. He threw Ambrose back so that they stood just out of blade's reach. No question now. This was no sham.

The imbecile had never intended to give a good account and then lose. Ambrose obviously held honor dearer than Jehan or any other thing. One had to admire the single-mindedness of that, even in these circumstances.

Henri knew that he must take charge of this and defeat the fool for his own good, as well as that of everyone else involved.

Immediately Henri assumed the offense, employing every lesson he had ever learned regarding swordplay. He set his mind to judge and strike, to use Ambrose's technique against him, to outthink and anticipate. But he discovered a worthy opponent, one whose abilities matched his own.

On and on they fought, until the muscles of Henri's arms fairly quivered with exhaustion and his legs wanted to buckle. He realized now how this would end. Unless there was a random occurrence of good fortune, one or the other of them would simply collapse in a heap.

He had the advantage over Ambrose, Henri reminded himself as he plied yet another leaden swing. He was used to France's warmer weather, and so was less affected by the day's unusual heat. Likely his opponent was even more sweat-soaked than he, thereby thirsty as hell. Henri's own sweat stung his eyes. How much worse it must be for Ambrose, with his head fully encased in that laughable excuse for a helm.

He'd no sooner thought that than Ambrose's blade

glanced off his own headgear. Stunned, Henri automatically extended in a quick and vicious thrust, gaining himself an instant's pause to shake off the blow.

That prompted an idea. If he could land a mighty, flat clout on that upturned bucket Ambrose was wearing, he might rattle the man's senses past thinking. He tried an overhead attack. Ambrose blocked, came off his blade and cracked Henri soundly across his rib cage.

Breath left him in a rush. Iana's scream echoed in his head. A flash of red skirts caught his eye just as the pain drove him to his knees. She was running toward them. "Hold her!" he thundered to Newell.

Desperately vulnerable on his knees, Henri lifted his sword to block, twisted to avoid Ambrose's cut, then came round in a sidewise arc whilst the knight was in close.

Ambrose jerked back his head just in time to avoid the full impact, but the tip of Henri's sword struck the eyehole and wedged. His own harsh gasp joined the general outcry of alarm.

Henri yanked back his weapon and with his free hand grasped Ambrose's wildly flailing sword just below the cross-guard, where the blade was quite blunt.

Disarming him from a kneeling position proved more difficult than expected, but Henri finally ripped the sword from his grasp and tossed it aside. Clenching his teeth at the agony in his side, Henri struggled to his feet.

With a hand to the shoulder, he grasped Ambrose. "Are you cut, man?" he demanded, then realized the knight could not hear him with the helmet on. Rob had rushed onto the field, and together they forced Ambrose to sit upon the ground, where they knelt beside him.

The helm's latch had been dented and would not release to unhinge it. The momentum of the blow, with the sword tip caught fast in the hole, had twisted the whole device. Henri now could see the top of Ambrose's ear through the eyepiece. "Speak, Ambrose, are you cut?"

"Nay," came the muffled answer. "I'm stuck!"

Henri laughed with relief and motioned for Rob to stand away. He then beckoned for Newell to come forward so that he could witness. He did so, clasping Iana's arm so that she accompanied him.

The assembly fell silent. Against the grassless ground, Hamilton's boots scraped, the sound interspersed with the more frequent patter of Iana's slippers as she rushed to keep up.

Henri waited on his knees, taking short breaths, pressing one arm firmly against his side, attempting to assuage the acute agony there. He prayed to remain upright until this was finished and the outcome proclaimed.

When brother and sister arrived at his side, Henri shouted to the sitting knight, who had commenced struggling with the helmet to right it, if not remove it. "Sir! You are unarmed and can no longer see. Do you concede the bout?"

They heard a muted grunt.

"Louder, *mon ami*," he urged, cuffing Ambrose's shoulder.

"Aye," came the all but inaudible answer. "I forfeit."

"Merci," Henri replied, and looked up at Newell. "There you have it, Hamilton."

Rob assisted Ambrose to his feet and led him away through the throng of observers.

Iana's brother watched his friend leave the field. Then he looked down at Henri with a flat expression. "To the victor, the spoils. She is yours. I wish you joy of her." He released Iana's wrist and quickly walked away, following Rob and Ambrose through the crowd.

No one moved or spoke. Henri saw that their audience awaited Iana's reaction to being awarded to him so bluntly. He supposed he would have to hear it himself, though he could guess what it would be and was in no way eager. His head felt light and his vision was blurred. But at least *his* helm was on straight.

Unable to rise, he shifted upon his knees so that he faced Iana, as if kneeling before her apurpose. She stood looking down at him. Her features shifted out of focus and he blinked hard.

"Oh, Henri." She breathed his name with a disconsolate sigh. He clearly heard her anguish and idly wondered if it was because of the drubbing he'd taken or because he had prevailed in spite of it. "You are hurt," she whispered.

"*Oui*," he admitted, "but I have…won you." She was his. Henri experienced a welling up of euphoria that conquered all his discomfort. His eyes closed tight with relief and the ground rose up to meet him.

"Help me!" Iana cried out as she dropped to her knees and cradled Henri's head between her hands. The words were no more out of her mouth than young Everand and four of Baincroft's sturdiest men surrounded them.

Iana quickly moved out of their way so they could lift him, then hovered as closely as she could while they carried him toward the keep. She hardly noticed the mounted party in the bailey until the horses blocked their path.

The men carrying Henri had to halt and lower him to the ground. His eyes were open, but he did not sit up. Iana quickly knelt beside him, afraid he was injured worse than she had first thought. He looked past her shoulder at the recent arrivals and grimaced.

Lord Trouville quickly dismounted and squatted beside his son. *"Pourquoi est-ce que vous ne nous avez pas attendus, Henri?"* he demanded, showing both anger and concern. *"Tu es endommagé?"*

"Bruises," Henri answered, and bared his teeth, more a wince than a smile. He spared her a reassuring glance before looking back to his father. "And I did not wait until you arrived because I thought you would stop me."

Trouville cursed and stood, drawing Iana with him as he stepped back. He motioned for the men to lift Henri again, but Henri objected. "No. Give me a hand up. I can walk."

His father reached down and grasped his hands. Without bending in the middle, Henri came upright with a pained grunt. *"Merci."*

"Do not thank me too soon," Trouville warned. "You might have more bruising ere this is done." He beckoned to two of the men. "Assist him inside."

They supported Henri's arms and began the torturous journey up the keep's steps to the hall. Trouville fell in step with Iana. "He won, of course?" he said to her, more statement than question.

"It was a near thing, *Monsieur le Comte.*" She kept her worried gaze fastened upon Henri's back. "But, aye, he did win." Though she did not intend it, a note of pride sounded in her voice.

"This pleases you, having two men so hot to have you?" he snapped.

"Not at all!" Iana argued. "I did all I could to prevent it! Ask my brother! I even agreed to wed Henri if he would call it off."

"So now you are bound to marry?"

She scoffed. "Nay. Newell offered my wardship instead."

Trouville nodded and sighed. "That will likely stand in a court if you challenge it. You need not bother, however. Henri will treat you fairly."

She said no more, for there seemed to be no point in doing so. Done was done. As angry as it made her to serve as chattel, she had no recourse but to accept.

They were already inside and more than halfway across the hall. Through the doorway to the solar, they could see the men carefully seating Henri in Lord Robert's cushioned armchair. "Meg, go and see to him, would you?"

For the first time, Iana noticed the three women who had followed them inside. They were now standing with Lady Mairi, who had just handed Tam to one of the nursemaids.

The woman who was more simply gowned than the others hurried toward the solar. Iana started to follow.

Trouville grasped her arm. "Remain here until Lady Margaret has assessed his hurts. Meanwhile, you should meet my countess, Lady Anne, and our daughter, Alys." To them, he remarked, "This is Henri's new *ward,* Iana, Baroness Duncan."

"My ladies," Iana murmured, and dropped a perfunctory curtsy, her mind yet upon Henri and how he was faring. "Is that woman a healer?" she asked.

"The best," the countess assured her.

Iana was relieved to hear it, but not willing to trust Henri's care entirely to another. "If you would please excuse me, I shall go and assist her."

"No," Trouville declared. "Henri must divest of his mail and undress in order to assay the damage. Your presence in there would not be proper."

Even as he said it, she watched the solar door close.

"Not *proper?*" Iana demanded, outraged that he held

her back. "I have tended him before and well you know it! Would you rather I had let him die to preserve propriety?"

He pinned her with a glare, one dark brow raised in admonition. "Then, it was necessary. Now it is not."

Iana almost defied him. He fairly dared her to try. It was just a look, but fraught with such intimidation she gave up the notion.

"My lord, please understand," she reasoned. "I wish to see to him because somehow I feel responsible."

He did not change his dour expression. "That, my dear, is because you *are*." With that, he turned about and went to go where she would have gone herself.

"You must excuse him," the countess said with a smile. "He dotes on Henri and is of a single mind when it comes to the welfare of his heir."

"Aye, I know that," Iana admitted, sighing with resignation. "When the *comte* was here before, he offered me the moon for saving Henri." She clicked her tongue. "Now he hates me simply for being, and causing *this*." Iana threw up her hands in resignation.

"Hates you?" Lady Alys said, laughing. "No! Papa quite admires you. He has said as much."

"He has," the countess agreed. "However, he is quite piqued that any woman would turn down the chance to be Henri's wife."

Iana released a slow breath through her teeth and shook her head. "It is not Henri I object to, it is any man."

"I know," the lady replied. "I once felt the same myself about Edouard." She took Iana's hand and held it. "Think you, Iana, what it is like for you, to be only a chamber away from Henri's side at this moment. Someone else will tend his hurts in future, as well, and you will not even know of them. Does that trouble you? Do you care for him at all?''

Iana admitted to herself that she more than cared. She loved him. She recalled how near to death he had been when she had first seen him. Today, when he had crumpled to the ground after waging such a long, arduous battle for her sake, she had felt pain herself. Even now that she knew he was not severely injured, she worried for him.

Lady Anne was right. In the years to come, she might not even know when he sustained a wound in war or in the lists. He could die if there was no one by him who was competent to tend him. And if he should die? She could not bear the thought of it.

Mairi looped her arm through Iana's and said softly, ''Come, let us have a cup of wine and something to eat.''

The four of them joined the many others who had come in from the outside to partake of the food and drink laid out upon the white-clothed trestles.

Everand came dashing out of the solar, hurriedly approached them and bent at the waist, smiling ear to ear. ''Father sends me to assure all of you that he will be able to attend the feast this eve. Lady Margaret has declared him almost fit to dance!''

''Feast?'' Lady Mairi asked, eyebrows raised in question. ''Did no one think to inform *me* that I am to give a feast?''

The other ladies laughed merrily at her feigned consternation. Iana could see their mood had lightened considerably with Everand's news that Henri would be up and about before the day was done. As for herself, she nearly dropped to her knees in a prayer of thankfulness.

That powerful feeling of relief—in conjunction with the ever-present memory of the passion between her and

Henri—threw a slightly different light over her determined quest for freedom. No matter how often or vehemently she denied him a hold over her, either as ward or wife, Iana knew full well in that moment that she would never be free of Henri.

Yet even knowing that as surely as she did, she could not bring herself to surrender to him outright. Not yet, and never at all, unless he agreed to her terms.

Chapter Eighteen

Iana took Tam to the nursery and left her in the care of the twins' nurse and the two maids who assisted there. As soon as she returned to the hall, she tried to bully her way into the solar to see how Henri fared. The men lounging around the doorway would not allow it, stating that Henri was bathing.

She managed to hear enough raucous laughter spilling from within to gather that no one inside there could possibly be in pain or in danger of dying.

"Come away, you worry-wit," Jehan urged her, tugging at her elbow. "Leave them to their splashing and bawdy jests. We ladies have a council of war to attend."

"War?" Iana asked, laughing with relief herself. "Who are we about to challenge?"

Jehan's bright eyes widened, as did her grin. "Why, the men, of course. Who else?" She leaned close. "Ambrose's pride is in shreds and he's hiding out in the barracks, where I am not allowed to go. I sent word that he will attend the feast today or I shall have him trussed up like a goose and delivered to me! I just know the dolt is planning to leave."

Iana laughed. "Then I wager he will if he's set on it. Will you not go out to bid him farewell?"

Jehan shook her head, sending her loose, dark curls bouncing. "He's not going anywhere. He'll never leave without his saddle. I hid it."

"You did not!"

"Aye, I did," she affirmed with a curt nod. "I knew the moment they cut him out of that helm that he would be dashing off to salve his wounded pride and gnash his teeth over his defeat. I intended to take his horse, but the beast would not let me."

They joined Mairi, Lady Anne and Alys fireside and pulled up stools to sit. Iana felt warmed by the women's acceptance of her. She was the outsider here, but no one seemed to mind. In fact, Lady Anne reached over and took her hand. "Henri is fine. His father came out to reassure us while you were taking your daughter up to the nursery."

Iana smiled. "I am glad to hear it. If he were hurt on my account, I should feel dreadful. Please accept my apology for causing all this uproar."

"Nonsense!" the lady said with a scoff. "'Tis not half the brangle that took place when Rob claimed our Mairi."

Claimed. That's what she was now, Iana thought. That should trouble her more than it did. She gently extracted her hand and clasped her fingers together in her lap. "I suppose I am officially Henri's ward now."

Lady Alys, Henri's sister, piped up. "Considerably more than a ward, I would wager. He wants you to wife."

Lady Anne shushed her, then regarded Iana with a keen eye. "Do not let Henri bully you, my dear. He is a trifle strong-minded, I admit. However, he is deeply in love with you. Rob is never wrong about these things. He believes that you feel the same way about Henri.''

"Love or lack of it is not the problem," Iana confessed.

Mairi clapped her hands. "See? There is more cause to celebrate this day than a piddling clash of weapons. We are to have a betrothal!"

"Two betrothals," Jehan corrected with a sly twitch of her brow.

"One," Iana argued, "unless…"

An expectant hush fell over the group. They waited for her explanation, and Iana felt they deserved to hear it. "I will not consent to marry Henri," she stated, "unless he agrees to my conditions."

"Good for you," Alys announced. "Put him in his place at the outset, Sister, for my brother is entirely too full of himself."

"What are your requirements?" Lady Anne asked. "May we hear them now?"

Iana sighed and shook her head. "I believe I should put them to Henri first. 'Tis only fair."

"Poppycock!" Jehan exclaimed with an unladylike snort.

"She is right, Jehannie," Mairi said. "Henri should be the first to hear them. However—" she held up one finger and continued with a sly grin "—I do think ye should state them publicly, Iana. At the banquet. With this horde of witnesses, there can be no chance of misunderstandings arising later."

"But how shall I? I cannot presume that he will ask."

Mairi interrupted. "I will charge Rob with suggesting to Henri that he propose a marriage between ye in front of everyone. I shall point out that ye can hardly refuse him without giving good reason, and ye must admit ye have none. I will hint that ye are secretly willing, of course.''

"Clever plan," Lady Anne readily agreed. She patted Iana's knee. "Any man's memory has a way of becoming rather selective as time passes. However, you will be reasonable in your demands, will you not? And open to compromise?" Her lovely gray eyes held the wisdom and joy of one long wed and happily so. "Believe me, that is the secret of forming and maintaining a successful union, child. Reason and compromise."

"And love!" Jehan added brightly. "Mustn't forget that!"

"And passion!" Alys interjected with feeling.

They turned an incredulous stare upon her.

"What do *you* know of *passion?*" her mother demanded tartly.

Alys shrugged, grimaced and wisely kept silent.

"Look, 'tis Ambrose!" Mairi announced, grabbing Jehan by the arm to keep her seated when she would have jumped up and run to him. The knight had just entered in the company of Newell.

Both men stopped, conversed briefly with one of the attendants setting up the tables, then strode purposefully toward the solar, where the other men were gathered.

"He has come to make peace, I expect," Mairi guessed.

"Or demand his saddle back," Jehan murmured with a giggle. "He looks a proper prune-face."

"Will you wed him, Jehannie?" Alys asked.

"Of course," she replied, "soon as his choler settles."

Mairi hurriedly turned the subject to plans for the feast, and a less intimate conversation resumed among the women. Presently they were caught up in the excitement, discussing the jongleurs who had been summoned from

Trouville's castle, and the elaborate concoctions the cooks were now preparing.

Yet Iana could not help but continue to contemplate the advice set forth by Henri's mother. What she said made sense. If the concessions worked both ways.

In truth, Iana had never known a man who bowed to compromise. But had Henri not given way on many things along their journey here? Did he not listen to her when she spoke of her concerns and give them consideration?

And she had to admit he did employ reason most of the time. Nothing he had done, save that horrid sword fight, could be deemed unreasonable. Aye, Henri used reason.

His making love to her she would not count, for her own unreasoning was as much to blame as his in that instance. They had been carried away, the both of them. Her traitorous body warmed with the memory of it. *Passion.*

He certainly cared for her; she knew that without doubt, just as she cared for him. They more than cared. They *loved.* As she had said to Lady Anne, love was not the problem. Nor was it enough. However, in combination with these other necessary things...

She supposed she would soon know whether they could accommodate one another for a lifetime. He had never given her cause to mistrust him, which she could say of no other man in memory. Aye, she would trust Henri to keep his word. If only he were willing to give it. Would he be, once he had heard what she required?

This was a test, she admitted. A harsh test of his resolve to make her his wife, if she was to be a wife again. She would never accept the lot she had before. Henri might as well know that from the beginning, if there was to be a beginning.

Henri and the other men were standing about waiting when the ladies descended the stairs just after noon. They collected a few ells away to one side of the stairs, surrounding Alys and helping her straighten her skirts.

His already unbearable apprehension increased when he noted Iana was not among them. Had she decided to remain secluded so that he would not ask her?

He firmed his lips to keep from frowning, locked his knees to keep from shifting impatiently, one foot to the other, and glanced at his father, who was wearing a rather smug look. Rob's merry smile encouraged him a bit. According to him, Mairi had spoken earlier with Iana and told Rob that she might now be amenable to a marriage. That seemed too good to be true.

Damn, but he did not like risking a rejection of his suit before everyone. However, Rob was right—Iana might be more inclined to accept him if they had an audience. And once she did so, the moment she made that promise this day, there would be no more of this vacillation on her part. All had been concluded, save for her words of acceptance. He shot a silent prayer heavenward that she would not refuse.

Rob nudged him with his elbow, and Henri's gaze flew to the lower curve of the stairs, visible at the bottom of the spiral. His breath caught in his throat. God's truth, a golden vision.

Iana seemed to float down the last three steps. The candlelight in the sconces above her caused shining glints in the rare, costly cloth-of-gold. Her long, flowing tresses seemed created of the same rich strands as the gleaming fabric she wore.

The soft white pleats of her chemise peeked above the magnificent overgown and clung enticingly to the smooth creaminess of her breasts. An amber jewel set in filigree of shining ore adorned her graceful neck, but it was as nothing compared to the treasure upon which it rested.

Her dark eyes sought his, and when their gazes locked, she smiled. The singularly sweet expression nearly stopped his heart.

"Breathe," his father said with a throaty chuckle, effectively snapping Henri from his trance. He shook his head and smiled back at her. On legs gone weak from their stiff position, Henri strode forward to take her hand and escort her to table.

Oh, interminable meal, would it never end? Course after course Henri watched delivered. The consuming of each seemed to take forever.

As the ranking guests, his parents held place of honor at the high table. Rob and Mairi flanked them to their left, with Jehan and Ambrose just beyond. Newell, as the elder baron, damn his eyes, sat to their right, with Iana sharing her brother's trencher. Though he had been placed beside Iana, Henri was stuck feeding his sister, Alys, on his other hand, who chattered nonsense throughout the entire feast.

As custom demanded, he fed the little minx. He broke her bread, cut her meat and offered their cup. She must have swallowed everything whole, he thought, for she never ceased her useless prattle.

To Alys's left sat the married priest and his wife, Father Michael and Lady Meg, Jehannie's parents. Thank God they had come today, for the good father would, if all went as planned, have duties to perform.

Henri turned to Iana to bolster his hope for that, and saw she was deep in conversation with Newell. Henri could not hear what they were saying, but at least they were not at each other's throats.

The players retained at Trouville's keep and the two who resided at Baincroft had combined their talents and were adding soft music to the clatter of the meal.

Henri's head ached with trepidation and his empty stomach roiled with unease. He could not force a morsel past his teeth. What if she said no?

At last the nuts, fruits and cheeses were brought out. Everand refilled the cup with sweetened wine. Appropriate to the course, but Henri knew it would not sit well. He prayed Alys would quaff it all, fall drunk upon the table and shut her busy little mouth. Suppose Iana had decided...

"Henri?" his father said, commanding his attention. "I would laud you upon your victory this morn. Let us drink to your prowess as well as that of your opponent, the worthy Sir Ambrose Sturrock." Trouville stood, cup aloft, and waited for everyone to rise. "Sirs, to your health."

Everyone acknowledged Ambrose and Henri, drank, then remained standing. Ambrose spoke, as was expected, and sounded quite sincere. "To the victor, Sir Henri Gillet de Trouville."

Henri nodded his appreciation and returned the salute with proper humility. "Fate took a hand, as you know, sir. I cannot claim superior skill, only a stroke of good fortune. God grant I never again meet an opponent with your august ability."

Again they sipped.

Now was the time. Henri glanced at Father Michael, then at Newell, and lastly at Iana. She met his gaze with one of daring, but she wore no smile of encouragement.

He reached for her hand and held it between his own.

The necessary formality of this was far from his liking. He would much prefer privacy to declare his feelings, but if she did not know by now how much he desired her and loved her, then she never would.

"My lady, now my beloved ward, I beseech you to hear a poor knight's plea. If you would accept me, I would be your husband."

Her beautifully arched brows rose slightly, as if she were surprised. He knew she was not. "Will you be my wife, Iana?" he added softly, trying as he might to inject what tender feeling he could into the formal proposal.

She looked around her at all those assembled, taking her time, making him sweat. Henri wanted to shake her. He wanted to kiss her. He wanted to get her somewhere alone and make her his forever.

"I might," she said simply.

"Might?" he replied, unsure what to say next. Was he to beg? Had he not done that already, in front of God and witnesses? What more did she want?

She tilted her head and met his intent gaze. "Sir, if you will meet my conditions before this company and swear to abide by them for a lifetime, I shall accede to your wish."

Henri felt a surge of something akin to anger. He carefully tamped it down. What would she demand of him? Something wholly impossible, most likely. Something he could never grant in a thousand years. She had told him clearly that she never wished to wed again. Now she would drive it like a knife into his heart. "Make your bargain, then," he said in a clipped voice.

"Three things," she announced, her soft words carrying like a shout within the silence of the great hall. "First of all, you must vow never to strike me, starve me or confine me."

Henri sucked in and released a deep breath of relief. "On my soul, I would not, even without such a vow. You must know this."

She nodded, glanced around them again and continued. "And I would have your word that we will reside in the country of my birth. Here, in Scotland."

Ah, so there it was, Henri thought with a sinking heart and a sigh of defeat. The impossible. His duty lay in France and she knew it. Unless he renounced his country, he could not have her. He wanted to shout unfair and demand she withdraw the condition, but knew she would not. She would only grow angry and use it as an excuse to refuse him altogether.

He cleared his throat, took a moment to think and then countered, "I know that you would never respect a lord who abandons those who depend upon him, as my people do in France. In lieu of said requirement, I offer this— we will spend three months of every year within these boundaries. What say you?"

She did not rush to decline. Nor did she hurry to accept. Instead, she lifted her cup and sipped. When she had set it down again, she nodded once. "Done."

Henri almost sat down in order to recover. One more condition, he told himself, taking hold of his composure. One more. "Your last condition, madam?"

She shrugged one shoulder slightly. "You must promise you will never gainsay me. That you will allow me to do as I will and say what I may with no thought to restrict me in any way whatsoever."

A collective gasp of disbelief issued forth from every man within hearing.

Careful now, Henri warned himself. His entire future rested upon how he responded to this outrageous stipulation. A simple "yea" and he might as well forgo his manhood and become her obedient hound. A "nay" and he would lose her for good.

He took her other hand, placed it upon the one he held and pressed them both between his own. "So long as I live, I vow I will heed your wishes, Iana. Your words I will hear and your wants I will carefully consider. Unless I fear for your safety and well-being, or that of those in our care, I shall not hinder your decisions. Only I entreat you to grant me the same favor."

"A compromise, my lord?" she asked.

"Let us share counsel, one of the other, in all important matters. I value your judgment and would hope that you value mine. I would take *you* as wife. Does that not speak well of my wits?"

She answered with a smile.

"Then you will take me as your husband and lord, Iana?"

"I will."

He squeezed her hands by way of thanks and drew her close. He turned toward Father Michael and watched him make the sign of the cross.

"It is done. We are wed," Henri announced, and kissed her soundly before she could object. Huzzahs broke out around them, a deafening sound that filled the hall. The musicians struck up such a cacophony, Henri could no longer hear his heart beating in his ears. He laughed against her lips, then kissed her again.

Fearing her protests at his gambit, Henri scooped her up and carried her through the throng of well-wishers toward the stairs and his chamber above. They were halfway up before he could hear her voice over the happy shouts and raucous music.

"You are mine now!" he announced. "No betrothal, no waiting."

She pounded his shoulder with one fist and threw her head back, laughing. "Foul trickery, you knave! I should have expected such!"

"You do not mind?" he asked in spite of his better judgment. He had not wished to anger her, only to seal their troth the moment it was made.

She kissed his cheek. "I have lived in Scotland all my life, Henri. No one knows better than I how easily one can assume the yoke of marriage. The priest was there. I should have guessed. All that was needed were willing words and a blessing."

"Even the blessing was not strictly required, but I am glad we have it," he rejoined. They had reached his chamber. He kicked open the door, entered and closed it the same way, leaning back against it with Iana still in his arms.

He looked deeply into her eyes, searching for her true thoughts. "Please do not consider this a yoke, Iana. Have I not vowed no constraints?"

She leaned her forehead against his lips. "Aye, you have the right of it. Not a yoke, then. Not the bonds of matrimony," she added. "Nor the shackles some would name it."

"Wedded bliss, we'll call it," he suggested. "For I am full of blissfulness as I have never been before."

"You are too easily pleased, Husband," she argued, then nodded toward the huge bed that rested upon the dais. "Should we not explore the boundaries of the wedded estate and see whether this bliss of yours has yet reached its limit?"

Henri released her legs and allowed her body to slide down the front of his, molding her to him with one arm while he barred the door behind him. Lifting her again, he swiftly carried her to the huge feather mattress and placed her upon it.

Then he answered her question with a question. "Did I not promise to give full credence to your every notion?"

"And you like this one," she guessed, smiling as she traced one provocative finger down his chest and tugged gently at the ornamental buckler that held his ceremonial sword.

Henri covered her hand and released the catch, grinning when the weapon crashed to the floor at his feet. He climbed upon the bed beside her. "You have always avowed how you wish to feel free, *ma chérie*. Why not make free with me?" he asked her suggestively. "For I am yours to command."

"Then give me your heart," she said in her most imperious voice.

"That has always been yours," he admitted. "Now you own other parts of more practical use." He sat up, shrugged off his tunic and began removing the rest of his clothing. "And I assure you they need using," he added, looking pointedly at her gown. "Which you cannot accomplish until I divest you of that dreadfully dear mass of fabric."

He did so, taking care not to damage the raiment in his haste to rid her of it. The chemise followed, billowing upon the floor beside the golden surcoat.

"The gown. I borrowed it from Mairi," she whispered, turning her face away and folding her arms across her breasts. "Do you like it?"

"*Mais oui*. It is charming, love." Henri traced her cheek with one finger and became serious on discovering her need for reassurance. She had given up her dream for him. What dearer gift could she give? And here he was making light of that in the joy of his triumph.

He ran his fingers through the length of her hair and spread it about her shoulders, letting his hand rest in the graceful curve of her neck. "You are so beautiful I could not draw breath when first I saw you so. However, your beauty is but a boon, Iana. It is your goodness and the sweetness of your soul that drew me to you and hold me fast."

She covered his hand with her own. "Thank you for agreeing to my conditions, Henri. I will not disappoint you."

He kissed her softly. "How well I know that. I would have promised you anything today, you know. Anything your heart desires. Castles in France? Treasure in abundance? These are yours."

To his surprise, her eyes twinkled with merriment. "Why, thank you! What a generous fellow you are. I would have asked for more, had I known."

"Ask now. What else do you wish, my heart? Make your list."

She shrugged one shoulder. "Oh, health, happiness…and mayhaps pleasures untold." She lifted her brows suggestively.

"Granted, granted and…oh, forgive me, there are those pleasures untold you are still awaiting." He caressed her with a heated gaze as he brushed the golden waves from her shoulders and took her in his arms. "Wait no more."

Epilogue

Iana snuggled next to Henri in their wee cabin aboard the vessel called *Ariadne*. "When will we put to port?" she asked him, drawing her foot along the length of his shin as she threaded her fingers through the hair of his chest.

"All too soon," he admitted with an aggrieved sigh. "Our captain would be a fool to agree to sailing around the isles until we have had our fill of each other. We should all grow old at sea."

Iana laughed at the thought. Two days aboard ship were not enough time to enjoy this bit of privacy they had been denied for the past fortnight traveling across France.

They were coming "home" for the first time since their marriage nine months before, sailing from the south of France, where Henri had ended their progress visiting the four estates he attended for his father. She looked forward to spending the promised three months of summer in Scotland.

The letters that had arrived made her even more eager to see everyone. Lady Anne had written that Jehan and Ambrose would be wed soon, now that he had inherited his father's title. Newell wrote that Dorothea had run afoul of the prioress in the convent to which she had unwillingly retired. And Mairi had implied in her last missive that she, Rob and the twins were eagerly awaiting another addition to their family.

Iana was eager to arrive in Scotland, but the journey there was such a delight. She stretched and sighed with longing to hold and be held.

"Our children must wonder if we are ill, we have tarried so long below deck. Though I cannot say I would have wished our time spent otherwise." Henri smiled appreciatively and drew her beneath him again on the feather-filled mattress.

"Ev will mind Tam. He adores his role as her protector."

"His role as *slave*," Henri corrected. "She stands him about as if she were the elder." He raised a brow. "Much like another female of my acquaintance does to me at times."

"Only because you both allow it," Iana agreed, laughing. "Ah, the family will not credit how tall Ev has grown these last months, will they? And how like you he is in every way that counts."

He shook his head ruefully. "Nor will they recognize our Thomasina, the magpie." Henri brushed the tangles from Iana's brow and kissed her forehead. His lips were warm, enticing, as he trailed them down to her cheek. "I do wish we could give Ev and Tam brothers and sisters," he said sadly.

"You have given up so soon?" she teased, moving provocatively, encouragingly. "Perhaps one further effort?"

"It is no laughing matter to me, Iana," he warned. "You know how I regret—"

"Then do not trouble yourself a moment longer. Have you forgotten so soon how you vowed to honor my wishes? I forbid you to frown."

He did, however. "By all rights, a woman should be able to have a child of her own. It is not fair."

"Oh, very well," she said, pressing a finger over his lips. "If you insist upon more, then I shall give you one. After all, compromise is the key to a happy union. Your mother told me so." She grinned up at him. "Can you wait seven months?"

His eyes went round, his brows high. "Iana? Are you...?"

"Aye, for certain," she declared. "I wanted to surprise you on your name day, but I could not bear to wait a moment longer."

After a long and passionate kiss, he held her as if he would never let her go. "I have never thought to be so happy," he admitted. "So very happy."

She moved sinuously against him and twined her arms around his neck. "Well, my happy lad, do not think for a moment you are now free of your duty."

"I was never the one to wish for freedom, my sweet," he told her. His body proclaimed his willingness to enslave her. "I wonder, do you yet wish for it?"

Iana smiled. "All my wishes have come true," she whispered with feeling. "Every one, except the most immediate."

And that, too, was granted without further delay.

* * * * *